THE GUARDIAN HOUND

THE SHADOW WARS TRILOGY: BOOK TWO

LEAH R CUTTER

KNOTTED ROAD PRESS

The Guardian Hound
The Shadow Wars Trilogy: Book Two

Copyright © 2013 Leah Cutter

All rights reserved
Published 2013 by Knotted Road Press
www.KnottedRoadPress.com

ISBN: 978-1-64470-303-8

Cover art: GetCovers.com

Reviews

It's true. Reviews help me sell more books. If you've enjoyed this story, please consider leaving a review of it on your favorite site.

Come someplace new…

Are you a traveler? Do you enjoy exploring strange new worlds, new cultures, new people?

Journey into the various lands envisioned by Leah Cutter.

Sign up for my newsletter and I'll start you on your travels with a free copy of my book, *The Island Sampler*.

I will never spam you or use your email for nefarious purposes. You can also unsubscribe at any time.

http://www.LeahCutter.com/newsletter/

CONTENTS

ALSO BY LEAH R CUTTER

Urban/Contemporary Fantasy Series

The Witch's Progress

Circle of Air

Circle of Fire

Circle of Water

Circle of Earth

Seattle Trolls

The Changeling Troll

The Princess Troll

The Fairy-Bridge Troll

The Troll-Demon War

The Troll-Human War

The Troll-Troll War

The Cassie Stories

Poisoned Pearls

Tainted Waters

Spoiled Harvest

Bloodied Ice

The Shadow Wars Trilogy

The Raven and the Dancing Tiger

The Guardian Hound

War Among the Crocodiles

The Clockwork Fairy Kingdom

The Clockwork Fairy Kingdom

The Maker, the Teacher, and the Monster

The Dwarven Wars

The Chronicles of Franklin

Franklin Versus The Popcorn Thief

Franklin Versus The Soul Thief

Franklin Versus The Child Thief

Epic Fantasy Series

Houses of the Dead

Houses Divided

Houses Fallen

Houses Reborn

Forgotten Gods

A Wind Blown Torment

A Stone Strewn Clash

A Sea Washed Victory

The Tanesh Empire Trilogy

The Glass Magician

The Desert Heart

The Ghost Dog

Huli Intergalactic: Science/Space Fantasy

Origins

The Strawberry Girl

Mysteries

The Purloined Letter Opener

Dancer in Darkness

Trophy Hunters

The Alvin Goodfellow Case Files

The Rabbit Mysteries

The Shredded Veil Mysteries

Mystery, Crime, and Mayhem

AUTHOR NOTES

I've always called myself a *gestalt* writer. When I get the idea for a novel, the entire book arrives at once. I see the first couple of chapters, some parts of the middle, and the ending. I have no idea how to get from one part to the other—that's the fun for me, figuring out the journey from point A to point Z.

While I was writing *The Raven and the Dancing Tiger*, about two-thirds of the way through, I sat down for my evening writing session and wrote two sentences. Suddenly, the entire novel of *The Guardian Hound* appeared, from Lukas' first nightmare to the final battle. There were many things I had to figure out, and the final path is slightly skewed from the original idea. However, it's very close to the original vision, complete, and now, in your hands. I hope you enjoy it!

Although this novel is a sequel to *The Raven and the Dancing Tiger*, it can be read on its own, without reading the first book, as will be the third (and last) novel in the Shadow Wars Trilogy, *War Among the Crocodiles*.

Leah Cutter
July 2013

Acknowledgments

A huge thank you to my first readers, Melissa, Heidi, and Irette. This novel wouldn't be complete without you.

SHADOWS' DOOR

Hans reached for the falling beaker, but it was too late.

Silence filled the lab after the sound of shattered glass, all the scientists at their stations standing perfectly still.

"Just a harmless solvent," Hans called out. No acid to eat through the pristine white countertop, no noxious gas to make them all flee.

However, the scent of the bitter chemicals overwhelmed his sense of smell: He wouldn't be able to scent or track anything for the rest of the day. Luckily, despite being a member of the hound clan, he didn't need to. They lived in a city now, not the country, and he didn't live by his nose, not like Grandpapa had.

"Hansel Von DeWhite!" shouted Master Koenig, striding from the front of the lab to the back corner where Hans had his equipment set up. "What were you thinking? You weren't, of course," Master Koenig blustered on. "You must be more careful."

"It was just a solvent," Hans said weakly as he

gingerly lifted away the pieces of broken glass, putting them into the waste container on the floor.

At least it hadn't splashed and stained Hans' white lab coat. Then he looked more closely and sighed at the splatter marks down his right side. He couldn't afford to get it cleaned so soon; maybe he could wash it in the kitchen sink at the house. After a quick glance all the way down, he breathed a bit easier: He hadn't ruined his shoes. Again.

"Yes, yes, we all know that, we all heard it. But what if your clumsiness had upset someone else's experiment?" Master Koenig paused and pulled his own lab coat tighter across his expansive chest. "I was with poor Wilhelm up front. What if your inexcusable noise had startled him at a crucial part of his process? Hmm?"

"But sir—" Hans started. He should have known better. Once Koenig got going, nothing short of an explosion would derail him.

"Now, I promised your father and his friend that there would be a place for you here at the *Laboratorium*."

Hans didn't groan, though he wanted to. Of course, Master Koenig would bring Hans' father into it. Hans continued to focus on carefully, *slowly*, picking up the shards of glass and disposing of them. *Clink*, *clink* they went as they broke against each other in the container, a soothing sound.

"And you do have a place here for the rest of the year." Master Koenig gave a dramatic pause. "But." He sighed.

Hans found himself holding his breath.

"Only until the end of the year. Then you should seek employment somewhere else."

Hans wasn't surprised. He'd known his position as a lab attendant at the *Laboratorium* was in jeopardy since the first week, when he'd misread the instructions for the experiment he was conducting, verifying a scientist's work, and the resulting acid had poured out over the shining white counters and all over the floor, ruining Hans' shoes as well as the work of several nearby researchers.

Still, Hans turned to Master Koenig and said, "But sir—"

Then he realized his mistake.

He'd just swept his hand through the remaining glass.

"Oh, for heaven's sake, man," Master Koenig said, grabbing Hans' hand and examining it. "You didn't cut anything major," he said sourly.

"I'll get a plaster for it, sir, then finish cleaning up," Hans said grimly. It didn't hurt, not really, but blood was already welling up and trickling across his skin. The salty scent threaded through the bitter chemical smells, faint but reassuring. Maybe his hound nose wasn't completely ruined.

"No. Leave. Get that seen to and don't bother returning until tomorrow."

"But—" Hans deflated at Master Koenig's stern look, the way his arms crossed over his barrel chest. Even the points of his white mustache quivered with disapproval and disappointment.

"Yes, sir," Hans said. He grabbed a towel from the cabinet and wrapped it around his wrist, holding his hand high so the blood flowed into it and didn't drip onto the floor.

Hans pretended to be busy with the towel and his hand as he made his way to the front of the room, past all the other attendants, so he wouldn't hear their sniggers, wouldn't see them laughing.

He still heard their comments in his head—he'd heard them all his life. *Dummer Hans. Gar kein Feingefühl.* Clumsy, awkward, no good Hans.

He'd always been a disappointment, to his father, the hound clan, and himself. He wished more than anything that there was something he could do to prove himself, or, at least, to stop making so many mistakes.

But what?

* * *

Hans hurried down the quiet *Luisen Strasse,* wanting to get back to the house ahead of Father. The row houses that lined the street were half-timbered, old, and falling apart. However, the front gardens they shared were often beautifully tended, full of the first spring daffodils, brilliant purple Prague flowers, and white crocuses.

None of those modern automobiles came down this quiet road; no one living here could afford one. It was one of the reasons why Hans and his father lived in this neighborhood—the smell of the smoke from the engines was noxious and gave them both headaches. Hans didn't know how the humans stood it.

Hans paused when he spied the leather-like leaves and light mauve blossoms of a Lenten rose. If they'd still been living at home, in the country, he would have made a point to tell Grandpapa about the plant. It was a good repellent for insects and rodents.

Grandpapa had taught Hans about all the flowers and plants. He'd been the village *Apotheker,* an old country doctor, not one of those city types with a degree who had no idea what they were doing. He had cases of books with recipes for potions, spells, and charms.

Hans and his father had moved to Hildesheim when Grandpapa had died, selling the old house. Father had always claimed that he had a better nose for numbers than for smelly plants and potions, so they'd come to the nearest large town.

However, they didn't have the family connections or money for Father to become a banker. Instead, he worked as an accountant, drinking more heavily every day and grumbling about other people's mistakes. He was too proud to go to the hound clan to ask for a recommendation for himself: He refused to go begging to the sight hounds. He'd used his own connections—a cousin's friend's brother—to get Hans a job at the *Laboratorium*.

Father and Hans were scent hounds. They would make their own way, as they always had. The court—composed of sight hounds—wanted nothing to do with them.

Hans missed the countryside, missed Grandpapa, missed his cousins and his uncles. He would have missed his mother if he remembered her, but she'd died when he'd been young. He only vaguely knew her scent from the kerchief of hers that Father kept.

Grandpapa would have made a joke about the lab today, telling Hans that he was just a pup who hadn't grown into his paws, giving Hans hope.

Hans paused, looking at the Lenten rose, thinking furiously.

Grandpapa's books had cures for everything: From wasting diseases to falling down sicknesses, from childbirth to passing stones.

Father hadn't liked Grandpapa's work, and he'd insisted that Hans be a true scientist instead of following the old ways. Not that Hans had wanted to become an *Apotheker*—he'd followed Grandpapa around out of love, not because he was any good at herbs and spells.

But maybe, *maybe*, Grandpapa's books held wisdom still, as well as a cure for Hans' current dilemma. There wouldn't be a spell for fixing his life, but if only he could be a little smarter, or braver, or something.

Hans hurried the next few blocks to their house, barely nodding to the two cross old women dressed in black along the way.

The row house had originally been owned by a pair of elderly sisters. Their children rented it out but hadn't bothered to redecorate it. While Hans wasn't a muscle man, the pink, white, and rose paint and wallpaper stifled him. He tried to be out of the house as much as possible. The backyard was acceptable, even though it was just a small patch of grass with roses and more roses growing along the edges.

Luckily, Father's coat didn't hang on the white-painted coatrack next to the door. Hans threw his own suit jacket on the rack, as well as his hat, not bothering to unlace his light, leather "dandy" shoes (oh, how he missed his field boots!). A narrow white staircase went directly from the door on the ground floor to the first floor, the walls decorated with framed, poorly drawn pencil sketches of the town, done by the sisters.

Hans raced up the stairs, then paused in the hallway. The first room was his, smaller and overlooking the street. The second, in the back, larger and more quiet, was Father's. More awful sketches lined the hallway, along with some truly hideous watercolors.

In the center of the hallway, a long black cord hung from the ceiling. It opened the trap-door to the attic. The ladder they used for access rested against the wall, skinny, shaky, and painted white, of course.

Hans had to jump for the cord, but he caught it first try. The smell of old paper, storage straw, and cotton batting drifted down. Hans placed the ladder carefully, making it as stable as he could, before he climbed up.

The attic was directly under the steep-pitched roof. Just the center of the room had a floor, composed of rough planks. The center was the only place Hans could stand straight up. Bare, coarsely hewed beams ran from underneath the small center platform to the edges, where the roof sloped down. A layer of cotton batting, serving as insulation, ran between the beams. The ceiling was bare wood as well, with nails sticking through.

Small windows set high in the peak of the ceiling on either side of the attic gave Hans enough light to see his prize: Grandpapa's old trunk. It was made out of green leather, with wood reinforcing the square bottom, and thin tin strips running across the domed cover.

Hans picked his way through the other trunks containing their winter things: jackets, boots, heavy blankets, and quilts. Hans grunted with pain when he closed his hands around the aged leather handles of Grandpapa's trunk. He ignored his injury and tried to pick up the trunk anyway, then quickly put it back down. It was heavier than it looked and the handles grated against his injured palm.

He looked at the chest, then at the opening to the downstairs. He'd never be able to carry it alone, particularly not injured. With a sigh, Hans sat on the cold, rough boards and opened the trunk.

The musty smell of dried rosemary, bitter geranium, and delicate lavender floated up. On top lay one of Grandpapa's old journals, hand bound in leather.

Hans eagerly opened the book, marveling at the perfectly preserved yellow pansy pressed between the first pages. He recognized this book. Grandpapa had written out his observations and notes on his experiments in it. He had been forever trying new combinations of herbs, flowers, weeds, roots, leaves—anything he found in the woods that he hadn't seen before.

It was a wonderful reminder of Grandpapa, but not the book Hans sought.

A packet of letters neatly tied together with red ribbon came next, followed by two more journals, and Grandpapa's military service record, recorded on heavy red and blue paper.

Finally, at the bottom of the trunk, Hans found the black book he'd been looking for, bound in thick leather with gold embossed writing on the cover: *Heilungen* —Healings.

Hans carefully put the other items back in the trunk, though he hesitated over the journals. Maybe another day he'd come and fetch them. He closed the trunk with regret. It was all he had left of Grandpapa. The ache in Hans' heart made his breath catch. He missed him so much.

Now, he had to make his Grandpapa proud.

With the book firmly wedged under his arm, Hans backed his way down the narrow ladder, breathing a sigh of relief when he reached the ground still holding it. Hans leaned the ladder back against the wall, then pushed at the trapdoor.

It didn't budge.

Hans jumped and pushed it, snapping it shut with a loud bang, making him jump.

"What's that racket?" came Father's voice from downstairs.

"Nothing!" Hans called, hurrying down the hall toward his room. If only he could get the book put away before his father saw it....

Of course, Hans' luck was never that good.

"What are you doing?" Father asked as he topped the stairs, his face as ruddy as if he'd already had three shots of brandy. He wore his office suit, black and formal, though his magenta tie was askew.

"I—" Hans started.

"What is that?" Father asked, striding forward and slipping the book out from under Hans' arm.

This time, Hans didn't try to explain. How could he? He was already such a disappointment to everyone. It had been a stupid idea, to think that one of Grandpapa's potions could help his mess of a life.

"Huh," Father grunted, handing back the book. "You worried about your hand?" he asked, indicating the bandage Hans had wrapped around his palm.

"Yes," Hans said instantly, relieved. He did have a good excuse to have this book! "It was just a solvent beaker, but it burned like acid," he lied.

"You take care of yourself, then," Father said, almost gently. "And don't go burning the neighborhood down with any concoctions you make," he threw over his shoulder as he marched down the hall, going to his room at the back and slamming the door.

Hans took a deep breath. Now, he didn't have to hide anything.

All he had to do was find something that would help.

Curled over the tiny desk in his frilly bedroom, Hans found the spell he wanted: Opening of the Mind.

It was like a *Kraftsuppe*, a "perfected" broth, but instead of fortifying the body, it was meant to heal the mind. It would make him open to possibilities, including the ability to learn what was needed.

However, it wasn't a simple culinary recipe. It contained more ingredients than any meal Hans had ever cooked. Not only infusions, tinctures, and herbal waters made up the potion, but spells needed to be performed both before and after a particular ingredient was added.

Hans had never been that good at magic; many in the hound clan weren't. Luckily, the spells seemed simple enough, and he'd only have to add a few charms to the corners of the kitchen, as well as memorize some blessings to be uttered over the herbs.

After reading through the steps carefully, Hans decided he could do it. It was no different than a complex experiment, like those he'd performed at the lab. He would just have to keep track of each step, and be more diligent than ever.

The biggest problem would be finding all the ingredients. Hans already knew not everything on the list was readily available. Plus, as he'd learned to his chagrin, the country names for things at the market were not the same as the town names. He'd have to figure out how to translate the names of some of the rarer herbs to something the people here would understand.

Hans sat back on the tiny chair and sighed, disappointed. He'd wanted to find a spell that he could use tonight, which would change Master Koenig's mind about him so it would be easier when he went back to the *Laboratorium* tomorrow. He'd have to explain it to Father, somehow, as well, when he started making potions.

But Hans was determined. He'd be ready by the end of summer. Time enough to prove to Master Koenig, his father, even the hound clan, that he could be something more than a clumsy oaf.

Hans looked longingly at the rabbits hanging at the butcher's at the market, but they couldn't afford such luxuries here. Rabbits hadn't been a luxury at home: He'd hunted many himself, his hound soul tracking the scent through fields and woods.

For a moment, Hans' felt his hound soul stirring. It didn't wake as often in Hildesheim as it had in the country. It nosed up to him, regarding him with pleading basset-hound eyes.

He would have to transform in the next week or so. They needed a run.

Homesickness washed over Hans. Maybe for the *Silvester* holidays he could go and visit his cousins, and spend a week running in the fields and woods.

Hans shook himself. He couldn't afford to daydream, not here, not now, with his hound soul so close. He bought what he could, a few cast-off bits of chicken, enough for a stew.

Then Hans made his way over to the northeast corner of the market, where the old women in black dresses and embroidered kerchiefs held court. They came to market with goods they'd made: Pickled onions and carrots, newly spun wool and thick sweaters, berry preserves and honey.

Hans had discovered them early in his search for ingredients. They'd been a gold mine of information as well.

Old Engel waved to Hans as he approached. Her plump cheeks were rosy, and curls of her iron gray hair stuck out from underneath her black kerchief. Her eyes were a watery blue, faded as if they'd stared at the sun too long, in her weathered, wrinkled, browned face. "Eh, got a present for you," she said, pointing behind her seat.

Hans smiled. Old Engel wasn't as disabled as she

pretended to be: He'd seen her stand quick enough when a bee came buzzing. But he indulged her and walked behind her seat. A large burlap sack sat on the ground. Hans picked it up and walked back around.

"What is it?" he asked as he opened it. It was full of pungent leaves, green but starting to wither.

"Thorn apple," Old Engel said.

"Really?" Hans asked, looking back at her, amazed. He couldn't believe it. It was only midsummer! Yet now he had all the ingredients he needed to create his potion and cast his spells.

"Farmer Thalberg had a run of bad luck, brought in some sheep to be slaughtered, and that as well," she said, nodding. "Now, you know to be careful with those, eh?"

"Yes, I will. Thank you, Grandmother," Hans said, using the honorific she'd gifted him with.

"I know you're a good lad, but those are powerful strong," Old Engel insisted. "You test them out first, you hear me?"

"I will. I will!" Hans promised. He already had the herbals waters prepared. If he could get the first batch of these leaves soaking tonight, it would only be a day, maybe two, before he could finish.

"Thank you, so much," Hans said, gladly counting out the coins into her calloused hand.

"Now, before you go, I want you to meet my granddaughter. Petra. Petra! Come here."

Hans stood with the sack clutched to his chest, his cheeks flaming.

Women his own age confused him, with their soft curves and sharp tongues. He was never certain how to talk to one.

Petra had a laughing smile, beautiful blond curls sticking out from the edges of her kerchief, and clear blue eyes. She didn't wear black, but a coarse brown apron over her old-fashioned, pale blue blouse and skirt. She curtsied as she held out her hand for Hans.

Hans shifted the bag to his right arm, then realized his mistake and shifted it to his left so he could hold out the appropriate hand. "Very nice to make your acquaintance," he said, stumbling over the words.

"The pleasure is mine," Petra replied. "Grandmama said you were making a potion."

"My grandpapa was an *Apotheker*," Hans explained. He'd given this reason a lot. "I'm just experimenting with some of his recipes. I work in the *Laboratorium*."

"How exciting!" Petra said with another charming smile.

After a few moments of awkward silence, Hans said, "I, uhm, must go now. Nice to meet you."

"You'll have to tell us how the experiment went," Petra replied.

"And be careful!" Old Engel called out, always having to get in the last word.

Hans found it appropriate that the night he was finally ready to cast the final spells was *Johannisfest*, Midsummer's Eve.

If they'd still been in the countryside, all his relatives would have gathered in the village square that night for a bonfire, though several families would also have their own celebrations on their farms. They would have ritually sacrificed dried hops to clear away any bad spirits. After the ceremonies, the teenaged boys would take turns daring each other to jump over the flames from farther and farther away.

Here, in Hildesheim, there was only the one big bonfire in the market. However, they also had fireworks.

Hans was disappointed that he'd miss those, but he really wanted to finish his spell. He'd taken to trying little spells, easy things from Grandpapa's books, slaving away at the hot wood-burning stove. He'd explained it to Father as practice for the lab, experiments with precise measurements and exact timing.

Father had been pleased that Hans was finally showing such an interest. And Master Koenig hadn't threatened to send him home early again, though Hans suspected that if this spell didn't work, come the end of the year he would be out of the *Laboratorium*.

Hans hated it all. He hated the hot stove and had burned himself frequently. While Grandpapa's concoctions had been pungent, Hans' frequently reeked. He'd never been good at magic, but he worked at it, determined to prove himself.

Father left to go celebrate with the rest of the town—and to drink himself into unconsciousness, Hans suspected. So Hans worked in an empty house that night.

Hans put on his white lab coat over his navy blue work shirt. He was already sweating in the tiny kitchen, but he wanted some protection from the splatters. The single tiny window looked out over the backyard and their square of greenery, but it didn't provide much fresh air. A white-painted kitchen table sat in the center of the room, its top covered with the various potions, herbs, and charms Hans had already prepared. In the corner was a stained copper sink, with a crotchety hand pump for bringing up water.

A black cast-iron stove hulked against one wall, already filled with burning firewood. Hans had two pots boiling on top, ready for the final herbs.

After sharpening his knives with a whetstone, Hans

started cutting up the peppermint, mugwort, and valerian. The cool scents mingled and reminded him of Grandpapa. Hans used the plain gray stone mortar and pestle to grind up the star anise and cloves, and to crush the periwinkle petals.

Hans moved as slowly and methodically as he could, going back to check the recipe more than once. He found himself rushing, though. Finally, the night was here when he could *do* something about his life. If this spell worked, his whole life could be different.

The first step of the preparation for the thorn apple leaves was already complete. Hans had pounded them with the mortar and pestle, covered them with water and lard, put them into an old earthenware pot, then let them sit for a day. When he lifted off the lid, he had to take a step back as the astringent, musty smell came rolling out.

Old Engel had been right. They were powerful. But Grandpapa had said two cups of the leaves, so that's what Hans used. He carefully lifted the pot off the table and set it on the stove. When the lard melted, Hans stirred it, not letting it boil. Once all the leaves were softened, he strained the liquid, carefully measuring out two cups of it, then adding fresh herbs to the liquid.

Now, for the final steps. Hans reheated the other potions, muttering more than one spell as he cooked and combined ingredients, ending with the liquid from the thorn apples.

Twilight had come and gone, and true night was setting in by the time Hans was ready. The *Kraftsuppe* smelled sour and bitter. He curled his lips back as he lifted it, stopping himself from taking a step away from it.

Even his hound soul wasn't sure this was a good idea.

Hans put down the bowl and walked over the window, looking out over what he could see of the garden, his hound soul looming closer. They both missed the country, so much.

He could never tell Father, but if they'd stayed, he would have applied as a teacher's aid. Not for *Gymnasium*, no, but for the little ones. In his dreams, Hans saw himself leading them through the green grass near the one-room school, a daisy chain of little lights, laughing at his clumsiness and marveling at how many things he could smell.

But Father never would have allowed it. Playing with children all day wasn't a worthwhile occupation for someone of the hound clan.

With a sigh, Hans turned from the window, walked back to the table, and lifted the bowl. With his hound soul at his side, he opened his mouth and poured down the potion.

The vile, foul potion gushed over his tongue, making him gag. It stank worse than anything Hans had ever smelled before, even the bloated duck corpse he'd found in the marshes. He forced himself to swallow, coughing, his eyes watering. Then he drank some more. His hands shook with the effort of keeping the revolting liquid down, but Hans persisted.

Before Hans could fetch himself a glass of water to wash out the taste of burnt hair and rancid oil, the world tilted to the side. Hans felt drunk all at once.

This wasn't right. According to Grandpapa's notes, a slow tide of awareness should rise through him.

What had he done wrong?

Hans raced to the open book, forcing his eyes to focus.

He'd done everything right. Made all the secondary potions correct. Then he'd mixed—

Hans sighed. He'd reversed the amounts of two of the

potions, and had ended up doubling the amount of the thorn apple liquid.

Darkness approached from all sides. Hans whined, but it was too late.

The door opened, and Hans fell through.

Hans stood under a gray cloud-filled sky. An angry sun burned at the horizon. Everything smelled dead, like dust from an ancient tomb. Nothing grew here as far as he could see in any direction—the land ran flat to the horizon, full of ashes.

Yet Hans knew he wasn't alone. Something pressed at him, first from one side, then the other. He couldn't see what it was, but he knew something was there.

When Hans poked at his hound soul, he screamed, a thin call that bled quickly away.

His hound soul was wreathed in shadows, black formless things that surrounded the basset hound, stinging his sensitive nose and pricking his shoulder, back, paws —everywhere.

"Stop!" Hans called, but there was nothing to hear him.

Now, shadows formed around Hans as well. Or maybe they'd been there all along, and only now could he see them, give them a name.

They wanted in. They wanted him. They wanted his life, his breath, his vision.

And they wanted out.

The shadows were trapped here, on this dead planet, a planet they'd killed.

They were parasites, with no life of their own. They needed the lives of others so they could continue to exist. They were dying, here, starting to eat one another.

They showed Hans the magic he'd be able to do with their help, such as confusing the minds of people like Master Koenig, so he'd always be able to stay in the *Laboratorium*. Father would be proud of Hans, and their family would be recognized, finally, by the sight hounds in the court. They showed him a charm he could imbue with a wisp of shadow so he could have any girl he wanted.

On and on came their honeyed promises as they stroked him, petting his hound soul now. Hans let himself be lulled with the tales and images—Father standing beside him as he worked, beaming with pride. Maybe even a medal or two for things he'd discovered through his experiments, properties and chemicals the shadows showed him.

Hans might have listened to them, and maybe given them a little of his own life essence. As far as he could tell, their words were absolutely true: These weren't empty promises. They could do everything they claimed, could help him in all these ways.

But the cost was too high. It wasn't his life they wanted, but that of his hound soul's.

Even giving away just a little would diminish both his hound soul and his own.

His hound soul begged him to run away from the pain and hurt, as far and as fast as they could.

Father might call Hans a disgrace to the hound clan, but he trusted his hound soul to do the right thing, to warn him of the danger.

The shadows drew back.

Hans and his hound soul stood firm. They would not help the shadows. Hans wouldn't hurt his hound soul that way.

The shadows attacked again, harder, trying to force their way through skin and fur, into blood and bone. They leached his life and energy by wrapping tightly around him.

Exhaustion slammed into Hans. He suddenly felt older than his twenty-two years. He hunkered over, wrapping his arms over his chest.

He just had to endure. The spell wouldn't last.

The potion would wear off at some point, and Hans knew he'd wake up, probably on the floor of the kitchen, with a sour head and a rumbly stomach.

Then his hound soul howled, and kept howling.

Hans tried to fight the shadows. But how could he fight something that had no form? He couldn't grasp them, pull them away, or even slam his fists into them. He kept telling the baying hound that it would be all right. He curled up around his hound soul, trying to comfort him, but the shadows continued their attack, their promises and threats buzzing like gnats, then bees, then loud freight trains through Hans' mind.

What if Hans just helped them a little? It wouldn't have to be much. Just give them a tiny corner of his magic. He wasn't using it all anyway. A single thread. They'd help him prove the worth of all scent hounds.

Hans resisted, but he felt himself weakening.

The shadows promised it would be something that only the scent hounds could do—those snooty sight hounds at the court would never be able to see the shadows, or find them, or use them in their magic.

Then Hans grew firm again. No. He and his hound soul could endure this. They had to, despite how his heart broke over the howls of his hound soul. Everything hurt, so much, and he was already so weak and tired.

The shadows renewed their attack with vigor, pushing, prodding, pinching and scratching—a thousand ants biting all at once—trying to get a foothold, to make either Hans or his hound soul accept them.

But something was different. When Hans opened his eyes and looked up, he realized he was floating up and away from the dead earth, into a velvet black night, stars like a ribbon of lights twining around him.

Just above Hans' head stood a doorway, with warm fire glow pouring from it.

The shadows now pushed down on Hans, trying to stop him from reaching the doorway.

Exhaustion overwhelmed Hans. He struggled to raise his arm, to break through the bonds the shadows had wrapped across his chest that were squeezing the breath from him.

His hound soul bayed, louder now, more urgent.

Hans didn't dare look. He kicked his legs as if he were swimming, trying to propel himself toward the light.

Take us with you, the shadows pleaded, the first real words they'd used. *Let us live. We will make you rich and powerful and loved and admired and respected and…*

Hans reached the doorway and shoved himself through in one swift motion.

A thread of shadow remained curled around his ankle. Hans slammed the door shut with a thunderous *crack*, catching the tail of the shadow in the door.

When he looked again, the shadow was gone.

Another *crack* rolled through the space, shattering the light and the illusion.

Hans found himself lying on the kitchen floor, the taste of rotten leather in his mouth, his head pounding and his stomach queasy.

A third *crack* echoed through the room. Hans jumped up and looked around the messy kitchen.

Bright light reflected through the window. The fireworks exploded over town square.

Belatedly, Hans reached out to check on his hound soul, who mournfully snuffled up to him, shaken and sore, his coat ruffled, but unhurt.

Hans couldn't tell if his hound soul wasn't as full as it had once been. He also didn't like the accusing look in the hound's eyes.

"Everything will be all right," Hans said. He'd make sure that it was all fine. They'd go out for more runs, as a way to make it up to his hound soul.

He creakily moved around the kitchen, as if he'd suddenly grown as old as Grandpapa when he'd died. Without hesitation, he threw out the rest of the potion. Then he lit tapers and checked every corner, to make sure no shadows lurked there or pressed against the windows from outside.

Hans had shut the door on them before they'd come through. He'd escaped.

Except…

Hans' hound soul stared at him sometimes, accusing and hurt, though Hans hadn't done anything to hurt it.

While Hans wasn't doing anything differently at the *Laboratorium*, Master Koenig didn't yell at him, even when Hans dropped something. "Ah well," Master Koenig would sigh. "Accidents happen." And Master Koenig started talking about what they'd do together in the new year.

When Hans met Petra again in the market, he suddenly remembered an old charm he could use to help him. It was nothing, really. Just something to nudge her along, make her like him more.

The charm turned out to be easy to make, easier than

any charm Hans had ever made before. By the end of the year, Hans and Petra were married.

It wasn't until Hans went searching back through Grandpapa's books, looking for something to ease the birth of their first child, that he went looking for that charm.

He never found it. He'd known that spell, but he didn't remember how he'd learned it.

Hans never created a charm for his wife, and never taught his child how to create them.

He never used magic again, for the rest of his days.

GERMANY, THIRTEEN YEARS AGO

LUKAS

Lukas was five when he began dreaming about the end of the world.

The first dream started in the garden just behind the castle, the one with the squares of different grasses locked between squares of cold hard rock.

Like the rest of the hound clan, Lukas loved the different scents—American blue grass, grass from high in the Alps, and even African plain grass. He sent his toy soldiers marching between the rough, tall blades so he could skootch down and get his face close to the earth and sniff hard.

He knew he couldn't really smell Africa. He'd been told his human senses couldn't match his hound senses. He didn't know just how different they were, though, since his hound soul hadn't risen yet. He still imagined he could smell the tangy marker of lions and the thin traces of water, and feel the hot sun beating down on him.

In the dream, it had started sunny, and Lukas had played in the garden with his soldiers. When it suddenly grew darker, he looked up, surprised. Was it time to go in?

But it wasn't evening, and a cloud hadn't covered the sun.

Instead, dark, frightening shadows filled the sky. They filtered out the light, turning it blue-gray and lifeless, taking the joy out of the day.

Another shadow stood in the gate to the garden, boiling with fury. The ivy on either side curled away from it, sickened and dying. The stone beneath it grew black, and Lukas knew that just by stepping on it, he would break it.

The stench of the shadows rolled out to him. They smelled like death, like rotting mice in the woods and apples soured on the branches, combined with the dry dust smell of crumbling bricks.

Lukas froze, afraid that if he moved, he'd become the shadow's prey. He crouched, terrified, as the shadow in the garden spread. It destroyed all the plants it touched: the rosemary the cooks used with his favorite potatoes, the slim maple with the red leaves that Mama liked, even the large oak that stood guard at the far corner, near the woods.

Suddenly, Lukas realized that the shadows were surrounding him. If he didn't run soon, they'd come and get him.

There was still an opening in the far part of the garden, opposite the woods. Maybe he could run, faster than he'd ever run before, and escape.

"Lukas!"

Greta, his older sister, called him from the long balcony on the second floor of the castle.

"Lukas! Come inside!" she demanded, as bossy as ever.

"Greta! Look out!" Lukas cried.

But it was too late. The shadows took her.

Greta's eyes grew glassy and her skin changed, becoming as pale and white as the formal plates in the dining room that Lukas was always afraid of scratching. Her golden hair curled perfectly around her face, and her clothes stiffened, like they were brand new.

She'd changed into a doll.

"Lukas!" she called again, her voice now hollow and mechanical.

Lukas wanted to go to her, to free her, but it was too late. The shadows were upon him, eating him all up, stealing his hound soul, until he was as black as they were, inside and out, and as aged and cracked as the oldest parts of the castle. Once they finished with him, they'd move on to Da and Mama and everyone in the whole world.

With a start, Lukas sat up, still choking back his scream. He was safe, in bed, in his room.

Oma, his grandmother, sat on a chair beside his bed, watching with bright eyes.

Lukas launched himself at her, wrapping his arms around her, grateful for how warm and solid she felt.

He didn't cry. Instead, he shook with fear. The shadows had been so *real*. They'd taken over everything, sucking the life out of the planet.

When Lukas stopped shaking, he pulled back, suddenly aware of how dark his bedroom was. He glanced around. His bed was snug up into the corner, the door opposite. At the foot stood an old, scarred desk that had been his father's and his grandfather's, where he sat on a booster chair and did his school work. Against the far wall stood a huge dresser that held his clothes, and next to that, a hamper for his toys.

Where shadows hiding inside it? Or layered between his formal shirts?

Maybe they hid under the bed, ready to snake around the legs of his grandmother?

Lukas pulled back further, bringing his knees up and wrapping his arms around them, pressing them hard against his chest.

"What did you dream of?" Oma asked. She hitched her light green robe tighter across her chest. It had felt soft and warm when Lukas had held her.

But she didn't reach for him now.

"Shadows," Lukas whispered, afraid to even name them.

"Yes," Oma said.

Lukas looked at the corner behind his desk. Could shadows boil there? Then toward the closed door. What if they waited for him, just outside?

Oma smacked his arm lightly, saying, "Stop that."

Lukas jumped, startled.

"Think, boy. Use your senses. Can you smell the shadows in here?"

Lukas paused. What had the shadows smelled like? Then it came to him. It had been a wet smell, like ashes grown moldy.

After taking a deep breath, Lukas shook his head, relaxing a little. "No, ma'am."

"Trust your nose. That's the one true test. Your eyes can be fooled."

Lukas blinked, surprised at that. Da was a sight hound. Surely he wouldn't be fooled?

Abruptly, Oma stood and turned to go.

"Wait!" Lukas called, his panic rising. "Don't leave."

Oma stopped and turned back. "I'm sorry," she said, sounding sad. She came back and sat down on the chair, taking his hand and holding it in her warm, soft ones. "I've lived with the shadows for so long, I forget what they're truly like, how frightening they can be."

"What are they?" Lukas asked, wishing Oma would sit beside him on the bed and hold him, but not sure if he could ask or if he needed to be a big boy.

"They're the dark part of hound magic," she replied. "Forever tied to us through our magical gifts."

"I don't understand," Lukas complained. How could those, those *things*, be part of him? Then he yawned. Despite the terror and the blackness of the shadows, he still felt tired.

"No one understands," Oma said. "That's why you can't say anything about your dreams. It would just upset your da. All right?"

"Okay," Lukas said, though he didn't really understand.

"This is our secret," Oma said seriously. "And you're a big enough boy that you can keep such an important secret, right? Just like you keep the secret of being a member of the hound clan. If you can't keep the secret of the shadows, though, that's okay. That just means you aren't old enough yet."

"I'm big enough," Lukas complained. "I won't tell anyone," he promised. And he wouldn't. Then he couldn't help himself: He yawned again.

Oma reached up with her other hand to smooth back his black curls. "Why don't you lie back down and I'll sing you a lullaby?"

Lukas snuggled under the covers again but he never let go of his grandmother's hand.

Oma sang softly, almost a whisper, about a faithful hound guarding his knight long into the evening after a battle. The guardian hound stayed true to his duty, and in the morning, light came back to the world and hound's knight was able to go to heaven.

Lukas dreamed of being the hound to the mysterious knight, walking in the sunlight through tall, golden grass, bounding at his side. They were celebrating, he knew, the slaying of the shadows. The knight's armor was bashed in, tarnished, but strong; the chest plate solid, the chainmail on his arms moving smoothly.

Though Lukas couldn't see the knight's face behind his great helmet that had only a slit for eyes, he knew his knight's scent. Oma whispered again that it was the one true thing, so he concentrated on that complicated odor, made up of warm bird feathers, the cool scale of armor, a wild-yet-steadfast heart, and other things Lukas could only guess at.

When the morning came, Lukas barely remembered the shadows, until they came the next night to haunt him.

But the knight—Lukas would never forget that scent, and would forever be seeking it.

"I dreamed of the shadows again last night," Lukas told everyone at breakfast a week later. He knew he was supposed to keep it a secret, but it was growing too big inside. He had to tell someone. Because they were all from the hound clan, they all shared that secret. This one was just his alone.

All of them—Mama, Da, Greta, and Oma—were gathered around one end of the long dining table that was usually reserved for formal dinners, sitting on heavy oak furniture and using the thin white plates circled in gold that Lukas was so afraid he'd break. The breakfast nook was being painted so they'd eaten all their meals here for the last two days.

"Shadows?" Da asked, folding down the top of the report he was reading to look directly at Lukas. He had his silver reading glasses on and was already dressed for the court in a dark suit and light blue tie. Greta and Mama stayed absorbed in the papers they read.

"Your grandmother always used to talk about the shadows," Da added, turning his piercing blue gaze to Oma.

Did Lukas look like that sometimes? Was his stare so direct? Everyone always said he had the same eyes as his da.

"No such thing," Oma said with a decisive sniff, not turning her attention away from her porridge.

"But—" Lukas started.

"You ever seen the shadows?" Oma shot back at Da.

"No," Da replied, shaking his head. "I haven't."

Lukas sat back in his chair and looked at the adults. Greta still hadn't looked up, but he could tell she was listening.

Da was the best sight hound of all the clan—it was why he was king, or at least that's what he'd told Lukas. Sometimes the title was inherited from father to son, but the court ministers didn't always choose an heir from the same family. There was no guarantee that the Metzler family would continue on as kings.

If Da couldn't see the shadows, maybe they didn't exist. Maybe they were only in Lukas' dreams.

But Oma had said they came from the dark side of hound magic. That made them sound real, and not just nightmares.

Lukas opened his mouth to ask again, then shut it when Oma glared at him.

She'd told him not to say anything. Told him that only a big boy would be able to keep the secret. That it was as big a secret as being in the hound clan.

Lukas wanted to be a big boy. He looked from Da, to Mama, to Greta, and then out beyond, to the far hall where he heard servants talking.

They couldn't help him with the shadows. Just like in his dreams, he was all alone.

Then Lukas picked up his spoon again, the silver cold and heavy in his hand, determined to eat and act like everything was normal, like he didn't have the hugest secret in the whole world weighing his chest down.

L ukas tried to sit still in the quiet classroom. Greta had gone to study history with her tutor while Lukas struggled with his letters. Normally, they weren't so difficult, but his fingers ached from holding his pencil, and his hand couldn't hold it steady, so instead of his words marching straight up and down, they fell down again and again.

Outside, it was high summer. The sun called to Lukas, as did the all the scents of the woods, the small chipmunks and the brave foxes, the steady trees and the cool streams.

The classroom smelled stale, too small and boxed in. The chalk and slate smells irritated him, as did the pulpy paper in his hand.

As another letter skittered away, Lukas swept his book, paper, and pencil box to the floor in frustration. "I can't stay here!" he said, standing.

Then he slapped both his hands over his mouth. What was wrong with him? He'd never said anything out loud like that before.

But he couldn't, he just *couldn't* sit in here anymore. Normally, he loved this classroom: it was full of books about soldiers and brave hounds, and his desk has always been a haven from the shadows who'd haunted him since that spring.

However, Felix, his tutor, didn't punish Lukas. Instead, he said, "I think we've done enough for today."

Lukas immediately jerked his gaze to the window. He was going out to the garden, then into the woods, and run and run and *run*.

"Can you stay here for just one more minute, while I get Tilgard?" Felix asked.

Lukas forced himself back into the classroom. The hound master? Why did he need to wait for *him*, when he could run…

Oh.

"The change?" Lukas breathed out. Was it that time? Was he about to change into his hound form for the first time? Was that why he couldn't sit still anymore?

"I would say soon," Felix replied.

Could he wait? Lukas rocked back and forth, his chest expanding, then contracting, already feeling the rhythm of a running as a hound at full sprint. "Hurry," he whispered, unable to say more.

Lukas tilted his head back, nose high, as scents poured in, traces he'd never noticed before: the eggs and honeydew Felix had had for breakfast; the lavender lotion Oma had used before she'd visited the classroom, late, the night before; and the twisted grass and twine charm that hung in the corner with its unexpected magic.

Tilgard's scent rolled before him, clean lemongrass soap mingled with the rabbit fur he always wore tied to his belt and the bacon treats he kept in his pocket.

Lukas whined when he saw the hound master, begging him to *hurry*. Lukas couldn't hold on much longer.

Tilgard hurried to his side, dropping to his knees in front of Lukas. "Sudden one, eh? You're young, too. Well, that's not unknown," he said brusquely. He spread his hands wide and placed them around Lukas' head, pressing in slightly.

Tension bled out of Lukas. He suddenly felt secure. He whined again as his head strained forward, as if he could help push his snout out.

"Open your mouth," Tilgard instructed.

Lukas did. He was panting, his tongue long and alive, drawing in more scents, like the fish the cooks were making in the kitchen; Greta pretending to work in her classroom but really reading some book with modern paper; Oma in her study, hidden there by magic and shadows…

Lukas shook his head, wanting to break free.

Tilgard held on tighter. "Almost there, son. Focus on the gardens."

Outside! Lukas jerked his head out of Tilgard's hands and looked out the window. He barked and shivered, thinking about how he could *run* now, really truly run, finally, if only he could get free.

Lukas shook himself again, finally shaking himself completely loose.

It was no longer his body. He wasn't connected to it at all.

Lukas retreated into black nothingness and curled in on himself. It was worse than the shadows—just endless darkness as far as all his senses could tell.

Then his hound soul rose.

Suddenly, Lukas was no longer alone in the dark or

afraid. Another soul curled in around his, warm and steady.

Hamlin.

Lukas was aware enough to know that not all hounds had a human name. For most, it was just a sense, a presence that was composed of odor and sight. (Not that the hound didn't have a name for himself, but that was a dog name, and not a human one.)

Hamlin had both a presence and a scent, the combined smells of wool warmed by the fire and the hard steel of a soldier's bayonet, as well as musty hound. He wasn't a puppy, or even a young dog. Hamlin already knew duty.

His job was to guard.

Lukas was surprised at how protective Hamlin was. No one would harm Lukas while Hamlin was there. Not even the shadows.

Lukas rolled back in the warm comforting darkness of Hamlin's soul, happy to let go of his fear. He felt a tiny thread of disappointment—not from Hamlin, no, but from the man with the rabbit fur.

Did he really expect either Hamlin or Lukas to pay him any heed?

Neither of them recognized his authority. He was not their master nor the leader of their pack.

Run? Lukas asked.

Faster than any others, Hamlin promised, and soon they shared the wind on their face as he galloped under the trees and across the fields.

Almost fast enough to outrun the shadows.

When Lukas came back to himself late that evening, he was crouching, naked, in the gardens near the woods. The ground felt solid and cool under his toes. The air carried the scent of sunset, while the sky blazed orange and pink.

Felix carried the traditional cloak with him, rich red wool lined with the softest rabbit fur. It marked that Lukas had made the change and was a full member of the hound clan.

Though Lukas understood now that his human sense of smell would never match Hamlin's, he could still tell something was wrong.

Felix smelled nervous. And where was Tilgard? Why wasn't he here, bearing the cloak?

"Welcome back, Lukas," Felix said, standing, unfurling the cloak for Lukas to step into.

Lukas slipped on the unfamiliar robe, scenting that many had worn it before him.

Felix asked the traditional words of greeting: "Did you have a successful hunt?"

How should Lukas answer? Hamlin hadn't hunted anything, or chased rabbits or squirrels. Instead, he'd checked the perimeter. Lukas now knew every wall, every gate, every weakness and strength in their defenses.

Hounds didn't all hunt first thing—it was acceptable to just run. But that didn't feel right. Finding all the walls around the woods, even the hidden ones, was kind of a hunt, wasn't it?

So Lukas said, "Yes, we did." It wasn't exactly what they'd done, but none of the traditional responses fit.

"We should go inside now," Felix said.

"Yes!" Lukas said eagerly. "I must go present myself to the court."

Felix shook his head as they started walking back toward the castle. "Tomorrow."

"It's custom—"

"Yes. But you are a prince."

Lukas didn't think that was right; however, surely his tutor knew best. "What breed am I?" he asked. He was sure he was some type of sight hound—Da was a sight hound. All the important ministers at the court were sight hounds. Chances were he was a sight hound, too.

However, that didn't feel right. It was part of Hamlin, but not all.

"We want to verify that," Felix said smoothly. "Don't want to get something as important as that wrong," he added with a wink. "There's why I'm here, and not Tilgard."

Lukas nodded solemnly, reassured, despite how worried Felix smelled. Even if Lukas wasn't pure sight hound, he was still a prince. He'd prove it later, in a couple of years, by changing into different types of hounds. He knew he could, and Hamlin assured him that they would.

The cold stone of the entrance way shot though Lukas' bare feet, and he pulled the robe tighter around him. When the first servant saw him and bowed, Lukas grinned and forgot how he was naked under the cloak, how it tickled his bare skin, how easy it would be to get lost in all the new smells.

Instead, Lukas stood taller, proud to be a full member of the hound clan.

This was surely the happiest day of his life.

Oma waited for Lukas in his room, of course, when he came back from his first transformation. She dismissed Felix abruptly, shutting the door in his face.

Though the room felt smaller suddenly, Lukas stood as still as a point dog while Oma circled him. He wished he had more clothes on than just the red robe.

"Those fools don't know what breed you are," she hissed at him. "Only I do."

Her laughter sent chills down Lukas' spine.

Hamlin drew near, wary and on guard.

Lukas turned to face his grandmother, feeling brave, daring to ask, "What breed am I, then?"

"You're a guardian hound," Oma told him. "You're as fast as a sight hound, with eyes as good as theirs, despite their blue color. Your coat is brindle, almost tiger-striped, gray and brown. Your nose picks up trails like a scent hound. But your rear quarters and canines confuse them — they're pure guardian — making you stronger than you seem."

"A guardian hound," Lukas said, delighted.

Guard, Hamlin agreed. *And fight.*

Lukas was surprised at how close Hamlin stayed. Most hound souls only came at the bidding of their human soul. They only rose on their own when the human had stayed in control for too long; the hound clan needed to transform regularly, at least once a month. A hound soul also rose in times of great need. But Lukas was safe here, in his room, with just his grandmother.

Unless—

"What do you mean, only you know what I am?" Lukas asked, afraid of the answer.

Oma looked at him, then shook her gray curls. "You must stay hidden—stay safe—until it's time. The court can't know your breed. You can't tell them. And neither will I."

"No," Lukas said. A begging whine crept in his voice. "Not another secret." Carrying his terror of the shadows alone was hard enough. It had only been since spring, but it felt like a lifetime to him. Now he had to hide what breed he was? Lukas started to cry. "No!" he wailed loudly. It was too much.

Hamlin rose all the way and Lukas heard himself snarling at his grandmother.

It wasn't a sound he'd heard before. Not even the largest soldier hounds sounded like that, with that deep rumble.

Some part of Lukas recognized where it came from: A sound from before hounds were civilized, before they'd grown tame.

He snarled again like a giant wolf, then he nudged Hamlin to the side.

Let me, he said gently, his tears forgotten.

Only then did he realize Oma hadn't moved. She'd gone as still as a field mouse.

"You are a wonder," she whispered, her eyes still bright with fear. "No matter what anyone else ever says. You are more than I ever dreamed for. Remember that. You are perfect, a marvel that the fools will never recognize."

"I will," Lukas promised, swallowing down the knot that still lingered in his throat. "*We* will," he added. He didn't want to accept the burden of another secret, but he knew he had to.

He also already knew what the next day would be like, and cringed, wanting to wail and stomp the ground, but he only wrapped his arms tightly across his chest and shivered.

The crier would only use Lukas' name to announce him to the court, and not include any lineage or breed, since they didn't know.

All the ministers would wonder and whisper. They'd always question him, his loyalty, his heritage. He'd never follow in Da's footsteps; the ministers would never let him be king, no matter how brave or strong or smart he was.

When Lukas turned seven, two years in the future, he'd formally prove to them he was a prince. Only royalty could take on other hound forms.

It would never be enough.

However, Hamlin would be there, and together, they would endure.

CHINA, 1940S TO PRESENT

MEI LING

Mei Ling didn't like the trader Mama and Papa invited into their little village hut. He smelled too much of *bailandi*—sour peach brandy—and his crooked smile never met his eyes.

But the last war had been hard, and the next one was already coming. Chairman Mao had just risen to power. He promised reforms and a great revolution, but according to Grandmama, nothing would ever change in their small village, and the peasants and farmers just needed to accept their fate.

So Mei Ling didn't say anything about the trader or his filthy shirt, though she could see the crawling lice from where she sat. That would have been disrespectful, and she'd been beaten enough to have finally learned that.

Mama and Papa had begged, borrowed, and gone into debt to lay a feast before the trader, trying to drive up their asking price for Mei Ling. On the pretty red and gold hunk of cloth (that they'd borrowed from Aunty Li) lay steamed bamboo leaves wrapped around rice and thick pork sausages, a huge wooden bowl (also from Aunty Li) filled with imported sweet cherries, and a pot full of fatty duck soup with new onions.

Mei Ling sat in the corner of the front room, reminding herself to keep her eyes on the dirt floor and not stare too much like Papa always accused her of doing. She wanted to bring good luck and fortune to the family, and not be the bad luck daughter Grandmama had always declared her to be. Her four sisters sat behind the wall in the other room of their hut, probably huddled together on the shelf bed that Mama and Papa slept on while the five of them slept on the floor.

At least the dress Mei Ling wore was pretty, made from sturdy flax and dyed a deep purple. It wasn't new, of course—she had four older sisters. But it was clean, and Mama had spent many nights fixing it so it fit well.

At the end of the meal, long after even the crumbs had been cleared away and the good tea had been served on borrowed china, the adults finally got down to business.

The trader promised Mei Ling's parents that she would have fine robes and plenty of food for the rest of her life, if they sold her to him. He promised to keep her away from the new war, the one brewing with Korea.

Mei Ling knew he lied. She'd work harder than all of them did now, probably to her death, like Xi Ban in the story of the ungrateful daughter. She'd clean floors in great houses only if she was lucky.

While Mei Ling wanted to live, she also knew that the gods had long ago set the path she was to walk along. Prayer and sacrifice might alter the course a little, but her fate, in many ways, was already written in stone.

However, Mama and Papa didn't know how sharp Mei Ling's teeth grew at night.

Grandmama had always declared that Mei Ling had evil in her soul.

Mei Ling felt like she had a twin swimming inside her, closer now than ever before.

In a little while, her other soul would rise.

Then the trader would have to beware.

———

Mei Ling knelt still and unmoving in the line with the other girls. The floor of the dingy warehouse was hard, cold concrete, and dust lay thick on the wooden shelves behind them. Electric lights buzzed far above them —the first Mei Ling had seen. She'd also used a toilet for the first time, and had been unashamed when the trader had had to show her how it worked.

The other girls also sat unmoving; however, many of them smelled like sweet poppies and their eyes were hazy.

Mei Ling had never cried or tried to run away. She'd always tried to do what the trader had said, so she sat with her senses still clear. The trader hadn't tried anything with her either; maybe he sensed her twin, or her bad luck.

Fear ran through Mei Ling as she knelt, but she trembled only a little, and only when no one was looking.

The trader had left her at the warehouse, and she'd seen more money change hands. That was all right, though. Mei Ling, and her twin, would always remember his scent. She would find him again later, when she was grown and her teeth were even sharper.

Half a dozen men and women, dressed in fine silk robes of brown, red, and blue, walked up and down the line. Though they looked closely at the girls next to Mei Ling, none asked her to stand, or asked her questions.

Was she marked with such bad luck that others could see it? What would the new trader do with her if none of these city people wanted her?

A tall man wearing a light-gray, Western suit and black tie came in as the others drifted away, their choices made. He glanced around the room, then walked directly toward Mei Ling.

His cheeks were pocked, and his beard grew in patchy across his jaw. But his hair was ink black, his eyes burned with intelligence, and his forehead was as broad as the sages in the stories Mama had told Mei Ling.

"You, girl. Stand," he commanded.

Mei Ling looked up, startled. His voice was more beautiful than any she'd heard. She wondered what he sounded like singing in the fields, then told herself not to be silly—this man had never worked in the fields, not a single day of his life.

"What's your name?" he asked, not unkindly as she rose steadily.

"Mei Ling, honorable sir," she replied, finally remembering not to stare and focusing her eyes on his very nice, polished leather shoes, peeking out from the sharp crease in his gray suit pants.

There was something about him, something different, and not just his Western clothes.

Her twin soul swam closer in his presence.

"I want her," he announced.

The feet of an assistant came into view. Mei Ling flicked her eyes up, then kept them on the floor. He wore a traditional Chinese jacket and pants, all in black, with black embroidery that only caught the light when he moved. "But sir," the assistant said, his voice breathless. "She's much younger than you usually like."

Mei Ling raised her eyes to the man's waist. She might be young, yes, but everyone, including Grandmama, had said she had an old soul.

"How old are you?" the man asked.

"I was born in the spring. Sir," Mei Ling said, glancing up at his face, then back down again. It was true—she didn't know how old she was. Mama had never told her.

"Ten, maybe, sir," the assistant murmured.

The man looked thoughtful and glanced around the room. The older girls sat at the far end. His gaze lingered there for a moment.

Mei Ling caught her breath. He had to choose her. He was the only one who had seen her. He didn't scare her, not like the traders with the poppies.

Also, her teeth had grown very sharp over the last week.

So Mei Ling raised her eyes, all the way to the man's face, staring defiantly at him, daring him not to choose her.

He would be a fool if he didn't.

When the man glanced back, it was directly into Mei Ling's eyes.

"Bold," he said, smiling. "Her. I want her."

"My name is Mei Ling," she repeated, still feeling daring.

"Mei Ling. You can call me Master Yon," he said.

Mei Ling nodded and followed him out of the warehouse, feeling as though fate and something else had just collided.

M aster Yon's house sat around the corner from a busy street, down a quiet alley, set back with a gate. Mei Ling knew the gate wasn't just to keep others out, but to keep those inside, in.

The great wooden door was painted a dark red, like the earth from the far-away mountains. A golden doorknob stuck out from the center of the door, watching, like a great eye. It, too, guarded the house.

Mei Ling's breath caught. She'd heard stories all her life about magic. She didn't know it actually existed. Maybe Master Yon would teach it to her someday.

The first room was dark and small, with a steep staircase going straight up. A second room stood just to the right. The wood in the house seemed blackened with age and more sturdy than brick. Paintings hung on the wall to Mei Ling's left, like the drawings she'd seen at the village temple.

An older woman helped Master Yon with his coat. She wore a dark blue uniform with long sleeves and a high collar, her black hair streaked with silver and pulled back into severe bun.

Without being told, Mei Ling took off her shoes and placed them on the rack next to the door, under the painting of Xio Gong, one of the eight immortals. She spread her toes and pressed down against the slightly warm floor. She'd never had to wear shoes before, and they had hurt her feet.

"First, a bath," Master Yon said.

Mei Ling caught him frowning at her toes, but she didn't try to hide them.

"Then, after dinner, you may present her to me."

The old woman's black eyes didn't change, but her face grew more stern. "After dinner," she promised.

Mei Ling didn't know what Master Yon meant by either of those things, but chicken flesh crawled across her shoulders at the way he said them.

Still, she was prepared for her fate.

The old servant led Mei Ling up the stairs, instructing her not to dawdle as she took them one at a time.

Mei Ling didn't tell her it was the first time she'd even seen so many stairs all in a row, let alone climbed them.

The bath was in a room filled with cold tile, painted colorful red and green. Water ran out of the pipes, already hot. Sweet soap lay on the sink, and colorful bottles filled with hair soap—shampoo—lined the tub.

Mei Ling knew Mama and Papa had never seen such luxury.

"Eh, you're a quiet one," the old servant said as she efficiently stripped off Mei Ling's dress. "That's good. But you can call me Old Miss if you'd like."

Mei Ling knew that the servant's name was some sort of joke, but it was an adult thing she didn't understand.

Old Miss showed Mei Ling how to wash herself, and helped her scrub her toes and her nails until they were clean. Her fingertips were all wrinkled by the time they'd finished, then she stood still while Old Miss ran more water and rinsed her clean.

When Mei Ling finished and stepped into the softest, thickest towel she'd ever known, she swore to take a bath every day. Surely this was heaven on earth.

The water had pleased her twin as well.

There were too many rooms to count, too many stairs, and too much food. Mei Ling's head swam with all of it. Old Miss finally showed her to a room that she claimed Mei Ling could have, all by herself, with a huge bed that would have fit all of Mei Ling's family.

But such luxury came at a price. Even Mei Ling understood that.

After Mei Ling slept dreamlessly for a while, Old Miss came and woke her up. The night was quiet and dark outside. No one else was around, all the other servants gone.

Old Miss had Mei Ling dress in a fine, green silk robe,

covered in golden embroidered dragonflies—her namesake. It had obviously been made for someone taller and been hastily cut down to fit her.

But that was all right. Mei Ling would have her own clothes, soon. Master Yon had promised her.

"After, you come back here," Old Miss instructed Mei Ling. "I'll be here if you want me to be."

Mei Ling smiled but didn't reply.

Master Yon wanted something from her, something Old Miss and the assistant hadn't approved of.

Mei Ling wasn't worried. She had secrets of her own.

Master Yon's room was lit by a single oil lamp on the dresser, making Mei Ling feel more at home. Like the other rooms, the walls and floor were made from old, dark wood, but the ceiling was made from sheets of embossed tin. A large rug of red and gold covered part of the floor. In the corner lurked a high bed, with a throne-like chair before it.

The room smelled of sweet poppy smoke and something else, something magical, like the doorknob out front. It brought her twin soul swimming closer.

Soon, she knew her twin would rise all the way.

Master Yon stood by the dresser, pouring himself a drink—something amber and sour smelling—from a fine cut crystal bottle into an equally fine glass. He wore a beautiful robe, also in green silk, covered in cicadas. The cuffs and placard were done in red, quilted material, and Mei Ling knew they'd be soft to the touch.

Only after Master Yon had taken a drink did he turn and look at Mei Ling, who still stood just inside the door.

"Good," he said.

Mei Ling didn't like how glassy his eyes looked, the intelligence hazed with smoke and drink.

"I need you to do what I say tonight," Master Yon instructed. "I won't hurt you."

Mei Ling heard the unspoken "tonight" in his promise. There would be other times, in the future, when it would hurt.

But she didn't say anything, didn't tremble in fear.

"Good, good," Master Yon said, walking to his chair, then sprawling in it. "Take off your robe."

Mei Ling froze. This was not something she was supposed to do. She knew that. Maybe this was why Old Miss had said she'd be there, waiting, if Mei Ling needed her, needed someone to soothe her.

"Now," Master Yon instructed.

Mei Ling saw the path forking in front of her.

She could do as he asked, and that would break her, hurt her in ways she couldn't yet say.

If she disobeyed, she'd be beaten, or worse, much, much worse, maybe even forced to take sweet smoke and never be free of it.

Then her other soul stirred.

She had a third path she could take. Everything beyond that first step lay shrouded in darkness, nothing sure, except that it was her fate, primarily because she'd chosen it.

Mei Ling turned her back to Master Yon. With steady fingers, she undid the frogs on her robe.

All the while, her other soul rose.

The room grew lighter, brighter. She'd always seen well in the dark; now, shadows no longer lurked in the corners.

Mei Ling felt her teeth grow sharper. Her face pushed out and her jaw grew strong enough to break bone. Her nails grew claws and she had to be careful not to rip the silk.

Master Yon's breath caught as Mei Ling shrugged the robe from her shoulders, letting it pool onto the ground around her feet.

This, too, was a power, her twin assured her.

Mei Ling took a long deep breath, then, finally, turned around.

Master Yon's lazy, cruel smile melted away.

Mei Ling took one step, then another toward him, ready to fight, to bite and scratch and claw if he tried to hurt her or make her do anything more.

But Master Yon didn't yell, or pull back in fear and horror at the sight of her twin, the soul her grandmother had called evil.

Instead, he laughed.

"I knew there was something special in you, something those idiots were too stupid to see. Something that only I have the ability to train."

His gaze traveled over her naked body, but before Mei Ling could do more than bristle, he told her, "Put on your robe. No one, particularly not me, will ever touch you without your consent."

Mei Ling did as she was told, surprised to find her hands wanted to tremble. She didn't let them, of course.

Master Yon kept talking. "You're a wild one, I guess. Born crocodile clan, outside the families. I'm surprised they haven't found you yet. But I will teach you better than they could."

Crocodile? Her twin liked that. And to learn—she hoped he meant magic.

With a last, comforting rumble, deep inside, Mei Ling's twin soul slipped back into the silent waters buried within them. The room grew darker. But Mei Ling knew that when she called, her twin would rise again.

She turned back to Master Yan once she was properly covered up again. His eyes had grown less glassy. "I will have to change my plans for you, now," he said.

Mei Ling had been trained to silence, to listen with patience. But a question had been let into the room, and Mei Ling felt compelled to ask, "Plans, sir?"

Master Yan's smile widened. "I had thought—never mind. Now, I have the perfect place for you."

When Mei Ling didn't ask anything more, Master Yan finally relented and said one word.

"Management."

After Mei Ling's twentieth year with Master Yon, she politely asked him for two weeks of time off.

"Family matters," she told Master Yon, standing in his study. She loved this room, with the books that lined the walls and the fine calligraphy scrolls that Master Yon had done himself hanging between the shelves. Sweet incense mingled with the scent of high quality tea and candied ginger that Master Yon treated himself with. The broad oak of his desk held the accounts for the week, and Master Yon was checking Mei Ling's numbers.

He wouldn't find any errors, she knew.

Charms clustered in every corner of the room, protection magic that Master Yon had trained Mei Ling to use. A window on the far side opened up onto the garden of the compound. They'd moved from the city, changing houses more than once as bribes stopped working, moving the rest of the girls when they could, setting them free if they had to.

The Middle Kingdom was changing, faster than any could keep up.

Master Yon finally looked up at her. Age had puffed out his cheeks and made his jowls sag. But he proved once again he was worth staying with, his intelligence matching hers. "You'll go regardless of what I say, won't you?"

Mei Ling merely smiled. Her quiet continued to serve her well.

"You have my leave, then. Just be careful."

Mei Ling nodded. Mao's Red Guard roamed widely. They'd escaped notice so far—through connection, bribes, and magical spells that made those eager for victims to look past their door. "I will be more careful than usual," she promised.

"Do you need any supplies?"

Mei Ling considered. She had the charms and spells he'd taught her, the weapons he'd trained her in, and her own wits. "No, thank you, sir. I will return at the next half moon."

Master Yon snorted. "Good luck to any who tried to hold you."

Mei Ling left quietly that night, hidden by a dark cloak.

It didn't take her long to track her prey: The trader who'd lied to her parents and sold her into what was supposed to be a life of prostitution and slavery.

Just because it hadn't turned out that way didn't mean she no longer wanted the revenge she'd promised herself as a child.

The warehouse was in a different city than the one she'd been originally sold in, but it still had the same feeling of age, with shelves covered with dust and no near neighbors.

Mei Ling had chosen it for that, and for one other

reason: The working industrial freezer.

The trader and his coworker were easily trapped by Mei Ling and her other soul. She killed them faster than they deserved, using the stiletto Master Yon had gifted her with during her training.

It took a full week to finish both men. But Mei Ling savored every meal her other soul indulged in, waking with her belly full and her clothes bloodstained.

She only kept a single bone from the hand of the trader, which she had whittled into a toothpick: A reminder to keep both her human and crocodile teeth strong.

Something stirred in the house, a whisper Mei Ling hadn't placed there.

Despite her many decades, her ears had never dulled and her nose still easily scented trouble.

Trouble enough to send her twin swimming closer, twisting up around her human soul, restless and angry.

Mei Ling had been warned by the fortune-teller around the corner of dark smoke seeping into her house and spoiling it. She'd assumed it had meant some kind of fire, and had made her servants check all the smoke detectors, making sure they all worked, as well as running tests on all the cameras and the security systems. Then she'd checked her protection spells and charms, but everything was in order.

However, the fortune-teller had never been wrong. She was a blind girl, young, who read tea leaves by sticking her fingers into a cup and feeling the shape of the future.

Mei Ling suspected that whatever had invaded her house had come from one of the new girls, not one of her regulars, whom she'd worked with and trained diligently.

None of the new girls had smelled of magic, but maybe one had carried a charm with her, hidden away.

Mei Ling made sure her stiletto was close at hand, as well as her garrote and her claws. Then, she invited her twin to help her see.

The dark study brightened, beyond what the modern electric lights provided. Her ancient desk—rescued from Master Yon's estate before the Red Guard could smash it —stood clean of account books, holding a tall computer monitor now. Shelves all around the room were full of ancient and modern books in Chinese, French, and English, all read and cherished by Mei Ling. An old fashioned Victorian fainting couch sat in the corner with the perfect lantern hanging over it. It had been her favorite place for an afternoon tryst, though now Mei Ling only tried out new authors, not new staff.

Mei Ling prowled through the first floor, then the second, then finally up to the third, to the dormitories where the girls slept. The new girls stayed by themselves at first, only joining the other girls in the big rooms once they'd found their way, accepting their fate or else leaving. Mei Ling worked them hard, but she never resorted to drugs to break the will of her girls.

They chose the work. Or they didn't.

As Mei Ling had suspected, her nose drew her to the room of one of the new girls. Mei Ling hadn't learned the girl's name yet—why bother until she'd settled in? She was pretty as a kitten, though, with an upturned nose and long, sleek black hair.

What Mei Ling hadn't anticipated was the shadow that hung over the girl, like a lover, provoking her, draining the life from her, turning her golden skin gray.

Mei Ling hissed, her teeth growing strong and her claws, stronger. She lunged at the thing, striking it.

But her claws passed through it like smoke.

She struck again and again, but the shadow barely moved, as if it didn't even notice her.

Only when Mei Ling stopped did she see that she'd sheared off parts of the shadow. Black tendrils clung to her scales, wriggling like sea worms, trying to taste her flesh. They dripped off her claws like oily, black water, disappearing when they hit the floor, dissolving in silent poofs of smoke.

Finally, the entire shadow pulled in on itself, drawing together until there was nothing left but the rancid smell of moldering ash.

What was that thing?

The girl settled into a peaceful sleep, her tormentor gone, her skin regaining its normal, healthy glow. Mei Ling knew that when she questioned the girl in the morning, the girl would know nothing—only that she didn't sleep well some nights, as attested to by the dark circles under her eyes and drawn lines across her face.

Should Mei Ling send her away? Or kill her? The shadows were the girl's problem, not Mei Ling's.

Her soul's twin paused at that, and turned them around. Mei Ling walked into the next room at her twin's prompting.

More shadows lurked there, tormenting the other girls, draining away their joy and vitality. But these weren't new girls, no. Bing Yu and Xiao Li and other favorites of Mei Ling's slept here.

Mei Ling growled softly. These things were *not* allowed to hurt *her* girls.

Slashing at the shadows with all her might barely bothered them, though. The charms she'd hung for protection and good health didn't affect them.

Mei Ling had always chosen her own fate. These

shadows would not get the best of her or her girls.

And were they only bothering the girls and the help? How many mornings had Mei Ling woken up tired recently, with no clear memory of bad sleep?

Eventually the shadows had their fill and withdrew.

Mei Ling returned to her study. She knew of no books that talked of these things, no myth she'd ever heard of described such shadow creatures. She did a little research on the internet while she waited for the dawn, but again, found nothing.

At first light, she'd go call on the fortune-teller, the one who had predicted the shadows. The girl would tell Mei Ling how to defend her house against them.

Or else.

* * *

The blind fortune teller sat on the stoop outside her shop, wearing a simple white blouse and Western jeans. Her black hair was neatly pulled back, showing her moon-round face. In the street beside her, other early risers rode their bicycles to the market or were returning with their baskets and hands full of bags. A group of old women chatted adamantly as they carried birds in cages; not to sell, but taking their pets for a morning walk.

Mei Ling had always thought the girl's eyes were deep, like black holes, but here in the morning light, they looked sewn shut with black thread.

"Good morning, old mother," the blind seeress called, lifting her face and looking directly at Mei Ling as she approached. She'd always been able to sense Mei Ling's approach.

"Good morning to you," Mei Ling responded, using more formal language.

It wasn't correct, an older person showing a younger person such respect. But Mei Ling knew the girl had power, and she felt she had to acknowledge that.

The girl smiled at the greeting, then grew serious again. "I do not know how to help you fight the shadows," she said without preamble.

Mei Ling nodded, believing her. "Who can help?" she asked, just as directly.

"The clan can."

"My clan?" Mei Ling asked.

Master Yon and the other human magicians she'd met had some knowledge of the crocodile clan that they'd been happy to share with her; however, Mei Ling hadn't bothered to correct any of them when what they'd told her was blatantly wrong. She'd only agreed to meet someone from her clan once, and this woman hadn't told her anything she didn't already know. At least as a wild one, born outside the families, she'd had Master Yon to teach her magic.

"No, not your clan. Another. Others."

Mei Ling pushed down on the spike of excitement that rushed through her.

Other clans? Had that been a birdman she'd seen at the market, five years before? She hadn't tried tracking him but instead, had slipped away into the crowds before the foreigner had seen her.

Maybe she shouldn't have been so cautious. But she'd only survived the decades of upheaval in the Middle Kingdom by being careful. And her twin had approved of her action as well.

"You must first find the hound prince," the seeress continued. "Only he can help you. He will battle all the shadows, before they grow worse and attack not just in dreams."

"Where is he?" Mei Ling asked. Were there finding spells she could use to locate him? Or would he be fully defended against such simple magic?

"The hound court is in Germany—Hamburg. You must go there. The hounds have the most contact with the other clans, so they won't kill you immediately, unlike the ravens or the tigers, if you happened into their temples."

"Thank you," Mei Ling said, bowing to the seeress. It was enough of a hint. She could figure out the rest. She bent forward and placed some hard currency in the girl's hand.

The girl's fingers were cold, but strong as they clung to Mei Ling's. "You will not see me again," the girl whispered. "Not before the shadows ruin me. I won't know you, then. But I have no regrets. You've always had the most interesting fate."

Mei Ling straightened up, then bowed again, taking her leave. Rage boiled through her. The shadows were disturbing her girls, sucking her own life, and now were going to ruin the best fortune-teller she'd ever worked with.

They weren't to be tolerated.

But Mei Ling calmed herself as she walked, making plans.

She'd have to close the house, of course. Sell the girls who couldn't buy their way out of their contracts. Some of Master Yon's friends, the alchemists and other spell workers, could help her find the hound clan, if her own nose didn't lead her to them.

Then this prince…well, he was a man, no?

Though Mei Ling had many decades on her bones, she still knew how to get what she needed from men.

And if not, her teeth were surely sharper than his.

GERMANY, ELEVEN YEARS AGO

LUKAS

Lukas stood in the middle of the classroom, naked, ready for Tilgard's instructions.

He had to do this perfectly.

Luckily, Oma had been working with him, training him behind locked doors, after dark and his bedtime, for the last two years. He wrapped all the secrets she'd imbued him in like a cloak, protecting him from the shadows.

The classroom was warm, and the window was shut, a feeble attempt to limit distractions. Lukas concentrated instead on the paper smells of the books, the musty chalk, and the new red ink Felix his tutor had used the night before when he'd sat and graded Lukas and Greta's homework.

Tilgard wore his traditional leather pants and jerkin, with rabbit fur tied to his waist and bacon treats in his pocket. He kept his head and jaw shaved, making his dark brown eyes seem like they bulged out and his nose and chin flattened. He didn't stare at Lukas, didn't try to challenge him. But he did stand in a position of command, and he demanded respect.

Finally, Tilgard made a signal with his right hand.

Sight hound.

Lukas changed swiftly, calling on that aspect of Hamlin's soul.

"Good," Tilgard said, tossing him a bacon treat.

Lukas knew he'd done it perfectly, and that he now looked like Da, a champion gray-and-white greyhound. His head was diamond shaped, his body long and lean.

But the form didn't feel right. His jaw wasn't strong enough, and his hind legs weren't as powerful as Hamlin's.

Lukas stood still and proud as he waited for the next instruction.

Tilgard gave him a mixed signal, *sight* with one hand and *sound* with the other.

Lukas and Hamlin wagged their tail once and flowed into the shape of a Rhodesian Ridgeback.

This shape felt almost right. His chest was broad and powerful, and his nose was large, able to catch more scents. He liked the ridge that ran down his back as well, knowing that when he was older, he could choose this shape as a hound warrior, and the ridge would become armored spikes.

But this form wasn't completely right either. His eyesight, while strong, wasn't as keen, and in this shape, while he was fast, he wasn't fast enough.

"Good, good," Tilgard said. Then he made one last sign, a *questioning* sign, meaning Lukas could take whatever form he wanted.

Generally, the final shape of the three forms that all royalty had to practice was their natural dog shape, what their true hound soul looked like.

Oma had prepared Lukas for this as well.

Lukas called on Hamlin to help. This had to be perfect, too.

With a great shake, Lukas shrank down, more and more, until he was a compact little black Scottish terrier.

Tilgard still told him that he was good.

Lukas knew he had the form correct—almond eyes, perky ears, long silky coat. This shape wasn't right, either, though it was the best compromise he and Hamlin could find. It was comfortable enough, with strong legs, a keen nose, and far-seeing eyes. It felt almost like Hamlin's natural form, just with all his senses dimmed.

Except his intelligence. Lukas and Hamlin were both sharp and aware as a Scottie dog, more than any other.

Tilgard gave the next command: *Change back into human.*

Lukas sat down and looked expectantly at the hound master, as if he should get a treat. He tried to contain his excitement at the challenge.

After all the training, the weeks of secret study with Oma, Lukas was finally putting their plans into motion.

Tilgard gave the hand signal again, this time with the spoken command, "*Verwandele!*"

Lukas swallowed. *Calm, calm, calm.* He made himself sit up on his hind legs, as if he'd confused the signal and was supposed to beg.

"*Nein,*" Tilgard said.

Lukas stayed on his hind legs and tilted his head to one side, fighting the urge to obey.

Hamlin pushed out and up in the little terrier body, filling all the space, his heart and courage bigger than the commanding presence in front of them.

When Tilgard spoke sharply, Lukas dropped down to all fours and yipped playfully, rear up, tail wagging, as if this were a game, though his heart raced and he panted.

If he'd been in human form, he knew he'd be sweating.

"Change back!" Tilgard commanded in English this time.

Lukas stopped playing and backed away, his eyes wide and his ears flattened.

"No, no, I won't hurt you," Tilgard assured them.

Lukas stayed where he was, wary.

"Please, change."

Lukas looked around the room, as if noticing it for the first time, sniffing the air.

"I don't know what you're playing at, but you need to quit, now."

Lukas continued to ignore the hound master, only looking at him when he said something sharply. Maybe he could go play outside soon. He teased apart the scents in the air, seeking even the edge of the woods, the metal gate miles away. When he was in Hamlin's form he could smell it; now, only his imagination supplied it.

Tilgard left and returned first with Felix, then with Oma.

Nothing would make Lukas change back, no pleas or threats, as he and his grandmother had planned. He watched her carefully, impressed with her fine acting. She still had much to teach him.

Finally, the three of them left him alone in the classroom. Lukas curled up in a dog bed in the corner, exhausted with the effort of disobeying, his little body shaking.

Relax, he told Hamlin as he closed his eyes. *No guard tonight.*

Hamlin shuffled closer and curled up with Lukas, glad for the rest.

When they awoke, Lukas was human-shaped again. The traditional cloak lay folded next to him, the one he'd worn two years before, the first time he'd transformed.

As soon as Lukas put on the cloak, Tilgard came back in the room. "Was that some kind of game, son?" the hound master thundered.

Shaking, Lukas turned to him, remembering to make his eyes wide and scared. "No," he whispered.

He must have gotten the play-acting right because Tilgard pulled him into a tight hug.

"My boy, my boy," he said softly, kissing the top of Lukas' head. "We'll think of something, eh?" he added, pulling back.

Lukas nodded solemnly, knowing they wouldn't. Oma had seen to that.

In two weeks' time, Lukas would have to show his forms to the court. Since Hamlin looked like a mongrel, the only way for Lukas to prove his royalty was by showing that he could take more than one form, on command.

And he would. He would easily go through all the breeds of hounds dictated by the court.

But then he'd *stick* in the last one, hiding in plain sight, away from the shadows.

His dreams, and Oma's, had foretold that there was the only way he'd survive into adulthood: By staying in hound form.

T he next time Lukas played at getting stuck, he stayed that way for over a day. Hamlin guarded him in his sleep so he didn't accidentally change back.

It was nice not to dream of the shadows.

The next morning, at breakfast, Lukas pretended to be shamefaced at the dining table.

It wasn't all play acting—Da and Mama carefully

didn't talk about it, or even look at him, as they buttered their toast or passed the orange juice. They all sat together in the new breakfast nook, just the four of them; Oma had taken her breakfast in her room—another test, Lukas was certain, to make sure he'd performed well.

Lukas wanted to tell his family, but he also didn't want to tell them. He'd grown so used to keeping secrets over the years—about his breed, about the shadows, about the hidden signals he and Oma passed, about the ancient stories of other guardian hounds that weren't in the regular recitations—and this was just one more.

After Da and Mama had left, Greta stayed at the table, stirring her tea. She wore a long-sleeved white blouse buttoned up to her neck though it was summer, along with a nice black skirt. Lukas had teased her when she'd first come in that she looked like a secretary.

"What's it like?" Greta finally asked, pushing her blond curls out of her face to stare at Lukas. "Is it scary, getting stuck like that?"

Lukas shook his head. "No. Being a dog…it's fun."

Greta nodded. She wasn't a full member of the hound clan; it was usually only men who could change. She'd never seemed jealous of Lukas' ability, though. "You always do seem happy," she said.

"Yeah." Lukas had read that only hounds experienced pure joy. Though disobeying was thrilling, staying as a dog and romping as much as he wanted was a reward by itself. No school or studying, either with Felix or in secret with Oma.

"You only have to change into other forms once more. For the court," Greta added, looking back at her tea-cup.

"It'll be fine," Lukas assured her, though he knew it wouldn't be. He only had a few more days like this, in his human form. Then he'd stay as a hound for a year, maybe two. Oma hadn't been really clear on how long he'd have to stay hidden. But it wouldn't be that bad, being a hound all the time. He wouldn't have to study anymore.

"If you do get stuck, I'll do everything I can to help find a cure," Greta said in a rush.

"What, as a secretary?" Lukas teased.

"Scientist. Idiot."

Lukas grinned at her, then made himself continue smiling, even when it started to hurt. He'd give anything to be able to really say goodbye to his sister, Mama, and Da.

But it wasn't safe. He had to pretend he was stuck, and he couldn't give away their plans.

If his family knew about the shadows, the shadows would take them, and Lukas would never be able to rescue them. Only by hiding his human form, staying stuck in dog form, could he keep them safe.

It was sometimes so difficult not to tell them.

L ukas followed Oma into her room, his little Scottish terrier body shaking, small whines creeping out of his throat.

Yes, there was joy in being a dog all the time.

But he was also a boy, and after two weeks, it was getting harder not to change back. Being a hound all the time wasn't any more natural than being a boy all the time. As a member of the hound clan, he needed to do both regularly.

Plus, Tilgard watched him all the time. Lukas couldn't change back, even for a night, when he was being spied on that way.

Lukas had dreamed of being a boy again the previous

night. He'd woken to find the hound master waiting patiently beside him.

It wasn't hard to figure out that Lukas' scent had given him away.

So he'd come whining to Oma, following her back to her room.

A tiny bed, more like a cot, was shoved into one corner near the door. It didn't look comfortable at all. A small, three-drawer dresser sat next to it. Smells of bitter herbs, moldy paper, and bright flowers flowed around him. Shelves filled the rest of the room, standing out from the walls at all angles, reaching all the way up to the fifteen-foot ceilings. Just a path lay between the shelves, wide enough for the crooked ladder Oma used to reach the top.

Not just books lined the shelves. Though Oma wasn't a hound, she had magic, more than any other human the hound clan knew. She'd created all the protection charms in the castle and had taught magic to generations of hounds. She'd said once it was why the shadows had come bothering her as well: They were attracted to her magic.

Lukas never liked it here. It was too closed in, too much like a library or a laboratory, not like a bedroom at all.

Oma sat down on the little dog bed she'd put next to hers, soft and dark blue, and smelling only of Lukas. He jumped immediately into her lap. Oma knew just how to use her nails along his back to soothe him, how to skritch along his ears where his hind legs really couldn't reach. It helped him settle into his skin, at least for a little while.

"I didn't want it to come to this," she whispered, bending her head to his, her nose in his hair. "But you need help, don't you?"

Lukas nodded. He was trying so hard to be good, to

always stay a dog and to act more like one, as though he only had dog thoughts in his head, but it was hard.

"I can make it easier," Oma said.

Lukas pushed harder against her chest. *Yes. Better. Now.*

"Normally, a hound soul circles the human one, rising only when called. For a while, I can change that. Make your human soul circle your hound soul."

Lukas shivered. It sounded scary, making his human soul go away.

Hamlin pushed forward, leaning on him, assuring him that Hamlin would keep them safe.

Lukas nodded.

"Good. That Tilgard suspects something. You need to hide better."

Lukas stilled. What was Oma asking of him now? Not that it mattered. He wouldn't deny her anything. They shared too many secrets.

"I'm going to smuggle you away, out of here."

Lukas dropped his head and gave a great sigh. Away from the castle, away from Da and Mama and Greta and everything he'd ever know....He'd be lonely, but he suspected it would be easier to stay in one shape, away from them.

Plus, if he and Hamlin were far from the hound master, maybe he could change back into a real boy at night.

Slowly, Lukas nodded, giving his consent. It would only be for a year or two, right? Though that now seemed like an eternity.

"Good, good. Rudolf Von DeWhite will be your guardian. I trust him. Rudi. Not with all your secrets, but he'll keep you safe. He's a scent hound, not a sight hound."

Lukas understood what that meant: Rudolf wasn't part

of the court. Lukas thought he remembered Rudolph from a visit once.

"There are others, too, whom I have trained, who will hide your true location, confuse the search," Oma continued, whispering. "So, first, a potion to put your human soul to sleep. Then, tonight, the full spell."

Why did Oma sound so sad at that? Lukas twisted in her lap, leaning up to lick at her nose.

Oma put her hands around Lukas' head and looked deeply into his eyes. "I'm only doing this because I must," she said almost soundlessly. "Believe me."

Lukas didn't know why she was so worried.

Hamlin didn't either, but he would guard them both and make sure nothing bad happened.

***

The potion stank of dank seaweed and bitter, early roots. Without being told, Hamlin memorized the signature, teasing apart the components so they'd always be wary of them.

Though Oma had added good meat broth, Lukas had a hard time lapping it up. The bitter taste curled around his tongue, slimy and oily, and even the large bowl of water that he lapped up next couldn't chase it away.

By the time Lukas finished the water, his little Scottish terrier body could barely stand. The room moved, even when he kept perfectly still, the floor tilting up.

"Sleep now, good boy, sleep," Oma crooned.

Hamlin rose up to guard them, and Lukas slipped into the comforting dark.

For the first time since he'd taken dog shape, Lukas dreamed of the shadows that night. He stood alone and human in his room, grateful to be a boy again, to stand and stretch. He could reach his bed without jumping, and wear clothes again.

Then the shadows attacked. Buzzing like gnats, stinging like nettles, they tried to invade him. He had to keep his mouth shut or they'd crawl inside him, and he had to breathe shallowly as well. There was no place he could go and hide; he couldn't outrun them, not in human form. They stole his life as he stood there, making him feel tired and old.

They talked to him, in the dream, told him lies. If only he'd let them in, just have a part of him, just a little. It would all be fine. They'd stop hurting him, and they'd never hurt anyone else, either.

But he knew that if he let them in, they'd take over not just him, but all the hounds, then all the world, turning everything dark and stripping away all the laughter and joy.

As soon as Lukas shrank back down to a little Scottie dog, the shadows left him alone. He shook them off and left, looking for Oma.

But the shadows were already in the castle, in every corner of the court, hazing the tall ceilings and staining the windows. Even the garden and the woods were infected with noxious mushrooms and web-like vines. Only after Lukas had squeezed through a hole under the wall and run away did the shadows leave him alone.

Lukas didn't really wake up the next morning. He knew he slept, but it was a comfortable, easy sleep. He sensed Hamlin was near, standing guard over them.

At noon, Lukas rose, seeing out of their shared eyes only for a minute or two before slipping back down into darkness.

At midnight, Lukas rose again. Like the last time, it was only for a short while, though it was long enough for him to wonder briefly if this was what it was like for Hamlin before sleep claimed him again.

The next day, Lukas woke at noon, then at midnight again. But this time, when Lukas rose up, Oma and a stranger sat before him. "Rudi will keep you safe," Oma said, over and over again.

Lukas nodded, catching a quick glance of the man. He had silver hair standing all on end, bushy eyebrows over dark eyes, a solid chin with a cleft in it, and a ready smile.

"I'll guard you with my life, Prince," Rudi said quickly.

Lukas nodded again before he went back down.

He woke next in a tight, closed-in space. A gate was immediately in front of his nose.

A crate.

But he smelled Rudi nearby. Peering through the slats in the side, he found Rudi sitting beside him.

Hamlin showed Lukas the crowds and the long passage they'd come through, how Rudi had more than seat, so Lukas was here and not on the floor.

Lukas knew from movies he'd seen that they were flying somewhere, far from the court.

Safe.

Before Lukas could be sad that he wasn't really awake for his first plane ride, he fell back asleep.

Lukas kept track of the days and the times he was awake better than Hamlin. His hound soul knew seasons; dividing them up into more pieces was a human thing. So Lukas knew that it was about two weeks before the potion started to wear off and he began to be awake longer than just a few minutes. It took almost two months before Lukas felt more like himself and could be awake for most of the day.

Rudi lived in a rambling house, all one story, with a

large grassy yard that sloped up a small hill. The fence was high enough that even Hamlin would have problems jumping it. But there were many trees, squirrels, and birds. Lukas spent as much time outside as he could outside, reveling in every scent the wind brought him.

Rudi did some kind of work on the computer, and sat in an office overlooking the backyard all day. But he stopped frequently to play with Lukas, throwing a ball or going for long rambling walks, often driving out of the city to reach the nearby woods. Lukas had his own soft bed and all the chew toys he could want.

It was the perfect life for a dog, but Lukas wasn't really a dog.

At night, Lukas took to prowling the house, guarding his territory, memorizing every scent so well he could run at full speed with his eyes closed from one room to the next—racing from the faint overlay of smoke from the fireplace in the living room, to the new-glue scent still attached to the dining room chairs, past the heady spices and rich coffee smells of the kitchen, into the metallic tang of Rudi's office, then back again.

One night, Lukas noticed that Rudi had left a magazine open on the coffee table. Lukas jumped up and realized that even in this form, he could read. It hurt his eyes a little, focusing on the small print, and he had to back up to see more clearly. But now he could keep track of what was going on in Germany beyond what he could catch on the radio and TV. Plus, it would pass the time on the long nights, when he missed his family and his home.

He didn't need Oma to tell him that he needed to be careful and always keep one ear cocked for Rudi, and that he needed to leave everything just as he'd found it.

Lukas waited another two months, scenting the air carefully every day and every night, making sure no hound or shadow was near, before he decided to try changing back into his human form, just for a break.

The night was quiet; only the occasional truck rumbled on the far-off highway. Rudi slept soundly and no neighbors were stirring.

Lukas stood behind the big elm tree in the backyard, hidden from the house and all the windows, before he finally let loose of his hound form.

It felt like stretching after a long night's sleep, standing up to his full height. His human form had grown, he realized, even though it had been only four months. He opened his arms to the night air, breathing deeply, his nose dull but his skin alive. The ground felt cold underneath his bare feet. How odd it was to wiggle his toes.

Then the shadows attacked.

Like in his dream, they buzzed around him like gnats, seeking to violate him. He shivered in shock, looking around the garden. Where had they come from, and so quickly? Neither he nor Hamlin had scented them at all.

Down, down, Hamlin commanded.

With a last desperate stretch, Lukas obeyed, wrapping his arms across his chest as he shrank down, changing back into his Scottie dog form, shedding shadows with a final shake. Even the short attack had exhausted him, and he stood on trembling legs, panting.

Hamlin held their nose high in the air, untangling the scent of the shadows.

It was still a wet smell, sand and mold and ash, but something else threaded through the scent, something he'd only smelled once before but had sworn to remember.

It came to him slowly.

Oma. The potion he'd taken.

Now he knew why she'd looked so sad.

She'd cursed him with shadows so he'd never be able to change back to human form, not until she lifted it.

Why had she cursed him with the one thing that he was destined to destroy? Was it to make him more familiar with them? Or had they tricked her, somehow?

Deep inside, Lukas howled, shaking with anger and fear.

It was unfair. All of it.

Yet, all he could do was wait.

L ukas waited ten years before he received the first sign that his banishment was nearing an end.

GERMANY, 1970S TO ELEVEN YEARS AGO

RUDI

Rudi waited, anxious and alone, in the magic practice room after Lady Metzler, the king's mother, had told the rest of the class they could go. He'd failed the latest test. Magic slipped through his fingers as if they were still paws. He couldn't hold on to any of it. He hoped he hadn't failed so badly he'd be sent home immediately instead of at the end of the summer. He'd already missed the big Fourth of July party at home, celebrating the United States bicentennial. To be sent there now, in disgrace...Rudi shivered.

His life couldn't get any worse.

The room smelled of rosemary, straw, twine, dried roses, and all the other boys from the hound clan, sent there for the summer to learn. It looked more like the chemistry lab at his high school back in Pennsylvania than what he'd imagined a room for learning magic looked like: It had porcelain sinks, stainless steel tables, and white cabinets with frosted glass doors lining the walls.

Magic had been nothing like his dreams, or his favorite books, like Andre Norton, Susan Cooper, or even Ray

Bradbury. It was like trying to catch a single drop of oil in a boiling pot of water.

His dad had been so hopeful, sending Rudi back to Germany to stay with his aunt and uncle, be presented to the new king of the hound clan, and spend the summer learning. The new king wasn't that much older than Rudi, barely out of high school himself, but he'd looked so solemn sitting on the great stone throne in the court, with curly black hair and eyes bluer than the summer sky. The carved hounds on either side had looked more fierce than the king.

Lady Metzler came back in the classroom finally. She wore a fuzzy pink cardigan, tan slacks, and gold aviator glasses. She looked like a librarian, with wild black curls going gray and soft, and amber-colored eyes, not like one of the few humans in the world who not only could practice magic, but who had enough skill that she could teach it.

"Are you going to fail me?" Rudi asked breathlessly, then looked down, ashamed. His dad would smack him for showing no discipline.

"Of course. You have no magic whatsoever. If fact, you seem almost like anti-magic. Weaker charms and spells don't work on you," Lady Metzler said dismissively. She walked over to her desk at the front of the room.

Rudi heard papers being shuffled, but he didn't look up from his feet. His sneakers still had mud around the edges from the forest earlier that afternoon, when the hound master, Klaus, and his new assistant, Tilgard, had laid scents between the trees for them to follow. He'd done well at that—like his dad, he was a scent hound; not a purebred, but from good fox terrier stock.

"Oh, don't look so sad, boy. There's good work for people without magic."

Rudi nodded, then looked up. "So you aren't sending me back to the States?"

"If I had to send home every boy who fumbled a spell, there'd only be three or four students left."

Rudi breathed a huge sigh of relief. "Is there something else you wanted?" he asked, suddenly realizing that Lady Metzler was staring at him.

"Are you good with math?" she asked.

"Yes, ma'am." While he enjoyed reading and getting lost in the worlds people created, he also loved the simple structure and clean dynamics of numbers. His dad was a banker, and claimed Rudi's head for numbers came from him.

"I may have use for a boy who's good with numbers and bad with magic," the lady said.

"How can I be of service?" Rudi asked politely, remembering to stand up straight, at attention.

"Not yet. You're still young. You need to prove to me that you can excel at keeping secrets, beyond the recitations and just being a member of the hound clan."

Rudi gulped. "Yes, ma'am." The mother of the king was asking him to keep a secret? Greater than just hiding his hound soul from the every-day world? "I'll never tell anyone a single word you say to me," he promised. No one had every asked him anything so important in all his sixteen years.

"You'll prove yourself later, son. For now, just keep this conversation between us. You can go."

"Thank you, ma'am. You won't regret it. You can trust me."

Rudi bounded from the room. He raced down the hall, grinning widely. Maybe she wanted him to be a spy, or act as a courier, or—

"Hey, Rudi," Stefan asked, coming up to him. "You okay, man?"

Rudi ground to a halt.

He couldn't let anyone know anything.

"Yeah," Rudi said, heaving a large sigh. "I failed the last test. Really blew it. But she isn't going to send me home," he added. He figured that was a good enough lie to cover why he was happy after being asked to stay after class.

"Rudi, Rudi, Rudi," Stefan said, punching his shoulder. "You just gotta relax, let the magic flow to you."

"Is that how it is for you?" Rudi asked, throwing his arm over the shoulder of his friend as they walked down the hall. "All glowing lights and rainbows?"

Stefan tweaked Rudi in the ribs, making him shy away. "No, nothing like that hippie stuff. I can help you later, tonight, if you want."

Rudi remembered that Lady Metzler had said it would be better if he was bad with magic. "Naw. Thanks, though. I'll just stick with what I know."

Stefan laid his finger along his nose. "Tracking scents?"

"Yep," Rudi said, nodding.

And keeping secrets.

Rudi did everything Lady Metzler asked of him: Studied math and the brand-new field of computers at college, signed up for the hound guard for two years to learn how to fight, then took a job at a small firm in Germany, where he learned about network security and hacking.

Their communication was always simple, but not

direct: He'd write letters and postcards to her, telling her about his life, and she would write in return. They never said anything explicit, as if they both assumed someone else was reading every word.

Instead, Lady Metzler would ask about his computer classes, commenting on how they seemed to be the future for a bright young man, or telling him stories about her nephew who had just joined the guard and how much he'd learned, or mentioning that she'd heard about this company in Germany, and what a great opportunity it would be for an ambitious young man.

Only someone matching words with deeds would see just how she'd directed his life.

When Rudi moved from the firm in Germany to one in the US, the letters still came, but less frequently, now. When he mentioned going back to Germany for a visit, Lady Metzler said she thought she would be away, and he wouldn't be able to see her.

Rudi spent a sleepless night in his Austin, Texas, apartment, wondering if he'd done something wrong, if he'd disappointed her. But in a few months, her Christmas letter came, full of casual news with no messages, and he knew she was just keeping him at a distance.

Keeping Rudi hidden until she really needed him.

Based on her initial guidance, Rudi stayed in computer security, becoming a "white hat" hacker. If Lady Metzler ever needed to communicate with him in secret electronically, he was prepared.

However, she never gave any indication of that, so they merely stayed pen-pals.

After decades of occasional cards and letters, the Christmas after the prince, Lukas, had been presented to the court as a full member of the hound clan, Lady Metzler mentioned that she hadn't seen Rudi in so long and that it might be nice if he came to visit.

Dutifully, Rudi arranged for a two-week vacation that spring, to see his relatives in Germany as well as visit the court.

There had always been a guardhouse just past the edge of the woods on the single road into the castle. However, when Rudi had been spent time in the hound guard, it had been a primitive hut with a plain wooden gate that opened and shut manually.

Now, it still looked like a shed, but Rudi could smell that it was reinforced with concrete and steel. There were sensors in the road, and cameras, too. A quick glance inside showed computers and monitors displaying live footage from earlier down the road and further up it as well.

Nothing could replace the guard, though: The finest noses had always been selected for the hut. Rudi knew they could easily trace his path there, from the hotel he'd stayed at the night before, possibly the airports he'd passed through, as well as what part of the States he'd come from.

He easily got out of his car, stretching as he did so. "Rudolf Von DeWhite," he introduced himself, handing over his passport to the first guard while his partner sniffed around the car.

The guard merely nodded, using a handheld scanner across Rudi's passport. It was real; Rudi didn't have to travel anonymously to the court. But he always kept other papers, with other names, just in case.

The guards wore a simple white and black security outfit, with his last name, "Fuchs," embroidered in red on the right. Rudi remembered laughing about his uniform, calling it "stripper clothes" because they were deliberately made to tear off so a hound could change and not get his legs caught in his underwear.

"Just visiting?" Fuchs asked, handing back Rudi's passport.

"Yes. It's been, twenty, twenty-five years since I was here last? When I was in the guard," Rudi added with a grin.

"Twenty-seven," the guard said, glancing at his scanner.

"Ah, thank you," Rudi said, a little taken aback that they kept such complete records now. The court hadn't always been so concerned with security. Had something happened?

The guard nodded and stepped back, saying, "Have a pleasant visit."

Rudi slid back into his rental car and drove slowly up the steep hill to the castle. It looked the same as it had, with brilliant green grass running up to it, immaculately trimmed. Tulips, crocuses, and daffodils bloomed in artful disarray along the walk. Beautiful Japanese maples, slender Cyprus, and hearty yews stood guard near the door.

The castle itself was solid gray stone, a Victorian fantasy of turrets and crenellations, the windows too plentiful and wide to provide adequate medieval protection. More cameras were mounted high on the walls, along with heat and motion sensors.

Was all that high-tech security necessary? Didn't the clan have the best senses to detect when something was wrong?

A bored young woman in a severe black dress with her hair pulled back in an equally severe bun looked up Rudi's name on her laptop, then showed him to one of the small tea rooms on the second floor, overlooking the formal garden in the back, telling him to wait for Lady Metzler there.

The room was done in different shades of cream and white, with subtle roses blooming in the wallpaper, the motif repeated in the moldings along the fifteen foot ceilings. The furniture was all heavy, old, and painted white, with gold-, white-, and beige-striped cushions. Outside, Rudi was glad to see that the squares of different grass were still there in the first garden. He'd always loved them as a boy.

Lady Metzler's scent proceeded her: Rudi recognized her familiar lavender soap, as well as the slightly bitter, chemical smell he remembered from her classroom. She wore a dark blue cardigan over black dress slacks, her curls all gray now, her eyes still amber brown.

"My lady," Rudi said, taking her hand and bowing over it.

"Rudolf. You have grown into a handsome one," she said, looking him over.

"Thank you," he said politely. He knew he was handsome, and one of his girlfriends had said he looked like George Clooney with his salt-and-pepper hair, cleft chin, and perpetually single air.

"You never married, did you?" Lady Metzler asked as Rudi pulled a chair out for her.

"No, ma'am," he said. He'd never found anyone he'd loved enough that he even felt tempted to share his secrets.

She merely nodded. "I've asked my grandson to stop by after his lessons this afternoon."

"I'll be honored to meet him," Rudi said, sitting down himself.

A young man wearing a plain black suit came in the room, carrying a tray with a rose and white china tea pot, matching cups and saucers, cream and sugar, as well as a cut crystal decanter full of dark apple brandy with fine glass snifters.

Rudi served them both tea to start. They talked of his work, his father, and his uncles. He listened while Lady Metzler told him about her most recent classes, laughing about the boys, though assuring him that none has been as bad a student as he had been.

They reminisced as if they were old friends, Rudi noticed, though they never had been. He wondered if the performance was for the cameras not so hidden in the corners, or if there was some other reason they pretended to be closer than they were.

After they finished their tea, but before they started the brandy, a young boy came in. He looked at Rudi warily, his gaze strangely assessing and more adult than a six-year-old boy's. He had the same black hair his father had had when he'd been a boy, the same startling blue eyes, the same very solemn air.

"Lukas, I want you to meet Rudolf Von DeWhite," Lady Metzler said, taking the boy's hand. "He's a friend."

The boy breathed in deeply, taking in Rudi's scent.

Rudi did the same. The boy didn't have the milky scent of a puppy, or even a new dog. He smelled like a grizzled hound, strong and mature.

"It is a pleasure to know you," Rudi said, curious.

"And you," Lukas said with a nod.

"Now, go play," Lady Metzler said, squeezing the boy's hand.

Lukas looked at her quizzically before he grinned and bounded off, finally acting like the boy he was.

"I worry about him," Lady Metzler said, picking up a snifter.

Rudi took the hint and poured her a finger's worth of

brandy, then himself. "What are you worried about?" he asked.

"He's different. Not a pure sight hound, like his father."

"Ah," Rudi said. He'd heard talk about the boy, how he looked like a mongrel. "Do you know what breed he is?"

Lady Metzler looked at Rudi sharply. "He's royalty. When the time comes, he'll take the forms easily enough." Only purebred royalty could take on any dog shape they chose. Most hounds, like Rudi, could only change into one form, that of their hound soul.

"That's good," Rudi said. And it was. "Though isn't his cousin, Oscar, also prepared for the throne?" After King Metzler had been crowned, he hadn't taken a wife for many years, and Lukas had been born almost ten years after his sister.

"Yes. And Oscar will do a good enough job, as king."

Interesting. So Lady Metzler didn't think Lukas would be king? Was his breed so off, then? But Rudi didn't ask— he couldn't, not unless he was certain they were alone and unobserved. He had the equipment with him to take care of that, but she hadn't asked for such privacy.

Interesting. So Lady Metzler didn't think Lukas would be king? Was his breed so off, then? But Rudi didn't ask— he couldn't, not unless he was certain they were alone and unobserved. He had the equipment with him to take care of that, but she hadn't asked for such privacy.

Lady Metzler nodded at Rudi, as if listening in on this thoughts and agreeing. "My dreams—my dreams make me worried for the boy. They've always guided me, you know. You may think I'm a foolish old woman, but they've always foretold the future." She turned her head and stared directly into Rudi's eyes. "They've given me time to prepare."

Rudi swallowed. He felt his spine straighten, and the hair along the back of his neck stood up. "We're all very lucky to have you, my lady," he said. "If there's ever anything I can do to help, please don't hesitate to ask."

They finished their brandy, and Lady Metzler announced that she needed to go to her next appointment.

Rudi stood and took her hand again. This time, he slipped a cell phone into it as he bowed over it, kissing the back of it.

Lady Metzler acted as if nothing had happened, sliding both her hands into her pockets after he let go.

The phone was a burner, unregistered, bought with cash from a dealer who kept his own secrets. Only one number was programmed into it, and it wasn't Rudi's usual number. It came with a program that automatically scrambled the signal. It wasn't unhackable—nothing was —but unless someone was prepared, a short call would be difficult to hijack or trace.

"It was so good to see you, old friend," Lady Metzler said with a sincere smile.

"You too," Rudi said with another bow as she swept out of the room.

On the way back to his car, Rudi smiled faintly, tamping down on his excitement and anxiety.

After all these years, all his training with security, he might finally be of use to the king's mother.

At last.

It was a little over a year later before the twin phone, the one matching the phone Rudi had given Lady Metzler, rang.

"Come and get my grandson. Come as fast as you can, and arrive near midnight. "

The call ended abruptly. Rudi dropped the phone on the floor, then stepped on it, cracking the case and all the electronics. Then he scooped it up, got a bowl full of water, and tossed the pieces into it.

After the last visit with Lady Metzler, Rudi had gone into freelance work. He could live anywhere in the world as long as he had a good internet connection. He worked under more than one alias, with more than one tax ID for his various companies.

It took him a single day to arrange everything: His belongings to be packed up and put into storage, his most recent job finished up, more than one set of tickets bought under different names. He knew he wasn't impossible to trace—no one was—but he made it as difficult as he could.

Rudi arrived at the castle late, as Lady Metzler had asked, close to midnight. The guards at the gate knew he was coming and waved him through. A young man waited in the entranceway of the castle, and Lady Metzler joined them soon afterward.

"Old friend, I knew you'd come," Lady Metzler said, greeting him warmly.

"What's wrong, my lady?" Rudi asked, holding her hand in his. Her skin buzzed with fear and excitement, and her amber eyes were dark. She wore an old robe like some housewife, not the mother of the king.

"Come, come," she said, tugging him along. She took him to a part of the castle he'd never seen before. Worn red-and-white Oriental rugs covered the wooden floors. Ancient portraits and paintings hung from the high ceiling almost to the ground, hiding most of the forest green walls. Bitter lemon and pine cleaners had been used recently, making Rudi wrinkle his nose. Humans slept in this section, not anyone from the hound clan—the latter would never stand for the strong chemical scents.

The room of Lady Metzler smelled sharply of herbs, lavender soap, and the acrid scent Rudi always associated with magic. A twin bed lay immediately to the left. Rudi assumed the room was as big as the other studies, but he couldn't see anything beyond the tall shelves of books that stuck out from the walls, looming overhead and blocking the view.

A small, black Scottish terrier lay curled up on a dog bed on the floor. He got up and wagged his tail, coming over to Lady Metzler as soon as she walked through the door. She dropped immediately to her knees, more supple than Rudi had thought a seventy-plus-year-old woman would be.

Rudi knelt down beside her.

Lady Metzler picked up the little dog, putting it into her lap, and crooned over it, "My boy. My boy." For the first time, her voice sounded weak and frail instead of commanding and strong.

Fright stalked up and down Rudi's spine, making him sit taller.

"He's stuck," Lady Metzler whispered. "My grandson. He can't change back."

"Ma'am, I'm so sorry," Rudi said, horrified. The little prince was insane? Trapped as a hound? Poor boy.

"His human soul only rises twice a day, at midnight and at noon," the lady continued. "He's almost all hound, all the time."

Rudi nodded, saddened. Most of the hound clan, even when wearing their hound form, still had a great deal of human intelligence and soul. They shared the body. It wasn't right that the boy's hound shape was so strong.

"You needed to meet him, now," Lady Metzler

whispered. "So his human soul will remember you. Unless it slips away forever."

Rudi hoped that wouldn't be the case. "Maybe his soul will come all the way back and he'll return to us some day."

"I hope so. I truly hope so."

The Scottie tilted its head to the side, looking up at Lady Metzler. It licked her nose once, then froze.

"It's time," Lady Metzler said, picking up the dog and placing it on the ground before them. "Rudi will keep you safe," she said softly. "Rudi will keep you safe." She kept repeating the phrase until the dog shook its head again and looked at both of them.

Clear intelligence shone out of the dog's eyes. Rudi knew he was looking at the soul of the boy.

"I will guard you with my life, Prince," Rudi said quickly.

The little dog nodded, and the light in his eyes faded. He looked up at both of them, puzzled for a moment, then he turned and climbed back into the little dog bed that sat on the floor next to what Rudi assumed was Lady Metzler's bed.

"I have everything prepared," Lady Metzler said, rising gracefully. She disappeared for a moment behind the bookshelves, then reappeared with a handful of papers that she shoved at Rudi. They declared that the little Scottie dog had all his shots up to date. There were also plane tickets, for them to leave in just a few hours.

"You want me to kidnap the prince?" Rudi asked, horrified. He'd never signed up to do anything like that.

"No, no, just take him away. The court will know he's with you. They just can't know where he is, not exactly. You need to keep him safe." The lady pulled Rudi closer and whispered very softly, "It isn't safe for him here. He's too vulnerable, particularly as such a small dog who can't change back."

Rudi swallowed. The hound clan had a history of assassinations among its leaders, though not for centuries; the rule had been civilized for a long while, with no one family maintaining all the power. Still, Rudi was uneasy. "For how long?" he asked.

"Not too long," Lady Metzler assured him. "I'll let you know when it's safe. Or you'll see a sign."

"A sign," Rudi said. How could he smuggle the prince out of the castle? Once he got to the car, he could keep the dog in the trunk, even though that wasn't safe. Maybe only keep him in the trunk until they got past the gate house? "If I leave now, the guard will suspect I have him," Rudi warned Lady Metzler as she handed him the Scottie.

"Of course they will. I'll also give them a false trail or two to follow. I have many students who owe me their allegiance, and the guard won't find you, I trust."

Rudi gave her a toothy grin. "I'll lead them on a good chase, I promise." It was exciting, in a way, to be doing this, though he was worried about taking the boy so far away from his family.

"I knew you'd come in handy some day," Lady Metzler said, some of the old steel returning to her voice. "Guard my grandson. Never trust magic. Always trust your nose."

She turned and picked up a dark cloak, casting it over them. It stank of sour herbs and dusky magic. "The fools will see you with a briefcase, that's all," she announced. "Throw the cloak away at the far end of the woods."

Rudi nodded. "Anything else?"

"Keep away from the court, and all the hound clan," she added. "And—try to make him happy." She pet the small dog, kissing it once between its ears. "Now, go."

Rudi slipped out the door and easily followed his own scent back to the front and out the door. The dog was almost asleep in Rudi's arms, but raised his head when they stepped outside. "It's okay," he whispered into the soft fur. "No one will harm you," he swore.

And no one would find them, either.

UNITED STATES, TEN YEARS AGO TO PRESENT

LUKAS

R udolf moved them often while Lukas waited for a sign.

Once, while they were walking down the quiet streets of a neighborhood in Georgia, the air soft and felted, smelling of wet, green growing things and old, old trees, Lukas scented another of the hound clan.

He stopped, standing very still, making Rudi stop as well.

"What is it?" Rudi asked. He scented the air. "You smell that, don't you? Good boy, Prince. Come on."

They went immediately back to the house and moved cities the next day.

A fter eight years, when they were living in the suburbs of Chicago, Rudi carried a large bag into his study, then called Lukas in and shut the door.

The room smelled of Rudi and all his electronics—computers, printers, and plastic cords. The bag Rudi carried smelled of cool magnets and cardboard. He'd been to a mall, or a big store: His shoes carried scents of industrial cleaners and the car.

Rudi himself smelled anxious and excited. He opened the bag and pulled out a white board, then he arranged rows of magnetic letters at the bottom, two full alphabets' worth. After he set the board on the floor, he sat in his chair and addressed Lukas.

"I was not spying on you, Prince," Rudi said clearly.

Lukas continued to sniff the board, as if he was uninterested, though he was suddenly wary.

"My new laptop came with a camera that automatically records everything. I didn't realize it was motion-sensitive."

Lukas finished sniffing the board and walked over to where Rudi sat, nosing his pockets as if looking for treats. He wanted to run far, far away, but he had to pretend he didn't understanding a word Rudi was saying. After all, Rudi was talking in a normal voice, not demanding attention or commanding obedience.

"It recorded you reading my magazines."

Hamlin rose up and pressed against Lukas. *Trust*, he said. *Pack. Of us*.

Lukas sat back and looked up at Rudi. He couldn't share his secrets, not even with his protector.

"If you ever want to talk to me," Rudi continued, nudging the board closer with his foot. "You can use this."

Lukas walked back to the board and looked at it again.

It would be so easy, so very easy, to reach out a paw and slide a letter. Even just the letter "K" to show that he understood.

But then Rudi would want more, demand Lukas say more, and Lukas couldn't take the risk. He merely nodded and wandered off, sniffing around Rudi's chair, teasing apart all the scents, trying to figure out exactly where Rudi's shoes had walked most recently.

"All right. Keep your secrets," Rudi said. "Lady Metzler would be proud of you."

From then on, there were always at least three different magazines open on the coffee table, set there for Lukas to read from every night.

And Rudi's computer was never close by.

T heir most recent city was Seattle. Lukas didn't mind the rain, and he loved the open dog parks. Grass grew all year round, but there were still seasons, which meant leaves to jump and play in. They'd arrived more than a year ago, and Lukas hoped they'd stay longer.

Summer was just ending, and the nights were turning cooler. Rudi had taken them to a different park, and they were walking home in the soft twilight when Lukas smelled it.

He sat down in the middle of the sidewalk, nose high.

What was that?

Rudi scented the air as well. "Clan?" he asked quietly.

Lukas stood and shook himself all over, pretending it hadn't been anything. He walked to the end of his leash, then looked over his shoulder at Rudi, who still stood motionless. *Well?* Lukas asked with all of his doggie spirit.

"All right then. Come on." Rudi started walking again.

The scent hadn't been clan.

That warm, wild heart that Lukas caught a whiff of was purely human, but strong enough to fight all the clans, and more.

It was the heart of the knight he'd dreamed of, so long ago. The knight who would defeat the shadows.

Lukas had to find it—*her*. He needed to be near her, bathe in her scent.

She gave him hope against the shadows. Finally, after all these years. Maybe, just maybe, he could be free of his curse. Oma would see that it was time, and would let him go back to being a real boy. Maybe she could explain as well why she'd cursed him with his greatest enemy.

Rudi always walked Lukas with a leash, but not because Lukas or Hamlin gave him any trouble. However, Rudi had been lulled into some complacency: Two of the boards in the corner of the fence around the backyard were loose enough that Lukas could squeeze through them.

And he did so, that night, as soon as he was certain Rudi was sound asleep.

It was the first time Lukas had been out in the city on his own. He transformed into Hamlin once past the fence and started to run. It thrilled his speeding heart to be in his native form. They raced through the empty streets, running at full speed past the dark houses and parked cars. They avoided the corner bars and young people smoking in the street, heading directly toward the old part of town and that scent, just there.

She lived on the first floor in a corner building, in the back, near the alley.

Lukas whined as he circled the building. There was no gate. The front door was old, and mostly glass, and the lock was ancient. The back door wasn't any better. Lukas could see where the doorjamb had been recently repaired —had it been kicked open? There weren't even bars on the street-level windows, unlike the building next door.

She was not safe there.

Somehow, he would have to find a way to guard her.

Every night, after Rudi had gone to bed, Lukas pushed his way through the fence, then he changed into another form and raced to the human's—Sally's—building. He wanted to confuse the scent, in case Rudi followed him, or anyone else.

The first week, Lukas let Sally see him as Hamlin, wondering how she would react to a very large, strange dog approaching her with no human nearby. It was on a quiet back street, full of parked cars, the houses and apartment buildings set back with fascinating smelling gardens.

Lukas walked directly up to Sally. She showed no fear, though he came up almost to her chest; she merely smiled at him with her warm brown eyes. She wore her hair pulled back in a ponytail, and a plain T-shirt and jeans. He blocked her path along the sidewalk, so she stopped.

"Hey, boy, do you live around here?" Sally asked, letting him sniff and lick at her fingers.

The salty tasted exploded across Lukas' tongue and he knew, *knew*, he was finally on the right path. She was the one, the heart of his knight.

"I can't take you home," she mourned after a final skritch around his ears. "My apartment will only take small dogs. And I'm sure you belong to someone. Go on, now. Go on home." She pushed past him and continued to walk down the street.

Lukas sat on the sidewalk and whined at her back. She had to take him in.

But she disappeared behind the unsafe door of her building and he could only guard her from the outside.

Two weeks later, Rudi walked into the living room carrying the board. He placed it on the floor, then stepped back, sitting down on the couch. He kept his tone conversational, though he smelled excited. "So who's the girl?" he asked.

Lukas looked at Rudi, then at the board. How had Rudi found out? He hadn't followed Lukas, that much Lukas knew. Was it because Lukas still carried her scent with him, after every visit?

He could walk away. Rudi hadn't taken him to his study and closed the door. He could go into the kitchen, or even out the dog door and into the backyard, though it was raining.

Trust, Hamlin said.

Lukas sat on the floor and looked at Rudi. Yes, he needed to trust Rudi about this. Sally was too important. He didn't know how she was part of the knight, how she would help defeat the shadows, but she would.

Slowly, Lukas walked to the board. With a single paw, he pulled letters from the edge into the middle, spelling out a single word.

GUARD.

Rudi nodded thoughtfully. "You need to guard her? Why?"

Lukas couldn't tell him, even if he'd been in human form. He padded over to where Rudi sat and sat down himself, looking up.

"Not much of a guard hound, are you?" Rudi asked.

Lukas cocked his head to one side and looked at him, his heart racing. Had Oma told Rudi his true breed? But Rudi was smiling casually, not as if the term had any importance.

"All right. if she's that important to you, Prince, I will guard her as well."

Lukas put his paws on Rudi's knee, then reached all the way up to lick his nose.

It was all Lukas could ask for.

Over the weeks, Lukas appeared to Sally as different breeds. He never appeared in the same place twice, but on different streets, at different times of the day, now that Rudi knew. He merely asked Lukas to be careful, and left the gate open for him so he didn't have to squeeze through the fence.

She seemed to really like terriers.

Lukas followed her endlessly through the streets, learning her patterns, where she went to lunch, where she shopped, where she worked. He couldn't follow her on the bus, but he knew it was the one going downtown, so tried to meet her there.

When he appeared to her as a Goldendoodle, she was walking with a friend, so she gave him only a quick pat on the head before walking away, saying to her friend, "I'm going to get a dog of my own this week."

Lukas woofed at her back. *Take me, take me!*

But she wasn't paying any attention.

It didn't take long for Lukas to track her scent to a nearby dog shelter, one she passed by all the time.

Lukas stayed in a strange dog's form, so Rudi couldn't follow his scent until early morning. Then he curled up on the step as a little Scottish terrier and waited for the shelter to open.

Rudi showed up a few hours later. "My Scottie ran off," he said, loud enough for Lukas to hear in the back pens. "I'd wondered if he'd shown up here."

The dogs who had been there for a while heard a friendly human's voice, not one of the regulars, and knew this was their chance, so they pressed forward, going up to the front of the cages. Like with Lukas, they knew Rudi was something different.

For the most part, the dogs had left Lukas alone, not trying to either befriend him or challenge him. Luckily, none of the volunteers had spent enough time in the cages to see just how odd their behavior was.

An older woman walked Rudi back to the cages, bringing him to Lukas' cage. But Lukas backed away from Rudi, shaking his head. He even growled.

"I guess that's not him," Rudi said, staring at Lukas. "Still, if I can't find my dog, I may come back in a few days," he warned.

Lukas turned his back on Rudi and wandered to another part of the cage.

He'd be gone before Rudi came back. Sally would come and get him.

That afternoon, Sally came by. Of course, she went straight to Lukas, as drawn to him as he'd always been to her. She put her fingers through the cage and he came right up and licked them, reveling in her complex scent.

"I've been seeing so many strays lately, it just made me want a dog of my own," Sally confessed to the volunteer, a dour young man.

"He does seem taken with you," the young man said.

"I know, but I shouldn't get the first dog I see, should I?" she asked.

Take me, take me! was all Lukas tried to say with his big doggie eyes and rapidly waving tail.

"If you think," the man said, leading her down the line of cages to the next group.

Lukas whined and stared after her. She had to take him. She just had to.

Finally, she did, and called him Pixie.

L ukas had discovered that a side effect of Oma's curse was that he could now see ghosts.

There had only been a couple of places that Rudi and he had lived in that were actively haunted: The old shotgun house in New Orleans, as well as a hobby farm in Iowa.

In New Orleans, the ghosts had wanted the place clean. Lukas kept all his balls and toys away from that side of the house, never marked his territory there, and even nosed along the leaves if they piled up.

At the farm, Lukas had never been able to figure out exactly what the spirits wanted, but the seemed to like the way he ran across the broad yard, so whether it was snowing, raining, or too hot to move, Lukas always ran from the front fence to the fields behind the house and back again, at least once a day.

At Sally's apartment, the ghosts wanted to be acknowledged, or they'd break Sally's dishes, make her TV just show snow, and once they even bunched up her dining room rug so she tripped.

So Lukas greeted each ghost as he or she came in, circling and barking, saying hello. Sally didn't seem to mind too much.

The ghosts wore old-fashioned clothes, suits and dresses, gloves and hats. They didn't smell like anything.

And the ghosts sometimes gave him treats, cold snippets of bacon that melted on his tongue like ice.

Fall and winter passed. Lukas protected Sally as much as he could, though he was trapped inside much more often now. He scented Rudi near the building more than once, so he knew that his protector was still looking out for him.

Sally loved dancing, and went regularly. Lukas watched her carefully when she practiced in the apartment. He was glad he wasn't human those times: It looked too complicated, and he was sure he'd trip over his own feet.

Just as spring had started, and the crocuses were pushing through the soggy earth, Sally came home one night smelling of feathers.

The warm feathers of the knight.

Lukas would have given anything to ask her about it directly. Either Sally, or Oma. Instead, he stayed just outside the bathroom as she showered, and he jumped onto her bed as soon as she climbed in.

"I met a guy," Sally told Lukas after she'd talked about dancing that night. "His name's Peter. You can't ever tell him, but I think he's the one," she confessed.

Lukas gave a soft *woof* of agreement.

This Peter was part of the one, part of that grand knight who could help Lukas defeat the shadows. Those warm feathers that lined the nest, that made the scent of the knight *home*.

Now, Lukas just had to find the others—those cool scales and biting sword.

Lukas tried not to stare too hard at Peter when he came in door of Sally's apartment. The human boy was tall, thin, with blond hair and dark skin.

Behind him stood a shadowy figure wearing a huge cloak made of raven feathers, marking Peter as a member of the raven clan. His scent was spicy and warm, and the cool feeling of glass swirled around him.

Lukas had been too young to be formally introduced to members of the other clans at the court, but he'd seen them all and been taught to identify them: The quicksilver scent of the tiger clan, the warm mushroom-and-earth smell of the boars, how the vipers glowed, while the crocodiles stayed in the shadows.

Peter stood quiet and still after Sally invited him into the living room. Lukas liked that about him. He sniffed around Peter's feet, teasing apart where Peter lived, where he'd been, in case he ever needed to find Peter in a hurry. Lukas ignored Peter's hand when he held it out—both Lukas and Hamlin already had Peter's scent firmly in their memory. Peter smelled cautious, but not afraid. He'd need that bravery when they fought the shadows.

Finally, Lukas sat down in front of Peter, sitting on his hind legs and looking up at him.

Hamlin surged forward, and they held out their paw.

Peter looked at Sally.

"I've never taught him to shake. He doesn't know any tricks. At least, not from me. I've never seen him do that before."

Peter squatted down so his eyes were at the same level as Lukas', then he reached out and took Lukas' paw.

Hamlin said quietly, *trust*, as he pushed forward.

Panic welled through Lukas as he watched his paw grow bigger, large enough to fill Peter's palm.

"You have the biggest eyes," Peter said.

Notice the paw, Lukas felt like shouting, pressing down harder with it. He restrained the urge to bark. Were all ravens this slow? He'd always heard they were the sharpest of the clans. Peter needed to see him, *now*, before Sally noticed.

Because she *was* sharp, and she would see the difference.

Hamlin lifted up his other paw, which Peter took.

Finally, the birdman looked down and realized that Lukas was something else, just like he was.

"And big paws, too, for such a little dog," Peter said, his eyes dark and wondering.

At least this Peter knew enough not to say anything more to Sally. Despite Hamlin's urging of trust, Lukas wasn't sure it was the right thing to do.

"You think so?" Sally asked as she picked Lukas up to take a look.

Lukas played the puppy, wiggling in her arms, licking her face and asking to be let back down. He couldn't have Sally looking too closely at him, not ever.

Laughing, Sally placed him back on the ground.

Lukas took a stand in front of Sally, staring back at Peter.

"You protect Sally, don't you?" Peter asked.

Okay, so maybe Peter wasn't too slow. He understood Lukas' role. Lukas gave a happy bark and padded back over to Peter.

"I will, too," Peter told Lukas.

If Lukas could have rolled his eyes, he would have. Sally didn't need Peter's protection, not while Lukas was here.

Then Lukas ambled off to get a treat, leaving the humans so they could talk.

When it grew quiet, Lukas walked back toward the vestibule to see what they were doing.

Peter and Sally were kissing.

Lukas whirled and snuck away so they wouldn't hear him.

Hamlin rose up again, curling around him.

A part of Lukas had wondered if maybe Sally, someday, would be his mate, not just someone he guarded, but who would be with him.

It wasn't to be.

S omething was going on with Peter. Was he in trouble? Sally smelled worried, but not full of tears—no, she smelled like steel and hard determination.

Lukas knew she was stronger than any other person he'd ever met, maybe even Oma.

"You be on the lookout for a woman with red hair," Sally warned Lukas as they went for their evening walk. "She's been bothering Peter."

Lukas didn't scent the woman on Sally, but he still spent as much time as he could looking up, not just watching the ground. He didn't smell anyone around Sally's building whose scent lingered, as if they'd been coming by and watching the apartment.

Why was Peter endangering Sally? He should know better. Lukas thought the ravens were more protective of their mates.

But Peter also smelled young. He was older than Lukas, but he carried the milky scent of a boy, not a man.

Two nights later, Lukas woke from a warm dream to the stink of shadows. He shook himself, coming awake instantly.

He was still in Sally's apartment, curled up in the living room on his end of the couch. Where was the smell coming from? He raised his head. It wasn't from the alley behind the apartment, or the sidewalk beside it.

No, it was coming from inside the apartment building itself.

Lukas growled and raced to the door, planting himself on the parquet floor.

Someone was there, outside, in the hallway.

When the doorbell rang, Sally walked into the vestibule, still drying her hands on a kitchen towel.

Lukas growled at her.

"Pixie?" Sally asked, wondering.

Hamlin growled, now, low and menacing. Lukas knew that he'd grown in size, and his hair stood on end, his hackles rising.

"Who's there?" Sally called when whoever it was rang the doorbell again. She didn't try to come closer, but stayed where she was, staring at him from the edge of the front hall.

"Tamara. You met me, dancing."

Lukas didn't care where she'd come from. She stank of shadows and some other clan, warm fur that had been matted and stained—not hound clan, maybe boar or tiger clan.

"I'm sorry, I can't come to the door right now," Sally said.

"But you must let me in," the woman wheedled.

Lukas planted his feet wide, staring at Sally, his teeth bared. Whatever was outside could *not* be allowed to come in.

"I really can't," Sally said, watching him wide-eyed. She smelled scared.

Lukas knew it wasn't because of the creature outside,

but because of him. However, he couldn't let her near the door. She didn't know that he wouldn't hurt her, and there was no way he could tell her.

"Not even if I have news about Peter?" the voice through the door asked, dripping with false sweetness.

"What about Peter?" Sally asked.

Lukas growled louder. That other woman was *not* coming in here. He didn't know if she lied about Peter, and he didn't care. She was tainted with shadows. He couldn't let them in here.

"He's going away this weekend, you know."

"Yes, he told me," Sally said firmly.

Leaving? Why was the birdman leaving? Was this why Sally had been sad earlier?

"You know he'll face his death, there, at Ravens' Hall."

"You're being ridiculous," Sally said defiantly.

Lukas couldn't let down his guard, couldn't let Sally get closer to the door. But he wanted to grin and wag his tail at her: There was that strong heart. Hot anger now underlay the scent of Sally's fear. She would stand up to any challenge, every challenge. He'd been right about her.

"There's just so much you don't know. About him. And me."

Lukas could tell from Sally's face that she also added him into the mix of things she didn't know about. He'd explain, or he'd have Rudi explain. Someday.

"You should just give him up now. It's hopeless, completely hopeless."

"You're crazy," Sally told her. She added a whisper, "Good boy for not letting her in."

Lukas nodded at her, but didn't let down his guard.

"No, my dear, you are." With a laugh, the other girl scratched her claws across the door and walked away.

"What was that all about?" Sally wondered out loud. "It's okay, now, Pixie, she's gone," she told Lukas.

Lukas scented the air. Something wasn't right. Something magical and tainted with shadows still remained. He gave Sally a woof and sat down right next to the door, determined not to let anything come through.

"All right, you stay there. Don't let her in," Sally added. "I'm calling Peter."

Lukas could still smell the fear on Sally. It would take her a while to forget, for her to accept him as her little Scottie dog again. However, he'd done the right thing.

The scent of the shadows increased. Lukas growled, low and deep in his throat.

Something was trying to get in.

"Pixie?" Sally came back, phone in hand. "What is it?"

He barked, pawing at the shadows that were seeping under the threshold. How could he stop them? His claws couldn't tear them to pieces. They were just like smoke, ephemeral and without true form.

Sally was already talking with Peter, but the birdman wouldn't get there in time to get her away.

Hamlin surged forward, and they grew in size just as the shadow began to take shape.

It looked like a ghost tiger, but its claws were deadly sharp, as were its teeth.

Hamlin charged at it, rising up on his hind legs to smash down against the beast.

He went right though it.

The beast came inside, heading for Sally. Hamlin tore after it, barking at it, harrying it, worrying it, biting again and again into the faint smoke that left a bitter taste on his tongue.

It couldn't reach Sally, not with Hamlin always standing between it and her. He bristled and lunged, barked and bit. Sally ran away, it chased, and Hamlin fought.

But it was just smoke. He couldn't tear it to pieces, no matter how he tried. How could he fight a shadow? That had always been his problem.

Finally, the thing dissipated, either the spell worn down or because it couldn't reach its target.

Hamlin shrank back down, and Lukas turned mournful eyes to Sally.

"You. Stay. There," she said, pointing a shaking hand at him.

Lukas whined and thumped his tail, his ears down. He'd just been protecting her. Couldn't she see that?

A knock on the door startled both of them. Lukas ran to it first.

"Sally? Sally? It's me, Peter."

Lukas sniffed. Traces of the shadows remained, but not coming from Peter—he smelled of warm feathers, hard glass, and fear. Lukas barked once in reply, and he let Sally open the door this time.

At least Peter recognized that Lukas was the one who first had to be appeased. Peter knelt slowly, letting Lukas and Hamlin get a good sniff of his hand, making sure no shadows clung to him before they stepped to the side to let Peter in.

Lukas hadn't expected Sally to slip out the door, closing it quickly behind her. He gave an unhappy bark.

"It's okay," Peter said. "I'm here with her. I'll stay with her."

There wasn't anything Lukas could do with the door between them. Not that he couldn't knock it down if he needed to, or crash through one of the windows if need arose.

Peter couldn't protect Sally, couldn't guard her as well

as Lukas could, but for now, she was safe enough with him.

He listened to their conversation. At least Peter told Sally that she should trust Lukas. He waited, frustrated, not letting Sally out of earshot, until the door opened again. Then he immediately stood between Sally and Peter. He trusted Peter, but Peter didn't know about the shadows.

It was good for Peter to acknowledge that Lukas could take good care of Sally.

And he would.

<hr>

Sally didn't trust Lukas after that. She was always staring at him as if she expected him to suddenly change form again.

He didn't know what to do, so he played at being more of a puppy with her. He carried her things out of his toy basket, looking expectantly for her to play with him. He also followed her everywhere, from kitchen, to living room, to bedroom, and back again, always hanging out in the same room with her. He kept alert to more shadows, patrolling the small apartment regularly.

Sally seemed wary of another attack. She took Lukas everywhere she went: To the office, to the store, for long walks. Whatever that shadow thing was, it had scared her more than he had.

"I'm off to get groceries," Sally told him one evening. "I'll be right back."

Lukas stood by the door, willing to go with her, but she told him, "Not this time."

Then Sally didn't come back.

Lukas fretted, waiting by the door, getting up every

time he heard footsteps, but Sally didn't return. Not for hours and hours.

Something was wrong. Was it the shadows? Was it Peter? Had she been in an accident?

Lukas decided to wait until midnight, then he was bursting out of the apartment. However, before he could go through one of the windows, he heard keys in the lock.

Kate, Sally's regular dog sitter, came through the door. She wore her usual oversized poncho, and smelled of her three dogs, four cats, and two canaries.

Lukas liked her. Kate always talked to him as if he could understand everything she said.

"Hey boy, I know you're worried," Kate said when Lukas came right up to her. "Sally went away with her boyfriend for the weekend. Unexpected death in his family. She said to be sure to tell you not to worry."

That other woman had said Peter was going away for the weekend to face his death. Now Sally was there with him?

Lukas was worried. There was only one thing to do.

When Kate opened the building door to take him on a walk, Lukas raced out in front of her. He paused, letting her almost catch up, but he kept running ahead, running straight to Rudi's house. It still looked the same, the yard well trimmed with healthy grass, the curtains drawn back showing the darkened living room inside.

Lukas sat on Rudi's doorstep, barking frantically, hoping upon hope that Rudi was there, that he'd come see what was happening.

"Ah, hello," Rudi said, finally opening the door. He wore a T-shirt and jeans, his feet bare, his hair messy. He'd probably been sleeping.

Lukas sat up and put his front paws on Rudi's thighs.

Rudi looked between Lukas and the sitter, just now catching up with him.

"Is everything all right, ah, Pixie?" Rudi asked.

Lukas growled and shook.

"Hello, miss," Rudi said, crouching down to pet Lukas.

"Thank you for catching Pixie. He seemed determined to see you," Kate said, a bit breathless.

"Where's Sally?" Rudi asked.

Lukas pressed up against Rudi's legs so Rudi could feel every shake and tremor.

"She went out of town—"

"With Peter?"

Lukas relaxed a little. Rudi had been keeping track of Sally, too.

"Yes. There was a sudden death in Peter's family."

Lukas growled softly, just a quiet rumble that only Rudi could hear.

"Is everything okay?" Rudi asked.

Lukas shook himself, though Kate said, "Yes, everything's fine."

"I thought Peter's family lived here in Seattle," Rudi said slowly.

Lukas wanted to wag his tail, glad that Rudi had learned so much.

"It was an uncle living in Wyoming," Kate said.

Lukas turned to stare directly into Rudi's eyes, pleading with him with his entire doggy heart. *We need to go to her. Find her. Guard her.*

"Wyoming, you said?" Rudi asked, nodding yes.

Lukas gave a soft bark. Yes! Rudi understood. Lukas stood there, looking up at Rudi, expecting that his next words would be an offer to take care of Lukas while Sally was gone.

"Okay. I need to go now," Rudi said, standing. "You

take care of our boy," he added.

Lukas whined. No! Rudi needed to take him with. He needed to go find Sally. Maybe he could run away again.

"You stay here," Rudi instructed Lukas. "I'm sure everything is fine."

Kate clipped the leash to Lukas' collar and started walking away. Lukas dragged his heels, but there wasn't anything he could do. He had to trust that Rudi would find Sally and guard her.

He'd never hated his curse so much in his entire life.

After the sitter had gone, Lukas dragged his dog bed out to the front vestibule so he could sleep next to the door. He woke up every time the hallway door opened or when someone walked by. But he didn't know what else to do.

Two nights later, a low growl in the hallway outside Sally's door woke Lukas from a sound sleep.

Was that a shadow? He didn't smell any, but then the growl came again.

Without hesitation, Hamlin rose up, and they transformed into his natural shape, much larger and more deadly than the little Scottie dog.

To all except the shadows.

Claws scratched the door, then a key.

Hamlin growled low and deep in his throat, a warning to any who would trespass.

The door sprang open and Hamlin tensed, ready to jump.

Rudi stood in the doorway.

Rudi, who could never know Lukas' secret.

"So, it is true," Rudi said.

SEATTLE, PRESENT DAY

RUDI

R udi stared at the hound in front of him, lit only by the hallway light, half in shadows. It was the prince, Lukas. The hound stood frozen in the entranceway to Sally's apartment, hackles raised, still growling. Though part of the prince stood in shadow, Rudi could still see enough to know just how big a hound the prince was: Not just a large breed, but giant class, like a Great Dane or an Irish Wolfhound.

This hound smelled different than the Scottie dog. Instead of a sweet, milky, young-dog scent, the prince now smelled more like a greyhound: musky, with a cooler thread running through it, like steel.

Rudi had heard rumors about how gangly the prince's true hound nature was, how he looked more like a mongrel than a purebred. It was the jaw that gave him that look, strong and out of proportion with the triangular, greyhound face. Maybe his nose gave that impression as well—Lukas had the nose of a scent hound, larger than normal, with the hanging ears, too, to help capture any scents. His eyes were the same startling blue as a husky's. He had a brindle color pattern, with gray stripes against a dark brown coat.

However, when the prince shook himself, turned, and walked away, he moved with the graceful gait of a hunter, silent and swift.

Rudi closed the door and asked, "Why have you been hiding so long?" He walked further into the apartment, switching on a light. "Why did you pretend to be stuck?" Because Rudi was certain that if Lukas could change from one hound breed into another, he could also transform into his human form. "You've been playing at this for ten years."

What had happened at the court that would make a boy —such a young boy—hide for so long?

The apartment looked comfortable enough, with a long, olive green couch that ran along one wall. The far end was where the prince, as a Scottie, generally sat. A large basket of toys sat next to the electronics cabinet, that the prince had mouthed and played with.

"You could have told me. I would have kept your secret," Rudi added. "I should have known, though, when you showed me you could read." He'd just thought the boy's soul had been rising more, maybe earlier in the evening instead of just at midnight, and had hoped the prince would come all the way back to them.

"Sally is fine, by the way. Her boyfriend, Peter—her fiancé, now—is a full raven warrior, and going to take over the Ravens' Hall. They were the ones who told me that you could change shape."

The prince returned to where Rudi stood with his leash in his mouth, then dropped it at Rudi's feet.

"Still not talking, eh?" Rudi picked up the leash. "I'll just carry this." He hoped that by showing the prince that he trusted him not to bound off, maybe the prince would trust him a little more.

Rudi would be able to track the prince if he stayed in this hound shape, or if he changed back into the Scottie. However, if he changed into a different form, Rudi would lose his scent. It explained why Rudi hadn't always been able to track Lukas when he slipped out of the fence: He'd never imagined that the prince could transform into different hound forms.

The night was cool—summer was still a few weeks away. Dark, quiet houses lined the streets. The prince led the way, walking quickly down the hill, moving with an unnatural directness.

Generally, only humans walked such straight lines. Dogs ambled, and as a Scottie, the prince had always emulated that behavior, wandering from one side of the sidewalk to the other, catching new scents.

Finally, the prince nosed open the gate to a pea-patch community garden, a place where people living in the nearby apartment buildings could have a bit of earth to grow things. Though it had rained most of the day, Rudi could still scent that the prince, as the Scottie, had been there many times before.

The garden itself smelled of wet ground and hearty herbs that had weathered the Seattle winter, rosemary and sage. Cedar chips covered the path. If it had been daylight, Rudi would have been able to see the brilliant begonias instead of just catching a whiff of their sour scent.

In the darkest part of the garden, away from the streetlights and hidden by ferns from the closest neighbor's window, the prince stopped, then turned and faced Rudi.

After sniffing the air again to make sure they were alone, Rudi encouraged his hound soul to come closer, both to chase away the darkness but also so that they'd both see.

The prince gave a great shake, then lowered his head.

Rudi caught his breath, waiting. What was the prince going to do?

The mottled fur melted away, revealing pure, pale skin underneath.

"Oh," Rudi exclaimed softly as the prince changed before him, regaining his human form, becoming Lukas.

If the prince has been gangly as a hound, Lukas retained that as a boy—no—a man, now. His hair was long, black, and curly, falling into eyes that retained that searing blue color. He was wiry, but he had a strong chest and powerful legs. He looked so much like his father, the king.

Lukas' expression was pure sorrow, though. "Remember their scent," he commanded.

"What—"

Shadows attacked the prince. Rudi automatically took a step backward, then swore and took a step forward.

Lukas held up his hands, indicating that Rudi shouldn't come closer. Then Lukas closed his eyes and pressed his lips together, twitching where the shadows spread across him, grimacing in pain.

Rudi had never seen such an abomination. The shadows were like filth, trying to stain the clean skin of the prince, to get inside him and taint him. They turned the pale pink skin gray where they lingered, sucking the life out of it.

However, Rudi did as he'd been instructed: He stayed still and breathed deeply so that both his human and his hound soul would recognize and remember the scent.

It was a wet smell, moldy and ancient, like a ruined graveyard sitting next to an apple orchard where the fruit had been left to rot. Bitter magic curled through the scent, reminding him of Lady Metzler.

This wasn't a natural attack. It was magical. Someone had cursed the prince.

After a short while, less than a minute, the prince shrank back down into his Scottie dog form. He shook the shadows from him, like a dog shedding water.

"Oh, my prince," Rudi said softly, kneeling down. "Who cursed you? Why? Do you know?"

Rudi had thought he'd been protecting the prince from the court, from any hounds who might harm him. He hadn't realized that the attack had already come and gone.

With a soft *woof*, the prince led the way to an old sewer grate. He swiped away the wet leaves with his paws, planted his feet deliberately, then gave another soft bark.

"What is it?" Rudi asked, guilt wracking him. He thought he'd been doing such a fine job. Now, he knew that he'd been barely adequate.

The grate had been imprinted with the words, "Property of King County."

The Scottie's paws framed the word "King."

With a horrified whisper, Rudi asked, "Was it the king who did this? Who ordered this done?"

The prince shook his head no. He nosed a leaf back onto the grate, partially covering the "N" in "County." Then he replaced his paws.

"Count?" Rudi guessed. Then he looked again. "Court. Someone at court."

The prince gave a soft bark and wagged his tail.

Rudi knelt down next to the little dog, his prince, whom he'd failed so badly. "I will go to the court and find out who cursed you. I will make them reverse it. I promise you this."

The little dog cocked its head to one side and gazed up at him.

The look was cute, endearing, and completely heartbreaking at the same time. Rudi grieved that any boy, let alone a prince of the hound clan, should be forced to stay in this form, unable to grow up as he should have.

Finally, the prince nodded once. Then he surged forward and licked Rudi's nose, as if he'd been forgiven.

However, Rudi knew he'd never forgive himself for not hounding the prince about this secret sooner, for not doing more for his charge.

The official story given out from the court about Lukas was that he'd been taken to a safe, hidden location to live out the rest of his days as a dog. Oscar, Lukas' cousin, had been training to be the heir since before Lukas had been born. The ministers in the court could, of course, decide to choose someone else, but Oscar was a purebred greyhound, an eloquent speaker, and well-liked.

Rudi has always assumed that the court knew that he had the prince, and that they knew Lukas was safe. That's what Lady Metzler had told him, all those years ago.

Still, Rudi took no chance, doing everything he could to hide his home so no one could track him. He didn't want to leave Seattle just yet, and he wasn't sure Lukas would leave without Sally.

On the first leg of Rudi's trip, to New York, he traveled with almost nothing: A paperback book and a burner cell phone, programmed to accept just one number, from Sally. Once he got there, he took advantage of a Turkish sauna, steaming and soaking all the scents from his skin, so no one could track him back to Seattle. Then he dressed in all new clothes, leaving the old ones in the locker he'd rented, not touching them again.

No trace of any scent of Seattle remained by the time Rudi boarded the plane to Hamburg. He traveled under his own name, on a direct flight. The hounds knew him, and any additional subterfuge would raise questions.

The flight was uneventful: No shadows chased Rudi, even in his dreams.

Only awake did the horror revisit him. When a cloud passed over the sun, he paused, startled, and looked up, afraid that shadows would now attack him.

Did Lady Metzler know? Of course she did. He smelled her magic on Lukas when Lukas had changed. Rudi tried to set up a meeting with her during a layover, but the helpful young man on the other end only said he didn't know, that Rudi would have to see if he could be fit in when he arrived.

The guards at the gate to the castle looked puzzled when Rudi climbed out of the car. He knew nothing smelled of him, not really.

While scanning his passport, the guard asked, "How was your trip?"

"They lost my luggage on the first leg," Rudi replied with an exasperated sigh. "Had to replace everything."

The guards relaxed after that and waved Rudi through.

The castle looked the same it had the last time Rudi had been there during the daylight hours: The grass in front of the gray stone building was beautifully trimmed, the many windows on the building gleamed in the sunlight, while the trees smelled of earth and hound and home.

More guards waited just inside the broad, wooden castle doors. Rudi detected not just more cameras, but heat sensors as well.

Were they there because he'd smuggled away the

prince? Lady Metzler had assured him that the cameras would be fooled. Maybe they thought more, redundant electronics couldn't be tampered with as easily.

The two-story ceiling leading up to an incredible fresco of a brilliant blue sky and white fluffy clouds was the same, as was the white marble floor and ancient tapestries showing scenes from medieval hunts and hounds.

It was beautiful and should have filled Rudi's heart with joy.

It stank of the shadows.

Rudi still smiled as he walked over to the huge reception desk. It was an antique, with carved hound paws for feet and intricate, inlaid swirling designs racing across the surface. "I'd like to see Lady Metzler, if that's possible," he asked politely.

"I need to see if she's receiving today," said the very prim young man sitting behind the desk, wearing white-framed glasses, a dark suit, and a thin blue tie.

"Has she been ill?" Rudi asked, worried.

"Yes," came the curt reply. "Please wait here."

Rudi hadn't heard anything from Lady Metzler since he'd taken Lukas, not a postcard or a letter. He'd tried not to worry, as she'd told him not to stay in contact. But he hadn't heard any news of her being ill through any other channels.

To distract himself, Rudi tried to pinpoint the location of the shadows: Did they lurk in the corners? Up around the ceiling? He couldn't see them—but then again, he was a scent hound, not a sight hound, and Lukas had told him to memorize the scent of the shadows.

When Rudi walked to the far end of the hall, he discovered another person waiting there, sitting on an uncomfortable-looking carved chair. She was ancient, tiny, and Asian. Her hair was more white than black, pulled back casually from her face and piled high on her head, held there by an elaborate set of jeweled sticks. She wore a Western-style jacket and skirt made from deep red silk, and seemed to be covered in darkness. Not like the shadows he was scenting, but like a curtain that hid her true features.

"Hello," Rudi said, nodding to her as he pretended to be interested in the nearby tapestry, showing a group of fox hounds running across a field.

The woman nodded in return and went back to staring straight ahead.

She wasn't of the hound clan. Rudi, like the others in the hound clan, had met many of the other clans when he'd spent time at the court. He'd gotten a lot more practice determining people from other clans when he'd gone to Ravens' Hall to guard Sally.

He couldn't figure out what clan the Asian woman was, though—he'd never caught such a scent before, something earthy, yet soft, slippery.

The shadows were stronger at this end of the hall. Rudi risked taking a deeper breath, nose toward the corner.

The woman got out of her chair and walked with clicking heels over to where Rudi stood.

"You smell them too, don't you, hound?" she hissed quietly in lightly accented English.

Rudi looked at her, shocked. Was she talking about the shadows? Did she somehow sense them as well?

"These fools—they do not see what has invaded the very heart of their home. Bah," she whispered, disgusted. "We will talk later. I will find you," she added before she walked away, the sound of her heels echoing through the hallway.

Who was she? What was she?

And did Rudi have an ally?

"**L**ady Metzler will see you now," the prim young man announced as Rudi walked back toward the reception desk.

The Asian woman was nowhere to be seen, but Rudi had enough of her scent to know she'd gone into one of the meeting rooms on the right, reserved for court ministers and visiting dignitaries.

The young man led Rudi through unknown parts of the castle, but he recognized the last hallway they entered, with the same worn rugs, old paintings, and closed-in feeling. They were going to Lady Metzler's rooms. He could smell the lavender and the chemicals used to clean the wood and the carpets here.

Relief cascaded over Rudi. If the lady had been really sick, wouldn't she be in the infirmary, and not in her own bed?

The receptionist opened the door and Rudi's sense of well-being flew away as the stench of shadows rolled out, mingled with old urine, musty books, and bitter magic.

Without another word, Rudi pushed into the room.

Lady Metzler sat up on her tiny bed, supported by pillows, the huge shelves of books that filled the room and blocked off the rest of it towering over her. Her gray curls flailed out from her head, and her amber-colored, normally clear eyes were dark and hazed. She wore a clean white nightshirt, but it was obvious she hadn't been dressed all day.

She wasn't sick with something easy to cure, like the flu.

"You have come," Lady Metzler hissed. "Why have you come?" Her voice sounded querulous and old, her former strength gone.

Rudi's heart fell to his shoes. His former mentor was no longer there; just her shell remained.

"To see you," Rudi said gently, walking further into the room. He glanced up. He couldn't see the shadows lingering in the tall corners, though he was certain they were there.

Along with more than one camera, which was easily justified by a sick woman who probably pushed away all company.

Rudi cursed himself, wishing he'd come more prepared to evade any electronic eavesdropping.

"Yes, yes," Lady Metzler said, nodding. "I've changed." She leaned forward, whispering, "It's those damn shadows. They won't leave me alone, won't leave my thoughts to myself. Yes." She reached out and grabbed Rudi's arm with surprising strength. "They're everywhere, you know. Filthy shadows. Trying to reach my boy."

"Your boy?" Rudi asked, confused. They'd already reached Lukas.

"The king. But I won't help them. They try to trick me, like they tricked me before. I've helped them too much, in the past. I only did it because I had to. I thought it would keep him safe."

"Keep who safe?" Rudi knew it was dangerous to ask. However, he had to know. Had Lady Metzler been the one to curse the prince? If so, did she still have the mental capacity to reverse it? He'd promised the prince. Was he destined to be such a poor guardian?

"Gone, now. Gone, gone," Lady Metzler sang out. "The shadows can't find him, can't take him, now. He's gone, gone, gone."

"What if he came back?" Rudi asked.

"No, no, not until he's cured. Cursed and cured, cursed and cured."

Rudi didn't want to give whoever was watching any more information. "Who is cursed, my lady? Who needs to be cured? I don't understand who you're talking about."

"So good, you are," Lady Metzler said, smiling at him. "To come and see your old pen pal. My dreams were right, at least about you. I need an old friend like you, now."

"And I am here, my lady," Rudi said gallantly while he thought furiously. Could he maybe take her out for a walk, in the garden, so they could talk more freely? Or should he build something tonight, some sort of jammer, and come back tomorrow?

However, this wasn't an American adventure movie: He didn't have the tools he needed, he didn't know where to get the parts immediately, not in Germany, and he also had no idea what frequency would work or if there were additional devices that he couldn't detect through the stench of sickness and shadow.

"Would you like—" Rudi started, when the door opened.

The prim receptionist was back, and the tiny Asian woman stood beside him.

"Lady—" the young man said.

"Please, bring her in," Rudi said, giving the man one of his more charming smiles.

The Asian woman walked calmly into the room, as if the looming bookcases and rolling miasma of illness were nothing new. "I am Mei Ling Wang," she said with a bow of her head. "I wanted to see you again before I go."

Rudi introduced himself and Lady Metzler.

Mei Ling stared at the lady, then glanced around the rest of the room. Though she didn't show her displeasure, Rudi felt it rolling off her in waves.

"The hound clan ministers claim there are no shadows,

that they are just the imaginations of a disturbed mind. Your mind," she said coolly.

"My son, the king, he can't see the shadows, so they must not exist, no?" Lady Metzler replied.

Rudi stood up straighter, recognizing the sly voice. Lady Metzler, the supreme puppet master, seemed to be returning.

"And what about you?" Mei Ling said, turning to Rudi.

"I've dreamed about them," Rudi said. "Attacking a boy." That was the closest he could get, in that room, to telling the truth.

"A boy. A prince? The hound prince?" Mei Ling asked, turning back to Lady Metzler.

"I sent my grandson away, ten years ago," Lady Metzler said sadly. "At first, I knew he was safe. But now he's hidden from me. My magic can't find him, though I've tried and tried over the years."

Rudi had wondered why the hounds hadn't pursued him more closely. He'd known the lady had thrown them off the track. But that meant they didn't know where Lukas was, that he was safe.

They'd kill Rudi if they ever found out he'd taken the boy.

"I've been told he can stop the shadows," Mei Ling said.

"I don't know where he is," Lady Metzler said, her eyes clearing. "If I did, I would bring you to him."

Lady Metzler didn't flick her eyes over to Rudi, or squeeze his arm suddenly, or give any sort of signal of the importance of what she'd just said.

Rudi knew an order when he heard it, though.

SEATTLE, PRESENT DAY

LUKAS

Lukas waited impatiently for someone, anyone, to come back and tell him what had happened.

If the apartment had felt too small before, now Lukas paced from room to room as if it were a cage: kitchen, dining room—looping around the table in the center—to the TV cabinet in the living room, then the couch, into and out of the bedroom, to the front door, then back to the kitchen again. His nails clicked on the hardwood floors. He would bend down to sniff the air under the door leading to the hall, just for some sort of distraction.

Every time Lukas heard someone out in the hallway, he raced to the door to wait, disappointed when they didn't smell familiar and didn't stop.

Finally, he heard a key in the lock and smelled Sally and Peter outside.

"Hi," Sally said, seeing Lukas when she opened the door. She stood awkwardly in the vestibule, Peter crowding in behind her.

"Hey," Peter said. He glanced at Sally, then transformed slightly, his eyes going raven-dark.

The hackles stood up on Lukas' neck.

They knew. They both knew that he was more than just an odd dog.

Of course they knew. Rudi's scent still lingered, subtly, on Peter, though it was several days old.

Lukas peered curiously at the birdman. What did he see? Could he, a raven, see anything? Or did the old curse still work?

"Rudi said your name was Lukas," Sally said quietly.

Lukas shook his head sharply.

"No," Peter squawked, his voice mixed and harsh. "That's his human name. Not his hound soul."

Lukas gave a yip. Exactly right. He walked closer to Peter, stood up on his hind legs, and rested one paw on Peter's knee. What did he see?

"You just look like a dog," Peter told him. "I can't see anything special or different about you."

Lukas nodded. Good. It was one of the things that had kept him hidden all these years: That to humans, as well as other clans, he appeared to be just a simple animal. The hound clan knew the scent of this shape, but they'd never found him. Other dogs knew the difference, but they were the only ones.

Were ravens the same? Did other birds sense the difference?

"I don't know what to call you," Sally said, breaking in, her voice sounding strained. "And I don't know what to do with you."

Lukas didn't know what he could do to comfort Sally. He walked over to her and butted his head against her calves, then sat back and looked up at her.

"I know you're more than just a dog," Sally said quietly. "I hope I get to meet your human soul, someday."

Lukas nodded. He hoped that time would come soon.

"There isn't anything we can do for now," Peter said, softly. "Rudi's gone off to your court, and we're all waiting to hear from him." Then he smiled. "Want to hear about the challenge and Ravens' Hall?"

Lukas nodded and led the way into the living room. He sat down, then lay down, his head on his paws.

Listening to stories was as good a way to wait as his constant pacing.

Because that's what Lukas still had to do: Wait, like he'd always waited.

T he next afternoon, Lukas was at the door an instant before someone knocked.

It was Rudi, and something—no, someone else.

Sally opened the door. Lukas barged past Rudi to see who traveled with him.

It was a small Asian woman, who smelled of silk and scales—the scales of the knight Lukas had dreamed of, that Sally and Peter were also a part of. Those scales made the knight's armor solid and strong.

He gave a delighted yip, sitting up on his hind legs so maybe she would offer her hand to him and he could better take in her scent.

The Asian woman raised a single eyebrow. "This? This is the hound prince?"

She sounded so disappointed. Lukas whined, dropping down to all fours, his ears and tail drooping.

No, he could show her. He gave another bark, turned, and walked back into the apartment.

"That's just his disguise," Rudi explained as he followed, closing the door. "It isn't his true form. I think it's part of what's kept him safe."

Lukas nodded. *Yes.*

But he was safe here, with these people. The heart and the feathers and the scales. Safe enough for a while.

Lukas turned in the middle of the living room and faced them. He gave a great shake, then Hamlin came forth.

Hamlin slowed down the process this time, enough so Lukas was aware of how he grew.

And grew.

Finally, Hamlin reached his full height. His head was easily level with Rudi's chest, lower than that with Peter, and he could almost look the Asian woman in the eye.

"This is the prince?" the woman asked, less disappointed now.

Lukas stood tall and proud.

"His true hound soul, yes," Rudi said.

"I am Mei Ling Wang," the Asian woman finally introduced herself.

"He's been cursed," Rudi said softly. "When he tries to take human form—shadows attack."

"Shadows?" Sally asked sharply. "Like that shadow creature who tried to attack me?" she said, addressing Lukas.

He nodded. Not exactly the same, but yes, that thing had been tainted with shadows.

"I went to Germany, to the hound court, to try to get the curse reversed." Rudi turned and stared at Lukas. "I'm sorry, Prince. I failed."

Lukas tried to hold himself absolutely still, not to let his ears droop or his tail fall. He didn't want anyone to know how disappointed he was. He'd thought it was time. That Oma would finally remove her spell, and let him be human again.

"Lady Metzler, his grandmother, couldn't help," Rudi explained.

Why couldn't she help? How much longer did Lukas have to wait?

"She's infected. With shadows," Mei Ling said, disgusted.

A sharp ridge of fear ran down the line of his back and his hackles rose. Oma was lost to the shadows? Was he stuck in hound form forever?

How long had she been infected with the shadows? Was that why she'd cursed him with them, so long ago?

"It is a curse? Some spell? That holds you?" Mei Ling asked.

Rudi said, "Yes," while Lukas nodded.

"I know someone. Here. Who may help," Mei Ling said, considering.

Lukas walked up to her, hopeful. Maybe this was why he'd dreamed of her, so long ago. Maybe not only was she part of the knight, but part of the cure.

"If I help you with this, you will help me with the shadows, yes?" Mei Ling bargained.

Lukas nodded without hesitation.

"Prince—" Rudi started, then sighed.

"Good," Mei Ling said, satisfied. "We go see him now." She looked critically at Lukas, then waved her hand and said, "Smaller, please."

Lukas looked from Mei Ling to Rudi, who merely shrugged and said, "You'll never fit in my car like this."

In the blink of an eye, Lukas transformed back down into a Scottish terrier.

Peter gave a cawing laugh. "I don't think I've ever seen anyone transform that fast."

"Me neither," Rudi said thoughtfully.

Was that something else Lukas should have kept

secret? Oma had never said anything. Did he need to hide this ability? There was no longer anyone to ask, not if Oma had been taken by the shadows.

Maybe he could free her, though he'd never been able to save anyone in his dreams.

Resolutely, Lukas walked to the door, then looked back at everyone still just standing there. He gave an impatient bark.

"Yes, Prince, coming," Rudi said with a grin. "Let's see if we can make you whole."

***

Peter and Sally stayed behind—Peter didn't want to risk Sally, if there would be any danger. Lukas didn't blame him. He didn't want any risk coming to Sally—or Peter, or Mei Ling, for that matter. They were in enough danger from the shadows already.

Rudi drove his little electric sedan, with Mei Ling in the passenger seat and Lukas delegated to the backseat. He tried not to resent it—Mei Ling had to give Rudi directions, but she didn't know exactly where she was going. She kept making Rudi stop so she could roll down the window and smell the air.

Lukas tried to follow the scent Mei Ling did, teasing apart all the smells of the International District: overly sweet incense, deep-fried pork, roasted barley tea, cheap plastic goods, and expensive silks.

Finally, Lukas caught a trace of the bitter chemical scent he associated with Oma and her magic. He gave a quiet yip when he scented it a second time.

Mei Ling turned in her seat and smiled at him. "Yes, that scent. You have a good nose. Better than mine, I think."

Of course he did. He was from the hound clan.

Mei Ling's smile increased. "But my teeth are sharper."

Lukas cocked his head to the side. He'd been thinking Mei Ling was from the viper clan. But no, she was from the crocodile clan. He nodded, slowly. Yes, her teeth were very sharp and strong. He could see that now. A shadowy twin imposed itself on her form for a moment, with golden eyes, a long snout, sharp claws, and wicked teeth. She was a fierce warrior, indeed.

Rudi had the scent now as well, and found a place to park in a nearby lot. Mei Ling led the way down the cracked sidewalk to a small side street. They passed a market with ducks hanging in the window, spiced red and smelling smoked; then past a merchant selling dusty tea that made Lukas wrinkle his nose; then finally to a "massage" studio, the smell of semen and baby oil wafting from the open door along with soft Asian Muzak.

Rudi didn't say anything, but Lukas knew he didn't approve.

Mei Ling looked at Rudi curiously as they passed through a side door. "You feel nothing?" she asked.

Rudi shook his head, then gave her a wolfish grin. "Not my style."

"Curious," she replied. She led them down a service hall and past the business doors to a narrow, dark staircase in the back. A rope hung across it, with a sign: "No entrance."

Mei Ling ignored it and they climbed to the top, third story. The walls up here were painted gray, dingy with age. The floor was wood that would have been pretty if it had been restored; now, however, it was streaked with gouges and stinky black stains, and was sticky along the edges.

The smell of age and decay overlay everything.

However, underneath it all, Lukas tracked that thread of magic.

They stopped at a door didn't look like a door: It looked like a large, eight-sided wood carving, covered in black painted characters. A black mirror that didn't reflect anything bulged in the center.

"What is that?" Rudi asked, pointing to it.

"Nothing. Just a test." Mei Ling looked from Rudi to Lukas. "I guess you're not demons," she said with a small smile.

Demons? Really? The hound clan had no tales of hunting demons. Lukas would have to remember to ask later.

Mei Ling pulled open the door, struggling with its weight. The tiny room she led them into had wood cabinets with clear glass doors crowding against every wall from floor to ceiling. A small red couch that stank of sweat crouched in the center of the room.

A large man, bald, with bulbous eyes, a fat nose, and ears that stuck out like the handles on a jar, sat in the corner behind a tiny desk, more like a black, skinny table. He wore a stained white robe and smelled like cheap wine.

But his eyes were sharp, and he greeted Mei Ling by name.

They spoke rapid-fire in some language—Mandarin? Cantonese?

Lukas didn't try to follow. Instead, he looked around the room. Glass jars filled with herbs and Asian medicine, pungent and dried, filled all the shelves.

The smell of magic came from the ceiling, above the couch. A round, golden lamp hung there. Lukas couldn't see anything about it, but it smelled...different. Was it enchanted, somehow?

"No," Mei Ling said firmly. "You may not." She turned

to Rudi and asked, "Your teeth will not grow back, correct?"

"They won't," Rudi confirmed. "Why?"

"Albert wants one from one of the hound clan for payment," she replied.

"What about a nail?" Albert asked, addressing them with a startling pure British accent. "Nails grow back, don't they?"

"You're not pulling a nail," Mei Ling growled. "Clipping only. You just want some blood."

Albert shrugged. "Didn't hurt to ask."

"Why do you want it?" Rudi asked.

"Albert wants one of my scales for his concoctions," Mei Ling replied for him. "Which I will pay. But if you ever consider using it in a spell against me, I will hunt you down and eat you."

Lukas knew she wasn't kidding.

"I'd never turn against you, madam," Albert assured her.

"You lie," Mei Ling said with the sweetest smile. "You'd sell your mother if you saw enough profit. But I can track you, anywhere you go. And I will."

"Understood," Albert said.

Mei Ling turned to look at Lukas. "And a clipping of your nails."

"He can have mine," Rudi said, stepping forward.

Lukas shook his head. There was no need for Rudi to try to protect him like that.

"He's the one who's cursed," Albert pointed out.

"You're going to use these in other potions or spells, right?" Rudi guessed.

Albert nodded cautiously.

"Like with her, I'll come after you if you try to use it against me. And I'll bring a pack," Rudi added with a wolfish grin. "But you should use mine, not his. Mine may be more interesting to you."

"Really? Why?" Albert asked, obviously intrigued.

Lukas was also curious. Rudi was just…Rudi. What did he have that was special about him?

Rudi took a breath, paused, then pushed forward. "I'm bad with magic. Very bad. So bad that often simple spells don't work on me."

"Ah, that's why the charms downstairs didn't make you uncomfortable," Mei Ling said.

Rudi nodded. "Natural defense against simple spells, like finding spells," he added, glancing at Lukas.

Lukas blinked, surprised. He had no idea. But it made sense that Rudi had secrets of his own. Oma wouldn't have trusted him otherwise.

"Done," Albert said.

"I'll go first." Mei Ling put one hand on the man's skinny desk. The hand grew, turning into a scaled foot with great, sharp claws.

Lukas sniffed with interest, trying to capture the scent of her crocodile soul: Fresh water and muddy marshes, mingled with silk and cold scales.

"Just a scale. No blood," Mei Ling growled. Her golden eyes glared at the man.

The man said something in the tongue they shared, his face alight with wonder.

Lukas increased a bit in size, then went and stood next to her. He growled as well when the man produced metal tongs that reeked of magic.

"Just to preserve it," the man assured Lukas. Then he did a double take, looking at Lukas carefully. "Not your natural shape, my lord, is it? Interesting."

Lukas knew he'd given away too much. Only the royalty of the hound clan could change shape. He didn't do more than give a soft rumbling threat, deep in his throat. He had this Albert's scent as well.

Rudi held out a paw-like hand next, submitting to having his black nails trimmed.

Albert placed both the scale and the clippings in a glass jar that fogged the instant he sealed it. Then he turned back to Lukas. "I will concoct a potion that will put you in the right frame of mind for breaking the spell. How long were you—has he been cursed?"

"Ten years?" Rudi guessed.

Lukas nodded.

"Ah. I will do what I can from my side, but then you, my lord, will have to do the rest."

"What does that mean? What's he going to have to do?" Rudi asked, sounding as worried as Lukas felt.

"Fight."

L ukas lay on the small couch in his true hound soul form, trying to ignore how the cushions beneath him stank. The golden lamp above him blotted out the rest of the room. The light was warm like the sun, and just as impartial, waiting but not judging.

Albert came into sight. He carried an oversized pair of shears, like garden clippers, made of red-hot steel, which he used to snip away strings that Lukas didn't see until they'd been cut. Then they fell from the dark, beyond the golden light, landing and curling, like fishing line.

When Albert cut the last one, Lukas lifted off the couch.

"Fly, Prince," the man whispered. "Fight and be free."

Lukas found himself in his human form, naked, on a battlefield made of mud. Soldiers all around him had fallen, their faces twisted in agony, then turned to stone. Black clouds marched across the sky to the horizon, where an angry sun boiled.

The smell of decaying corpses, bitter magic, and the wet taint of shadows was bad enough to make Lukas gag. He reached for Hamlin, but found him curled up, far inside their shared body, sleeping heavily.

Worry stirred and danced up Lukas' spine.

Hamlin, sleeping?

Lukas asked Hamlin to rise, to come forward, to wake up and join him.

But his hound soul slept on.

Lukas shouted, begged, pleaded, but he couldn't wake Hamlin.

He didn't know where he was. He suspected that unless he could get away, he'd never wake Hamlin again.

The field of bodies stretched out as far as Lukas could see on all side. There was nowhere to go. Still, maybe there was something more, something better, somewhere.

With the first step, Lukas knew he was in trouble.

Shadows mingled with the mud.

When Lukas moved, he'd alerted the shadows that there was yet something alive, something they hadn't sucked the life out of.

The shadows, as mud, crawled up Lukas' bare legs, slimy and cold.

He knew he had to fight them and get them off of him, or he'd die like everyone else here, a lifeless husk turned into stone.

Was this the place where the shadows were born?

Lukas ran as fast as his human legs would carry him, but the shadow mud was already circling his ankles and streaking up his calves.

There was no end to the field, no end to the bodies, the carnage, and the stench.

Lukas howled as he ran. It occurred to him, though, that he'd always run in his dreams, always tried to get away from the shadows, but he'd never succeeded—the shadows had always caught him, taken and drained him, when he'd run.

This time, Lukas was determined to stand and fight. He remembered the knight, made up of Sally's heart, Peter's feathers, Mei Ling's scales, and more—the poisonous bite of a viper, the magic of a tiger, and the eyes of a boar.

Somewhere above Lukas shone that golden light, the one that had sent him to this place, the birthplace of the shadows.

Lukas stopped, spread his legs wide in a fighting stance while forming his hands around the haft of an invisible sword.

Let them come.

The mud leaped on Lukas, sliding down his back before it grabbed hold. It danced around his knees before surging up his thighs.

As the mud solidified, Lukas willed the sword of the knight into his hands.

A golden beam shot up from his cupped hands, warming them, bringing a whiff of hope: fresh mint and Seattle cherry blossoms.

Lukas struck down at the ground, freeing his left foot. The shadows shattered like ill-baked clay. Then he freed his right foot, flexing his ankle to shake the rest of the clinging mud away. Very carefully, he scraped the mud away from his back.

But he was never truly free of it. The shadows kept coming back and there was no end to the field, no end to the atrocities, no end to their attack.

Lukas pleaded again with Hamlin to wake up, but his hound soul wouldn't wake.

Exhausted, Lukas stumbled and slowed. It wasn't just the battle; the shadows sucked the life out of him where they lingered.

As he paused, the shadows crept higher.

Lukas swung at them with all his might, even jumping into the air—but he wasn't a raven. He couldn't fly away. He wasn't truly a knight, able to fight. He was just a hound. He could only be loyal, and endure.

Lukas let the sword fall to his side as he stood, panting.

The shadows saw their chance. This time, they didn't creep. Like an unstoppable ocean wave, they flowed up and over Lukas, encasing him, blackening his world until all was dark and full of filth. They siphoned off as much of his life, his energy, and his joy that they could reach.

Lukas resisted, hanging on. The shadows couldn't get it all. They couldn't touch Lukas's true self, or his hound soul still sleeping so deeply inside of him.

The shadows hardened around Lukas' body like a great shell. They exhausted themselves, drained of what energy they'd stolen from him.

Now, all Lukas had to do was break free. He knew he could. He had been brave and strong and true, all these years.

Lukas had the greater heart, and he still carried the true joy of being hound.

First, Lukas focused on breathing, flexing his chest; then, with a great snarling roar, he swung his left arm up and free. It felt as if it were made of lead, heavy and no longer supple.

However, the mud broke away. It fell off slowly this time, like partially set paint flaking off.

Lukas shook his head like Hamlin would, breaking his face and neck out of the mud.

This time, when the mud fell, instead of falling in pieces, it collapsed into dust, unable to reform.

Limb by limb, Lukas broke himself out of the shadow mud. He panted as he finished, exhausted to his soul, covered in dead shadow dust.

But he was free.

In triumph, Lukas raised his sword again, holding it above his head. The golden light pierced the clouds above him, and the true sun broke through, bathing him in light and blinding him.

When the light receded, Lukas found himself curled up on Albert's couch, the stench not as bad as it had been. It took him a moment to realize that he was in human form.

Lukas tensed, counting the seconds.

The shadows didn't attack.

Slowly Lukas sat up.

The shadows still didn't surround him.

Lukas took a deep breath—his first truly deep, human breath for ten years. Grinning, he turned to Rudi.

"Hi."

INTERLUDE 1
PROPHESY IN SHADOWS

Guatemala, 1947

Bernardo woke early, as always, before the singing of the chickens, as his friend Olan had jokingly described their noise. He rose from his simple cot and walked directly across the dirt floor to the porcelain bowl in the corner, not stumbling, though the sun hadn't yet broken past the horizon. He splashed a little water from a cracked pitcher into the bowl, splashed the sleep out of his eyes and the corners of his mouth, then knelt down on his prayer mat in the center of his room with the ease of habit to start his morning meditations.

First, Bernardo spoke to the gods, big and small. He thanked Q'ukamatz—Plumed Serpent—and Itzanam—Grandfather Iguana—as well as the nameless Christian god and his son. He thanked Saint Lonrad for the thick jungle surrounding the temple, and Saint Patrick for leading the viper clan to safety here in the highlands of Guatemala. He asked the gods to keep his feet on the

Green Road and to turn his steps away from the Road to Xibalba, harm, and death.

He also asked them to be kind to Olan, who'd just joined them in Heaven, to ease his friend's way along the Unending Dagger and the Star Road, and not to play too many tricks on him.

Bernardo paused. Tears pressed against his eyes, but he was also smiling. He missed Olan more every day, but the memories of his friend were warm and bright. As Olan had promised him, Death hadn't ended their relationship, just made it more complicated.

With a quaking voice, Bernardo sang a joyous hymn to the morning, thanking the gods for another day.

He ended his prayers as he always did, asking the gods to put him to service, to use him as they saw fit.

They had yet to answer that part, leaving Bernardo to chose his own path to duty.

Bernardo stood easily. Despite the age hanging off his bones—he'd been born in the previous century—he was still strong enough to do his share of the temple work. He quickly folded up the rough, handwoven mat and placed it on the foot of his cot so that when he went to bed, he'd remember to spread it out for the next morning's prayers.

The smell of frying dough coated in honey greeted Bernardo as he stepped out of his cell. He wrinkled his nose in annoyance. The cooks were still trying to impress the new recruits with fancy, sweet dishes instead of what they usually served: Tamales with pork, hen soup, beef stew with potatoes and carrots.

The cooks didn't realize it was hopeless. Few of the viper clan came to the temple anymore; even fewer of the young would stay. Just over a dozen lived there full time anymore.

The mystics had predicted that long ago, after the treachery of the raven clan that had decimated their people.

Still, Bernardo didn't blame the cooks for trying. Didn't he still petition the gods daily, asking for his fate?

A dull green canvas awning had been stretched from the squat building containing the kitchen to tall, wooden polls a few feet away. Half a dozen wooden tables with benches were scattered under it, with the students huddled around one.

They used to fill all of the tables every summer. Now, so few gathered.

"*Buenos días, Diácono* Bernardo," called the students, using the polite term that referred to all the temple workers.

Bernardo nodded and waved at the students, though he didn't stop; instead, he walked directly into the sweltering kitchen.

Rafe stood in front of the wood-burning stove in the corner, his long black hair braided, a stained white cap absorbing the sweat on his bronzed brow. He flipped the frying dough with a deft flick of his wrist, giving Bernardo only a nod while he sprinkled cinnamon and sugar across the pan.

Bernardo opened the tall wooden cabinets next to the squat icebox. At least the cupboards were fully stocked— the viper clan might not come in person to the temple anymore, but they still knew their duty, and they tithed.

"May I help you?" came the annoyingly smooth voice of Gezane.

Bernardo bit back his rejection. He didn't trust Gezane, an American. Gezane was always looking for a way in, wanting to advance himself, insinuate himself in the elder council. Like all youth, of course he knew better than they did.

"Certainly," Bernardo said, swallowing down his disapproval. He directed the young man to pour the grain for the porridge the mystics liked to eat, while he cut up plantains.

Gezane focused on his work, his tan face serious, his long, silky black hair pulled back. He wasn't a handsome man—his cheeks were too broad, his eyes set too far apart, and his lips thin and miserly, as if he hoarded laughter and smiles.

After they'd assembled the trays and poured the *xocolati*, a cold chocolate drink made with vanilla and peppers, Gezane volunteered to carry a tray to the temple.

Bernardo knew what the young man was doing. He'd thought that way himself, when he'd been younger: If he were near the mystics, maybe a prophesy concerning him would suddenly materialize out of the sacred smoke.

But Bernardo had sacrificed his entire life taking care of the mystics, while fewer and fewer prophesies formed, waiting to be read.

He'd thought, once, that maybe he could become a mystic; the smoke had spoken to him, telling him to stay here, at the temple.

But the smoke told almost all to stay. Only a few obeyed.

The usual calm filled Bernardo as he walked from behind the kitchen, along the white road that wound through the thick jungle, to the gray stone temple. Brilliant macaws flashed through the green canopy, screeching their disapproval. Monkeys chittered from the edges, not drawing closer until after the meals when the temple would throw the remains to them. Small voles and mice scattered through the underbrush, the sound of rustling leaves like rushing water.

Dawn broke around the edge of the temple just as they

stepped clear of the jungle, bathing the open air with a golden light. Bernardo paused, smiling, wondering if this was Olan saying hello.

The pyramid rose far above the tops of the trees. Bernardo had seen paintings from when the temple itself had been painted, and covered in murals of blue, red, green, and yellow, depicting stories of the gods and heroes, while lifelike vines had crept up the sides, with flowers that never faded bursting on the edges.

The only paint that remained were the names of viper clan's heroes and saints, painted on the flat rise of the stairs. During the Festival of Remembering, in the autumn, the names would be repainted, and possibly repositioned, if there had been a recent hero.

Bernardo couldn't remember the last time the names had been changed.

Gezane stood behind him, shuffling from one foot to the other, impatient as always.

Bernardo stayed where he was, breathing in the morning for another long moment, trying to show the young man patience. His viper soul rose up briefly, circling around him, as if basking in the light as well.

Then they walked into the cool pyramid. The thick stone held in the night's chill and would stay cool all day. The songs of the four mystics floated through the air, harmonious for once. Bernardo paused, widening his eyes so he could see in the dimly lit outer hallway that circled the entire temple, then he led the way through a dark, narrow passage into the inner sanctuary.

The sun had found its way through the high windows on the slanted walls of the four-sided pyramid, staining the air with its golden glow. Dust motes danced through the beams, weaving through the sweet smoke of sacrifice.

Each long side held a carved seat, but the mystics weren't at their places.

Instead, the mystics slid gracefully across the center of the open space, stepping lightly in the cool, beige sand, their plain robes stained with neglect. They danced with blind, white eyes, their faces turned toward the apex at the top, singing their wordless songs. They never touched each other, never spoke to each other, yet always seemed to be in wordless accord, weaving esoteric patterns around each other.

Bernardo didn't know why the mystics sometimes danced, what it meant. Prophesies would come regardless if they sat or walked, slept or sang.

Gezane came closer behind Bernardo, then stood still for once. It occurred to Bernardo that few had seen this graceful dance of the mystics.

"We will wait," Bernardo said softly, "for a little while." There was no way to know how long the mystics would dance, but they wouldn't eat until afterward.

Bernardo let himself be carried away on the high, soaring notes, floating with the song and the smoke, until he heard Gezane sigh. He took pity on the impatient young man and said, "Let's go. We'll come back with lunch."

Bernardo turned around, ready to leave.

Gezane stood stock still, staring over his shoulder.

"What is it?" Bernardo asked, half turning.

The mystics had aligned themselves into a straight line, their eerie white eyes all staring at him. Their song continued, suddenly clashing, as they raised their left hands to point at him.

Bernardo felt himself falling to the ground in slow motion, the breakfast porridge spilling over his shirt as his feet dissolved in smoke.

He tried to tell Gezane, "This isn't supposed to happen

to me. I'm not the one supposed to have a prophesy." He wasn't certain if his mouth even contained a human tongue anymore, or if he spat venom instead.

Or maybe the gods had finally decided to use him, to make him of service at last.

Shadows stalked the earth.

Bernardo saw a rich man, locked away in his house of a hundred rooms, with lights on in each. The shadows still slipped under the threshold, around the window sill, stalking the man until they surrounded him and sucked him dry, leaving behind a husk of darkness.

Fruit rotted in the orchards, while black blight swept over green fields, turning them barren overnight.

Soldiers shot their weapons into nothing, killing only their friends around them.

How could they fight a shadow? It had no form, nothing to grasp.

Even the brilliant light of mankind's worst bombs couldn't kill them.

The temple fell as shadows overtook the mystics. They spewed blackness over the jungle, killing the parrots, the monkeys, the iguanas, then the trees.

Soon the world was sucked dead, the mountains flattened, the oceans boiled dry.

And the shadows moved onto the next world.

To stop them, Bernardo had to stop a girl—no, a clan —from mingling the shadows with their magic.

The tiger clan.

Members of the hound clan were already infected with the shadows. But no matter how the shadows pushed, the hound clan didn't, and never would, practice enough magic for the shadows to grow stronger.

But the tiger clan…they were the most magical of the clans.

Through them, the shadows could take hold and move from the clans out into the world.

Bernardo saw his chance with the tigers, as if through a peephole. It was slim, like a single beam of light through solid clouds. Just for an instant, a single day, would he be able to stop the shadows from mixing with all the magic from the tiger clan.

Just one chance to turn the tiger warriors away from darkness.

Bernardo saw his path: from the highlands of Guatemala to the coast, to a ship south to Panama City, where he would take another ship west to India and Calcutta.

If he delayed, even a day, the world might be lost.

Bernardo wept as he watched cities turned to ash, vile filth spewed over all things green and good, the chilled Road to Xibalba the only path to take.

He would find this girl. And stop her.

Before the shadows took over the world.

Cold, gritty sand pressed against Bernardo's fingertips, as slippery as the shadows he'd tried to grasp. The world was fading, eaten by darkness. Bernardo had to find his way back into the light. But where was it? He couldn't see or taste it.

Then he heard the songs of the mystics, floating ahead of him as if they were walking in front of him through thick jungle. His viper soul rose, gliding along the melody, undulating through the air as if through water, leading Bernardo back to the real world.

Wet, slimy porridge slid from Bernardo's shirt, up along his neck and dripped onto the ground. Golden light still poured through the windows set high on the temple's slanting walls, and sweet traces of incense mingled with the smells of spilled plantains and *xocolati*.

Gezane popped into Bernardo's view. "*Diácono*," he said, relief in his voice. "Are you all right? You had a vision," he added, awe making his voice breathy.

Bernardo nodded cautiously, though his head felt like a leaf fluttering in a breeze, attached to his body by the merest thread.

"Can you save us from the shadows?" Gezane asked.

Bernardo wondered how much of his vision he'd shared as he'd experienced it. The mystics sometimes spoke everything out loud; other times, they merely gibbered and could only explain later what they'd seen.

In reply to the boy, though, Bernardo carefully shook his head. All he could do was stop the spreading of the shadows. They'd still live on, and they'd try to attack the other clans.

Bernardo sat up slowly, Gezane coming to his side to help. He rubbed his hand over his chin, across his cheeks. They felt as numb as when the coals of Olan's funeral pyre had grown cold and he'd found warmth in the local firewater.

"Do you have to go alone?" Gezane asked. While the tone of his voice was innocent enough, his face shone with hope. The boy desperately wanted to go with Bernardo, to be part of this vision, to maybe have his name written on the temple stairs.

If it had been Olan asking, Bernardo would have gleefully agreed. They would have driven each other crazy

—Bernardo planning every aspect of the trip, setting timetables and packing with care, while Olan would travel with whatever he'd thrown into his pack the morning they left, then talking Bernardo into abandoning his plans for shortcuts or adventures.

But Olan wasn't there.

Bernardo's viper soul stirred. Did he not trust Gezane? Or was his viper half merely anxious to go?

Gezane had spent his life in the outside world. He knew how to navigate it. Maybe he could be a good guide.

And maybe Bernardo could teach him some things as well, like patience and prayers.

Slowly, Bernardo replied, "I don't have to travel to Calcutta alone," his voice full of gravel.

The young man's glee was as bright as the golden light still streaming through the temple windows, bright enough to dim Bernardo's questions and regrets.

The sound of a great crowd floated above Bernardo and Gezane as they approached the market. When they turned a corner, the noise exploded into a cacophony greater than the jungle during the growing season. Everywhere Bernardo looked strode the people of Guatemala City: grandmothers with their loaded baskets, young mothers riding herd on their passel of children, even packs of young men on the prowl.

"Why are there so many people?" Bernardo asked Gezane, stopping in the middle of the street. He was disgusted by the quaver in his voice. When had he turned into this querulous old man? He tramped down on his fear, but it kept rising back up, like a boiling pot with an ill-fitting lid.

"This is a normal crowd," Gezane said derisively.

Bernardo flinched, but he kept his hand wrapped around the young man's biceps. Gezane's pulse fluttered under his fingertips, and the young man kept starting and looking over his shoulder.

He was nervous as well, though he'd never admit it.

Bernardo had no idea what Gezane could be scared of here. But he knew better than to say anything. Gezane would just push him away, maybe abandon him here amidst all this chaos.

They walked ahead through the crowded street, bypassing the market and going directly to the docks beyond. The tall buildings made of brick with grand windows and stonework gave way to squat wooden sheds and the stench of open sewers. Automobiles roared on the next street. As if in response, the lone wail of a train called out. Long piers ran out into the water, with great ships, large and angular, waited like floating temples, accepting their acolytes and their tithed goods.

"Which way?" Bernardo asked, looking up and down the waterfront. Their boat, heading down to Panama City, was docked at pier fifteen.

"How should I know?" Gezane snapped. Then he turned and looked at Bernardo. "I'm sorry, *Diácono*," he said softly. "I don't know why I keep saying things like that." He looked scared, pale under his tanned skin.

"We are neither of us ourselves," Bernardo said. He'd felt an uncomfortable pressure, as if his skin was too tight and needed to be shed, since they'd left the temple.

Gezane looked up and down the street, taking a deep breath, then he flashed a grin at Bernardo. "Let's ask," he said.

Bernardo shook his head but followed after Gezane,

who'd been adamant that they never ask anyone for help for most of their trip.

When they inquired which direction their dock lay with a pair of day laborers who were slopping whitewash on a decrypted store front, they were directed further north.

Bernardo heaved a huge sigh upon sighting the faded, weathered sign for their dock. "We made the first leg," he said. He felt a smile crack his face, and realized the good humor had recently been as rare as sunshine during the rainy season.

"We did," Gezane said. "The ship should be easier," he added quietly.

Bernardo nodded. He paused, then made himself ask, "Do you feel it too? The pressure?"

Instead of snapping at him, Gezane gave a sharp nod. "As if the air fights us."

An involuntary shiver passed across Bernardo's shoulders, as if cool vines were suddenly drawn against his bare skin. He'd thought it had been only him, out of his element, traveling so far from his home.

Suddenly, Bernardo's viper soul rose and twined around his human soul. He stopped and looked around. Was there something on the pier? Something threatening?

No one was close enough to see, so Bernardo encouraged his viper soul to rise more. Color drained out of the world and the broad wooden boards beneath his feet grew gray like driftwood. The smell of salty water and dusky seaweed rose, overwhelming the scents of the unclean city.

Horror slammed into Bernardo, as solid as Olan's fist, when the darkness near the entrance to the ship resolved into wisps of shadows, wrapped around the raised stumps decorating the edges of the pier.

They were waiting for them—watchers. Scouts.

Bernardo glanced behind him. No, not scouts. Shadows pressed in, all around him.

Had he opened the door to them with his prophesy? Is that why they hounded him, unseen, unbeknownst to him?

And Gezane, he amended, when he saw the young man looking back at him, his fear as dark as the shadows draped over his shoulders.

Bernardo sent a quick plea to the gods to help them both.

But he knew that the gods rarely answered anyone's prayers.

Bernardo shook off his viper's gaze and marched down the pier. The fear and age he'd been feeling weren't his. They came from his enemy, the shadows, who were trying to cloud his mind, distract him from his mission.

"It's going to be all right," he assured Gezane, his old strength returning. Seeing the shadows—knowing they were there, that it wasn't just him—had helped him return to himself.

Gezane stood up straighter, the cruel lines leaving his face, the cunning returning. "Yes, it will be," he said, squaring his shoulders.

They were going to have to fight off the shadows, who were watching their very thoughts.

Though he couldn't see them, Bernardo knew the shadows had drawn back. They were all right, now.

But for how long?

Bernardo's stomach rolled with the ship, feeling unmoored in his body, empty and adrift. However, the smell of the rice from this morning's breakfast made his nausea rise and his mouth flood with bile. He could barely manage even a few mouthfuls of water.

Another wave splashed against the bow. Bernardo couldn't contain his groan.

"Shut up, old man," Gezane snapped.

Bernardo focused on the young man, grateful for the distraction. "What do you know of suffering? You're too young to know anything." He regretted the words as soon as he said them. They were fueled by sickness and shadows.

But the journey on the ship seemed like an endless road through the dark underground world of Xibalba, with no stars to guide his way, his viper soul drowned by the endless water surrounding them.

"I know enough to enjoy life. To live it. You didn't have the *cojones*. You stayed locked away like a delicate flower behind the thick walls of the temple."

"I wish I'd never left it," Bernardo groaned as the ship heeled over again. They were staying close to the coast, never really leaving the sight of it, which meant the ship was in constant motion.

"Then go back! I can finish the mission." In the dark of their tiny room, Gezane's eyes took on a strange gleam. "Let me do it. I can see out your prophesy. Alone."

"No," Bernardo said, shuddering. He made a feeble attempt to push himself up on his bunk bed. "Don't you see? That's what they want. The shadows."

Gezane shook his head. "No. It's you. You don't want to be an afterward when they teach the children of our journey. Just a footnote."

"I don't care about fame," Bernardo protested, swaying with the ship. "I just want to help. To be of service to the gods."

"You've done your part. You *saw*," Gezane said.

"And I must finish it," Bernardo said stubbornly.

The vision had shown only him warning the tiger clan. Not Gezane.

"If it doesn't finish you first," Gezane said, pushing himself off the wall where he'd been slumped. He walked over to the door of their room and opened it.

"Wait, where are you going?" Bernardo asked, hating the quiver in his voice.

"Out. Into the fresh air." Gezane paused, his dark eyes still flashing that odd glow. "Smells like death in here," he added cruelly, slamming the door.

"No, wait," Bernardo said, shivering and afraid. He wanted to get up to follow, but he couldn't hold himself up anymore; instead, he fell back onto his bunk.

The shadows were eating them alive, here. Bernardo could see them now, even without his viper soul.

They were determined to stop Bernardo from reaching the tiger clan in time.

But Bernardo was just as stubborn. Seasick or not, with Gezane's help or not, he'd make the journey.

Though he'd come to realize what happened afterward no longer mattered. Gezane had been right: It did smell like death in their room. Bernardo would never survive the trip back up the mountain to the temple. His ashes would be scattered far from his home, and never mingle with Olan's.

Bernardo woke again to blessed stillness and quiet. Even after a week off the ship, he still marveled at it. Golden morning light filtered by white lace curtains splayed across the foot of his bed. The viper clan had paid for a luxurious hotel after the elder living here had seen how ill Bernardo had become.

Bernardo stretched, satisfied. The bed was soft and the room was full of heavy, dark furniture. It weighed Bernardo down; he didn't understand the need to possess so many things.

But they were leaving that day, at dawn, and Bernardo wanted to savor every moment on ground that didn't shift with the waves. Plus, the elder clan leader had provided Bernardo with a charm to help him fight his illness. Maybe it wouldn't be so bad this time.

Bernardo stretched again, enjoying the light, comparing how weak it looked to the light in the temple, up the mountain, closer to the sky, when it finally occurred to him: This wasn't dawn light, but mid-morning.

The trunk that the elder had provided Bernardo no longer sat next to the door.

Bernardo sprang out of bed and raced to the desk. The leather wallet with the money, tickets, and papers was still sitting there, but instead of being plump with purpose, it was hollow and empty.

Quickly, Bernardo slid on light, drawstring pants, a striped shirt, and sandals, then raced out the door. The laborers were no longer in the streets; they'd already all gone to their jobs. Instead, it was just the idle folk, with time on their hands, strolling to the market or the park.

Bernardo pushed through them, the inevitable crowds of the city, racing to the docks.

The pier looked empty, but still Bernardo ran on, all the way up to the edge of the water.

Nothing waited for him there. The ship was gone, with Gezane, corrupted by shadows, on it.

The next ship to Calcutta wouldn't leave for a week or more.

The shadows had won.

Bernardo would never get to Calcutta in time, would never be able to warn the tiger clan. Adrian couldn't fulfill Bernardo's prophesy, but in his arrogance and clouded mind, he thought he could.

Old man tears rose to Bernardo's eyes, futile as age. He'd wasted his life at the temple, and now, he'd killed them all. He was a disgrace. Olan would be ashamed of him.

Bernardo turned to go…and felt himself crumbling to the ground, the smoke of prophesy rising.

A second vision, one of Gezane, filled Bernardo.

Gezane had ruined this chance with the shadows. He'd have to give his own life to remove the disgrace from his name, his family's name.

But he couldn't be told the entire vision.

Gezane had betrayed them to the shadows. There was no guarantee he wouldn't do so again.

Then another vision attacked Bernardo as he lay drooling and gasping on the pier, showing him the end of his own days. Sailors would find him and lock him away in a cell for the insane, mumbling prophesies to himself until the elder of the viper clan found him, much too late.

Bernardo would die in that cell.

Gezane would carry a cup of Bernardo's ashes back to the temple, to mingle them with Olan's, as Gezane sentence was laid out, spells cast upon him, the fate of the world resting no longer with them, but with a hound prince yet to be born.

SEATTLE, PRESENT DAY

LUKAS

"How are you feeling?" Rudi asked.

Lukas considered the question. "Human," he said with a grin. "And...and good. I guess." He didn't really know how he felt. How was he supposed to feel? He hadn't been in this body for more than a minute in ten years. Albert's couch felt scratchy under his thighs, and the air seemed dull, no longer swimming with scents.

"Do you know who cursed you?" Albert asked quietly.

"Yes," Lukas replied, then he looked down at his feet, at the long human toes that seemed foreign, yet familiar. He wiggled them experimentally. Very strange.

"This person—they might be very ill now. Weak. They drew power from the spell, from *you*," Albert said.

Lukas looked up at Rudi. "*Wir müssen nach Deutschland zurückgehen.*" He had to go see Oma. Immediately. And the rest of his family too—Da, Mama, and Greta.

Rudi gave him a curt nod. Then he smiled. "First, we need to get you some clothes."

Lukas looked down at his odd human genitalia, nestled

in black curls. He knew Rudi was right: As a human, he would have to go around dressed. He remembered being told that, that he shouldn't walk around in just his skin, without his fur, but it was an old memory, from long ago.

"I'll just pop down to the shop," Albert said.

"Thank you," Lukas said. Should he put his hand in his lap and cover himself? Hamlin didn't care, but he was a hound, always covered in his own coat.

After Albert had gone, Lukas turned to Mei Ling. "Thank you for bringing us here," he said formally.

"You're welcome," she said, a smile breaking across her face like the sun peeking across the horizon.

Lukas was stunned by her beauty. Though she was old —maybe as old as Oma—her skin was still as translucent as a rose petal. Her dark eyes seemed endlessly wise, and her long white-and-black hair fell like a silk curtain.

"You will help me with the shadows now, yes?" Mei Ling asked.

Lukas paused, blinking. The glow around Mei Ling faded. She was still beautiful, but he could see through the casual magic she used.

"I don't need to," Lukas said, puzzled. Why had she thought she needed to charm him? "You are part of the knight who will destroy the shadows for good."

"She's what?" Rudi asked sharply.

Lukas jerked his head around to see Rudi, then back again to Mei Ling. He'd been thinking these things for so long, but he'd never had a tongue with which to say them.

Did he need to keep all his secrets still? Could he finally tell someone what was going on?

"What do you mean, the knight? *Ritter?*" Mei Ling asked, using the German word.

Lukas nodded. He looked at Rudi, helpless. What secrets could he tell?

"Do you trust her?" Rudi asked softly.

"Yes," Lukas said without hesitation.

"Then you can tell her what she needs to hear," Rudi replied.

"I am the guardian hound," Lukas said, standing, then turning to face her.

He towered over Mei Ling. And Rudi. He had no idea he'd be this tall as a human.

"Oma—my grandmother—told me that one of my breed only comes when the need is dire. But I am…" Lukas paused.

The words had been so hard to hear as a boy; now, after so many years in hiding, they were still difficult to say.

"I am not part of it. A member of the knight. I can't defeat the shadows myself. I merely search out the people who are necessary to save the world. You. Sally. Peter. Others."

"And what will we do, after you've brought us together?" Mei Ling asked, skeptical.

"Amazing things," Lukas assured her. He suddenly felt the solid warmth of the knight's sword beside him. "You will defeat the shadows. Drive them from the earth."

"How?" Mei Ling insisted.

"There's a knight, and a sword…. You are part of the knight. Your scales are part of his armor." Lukas said, looking down, pressing his lips together. Such an odd feeling, to press his teeth against his lips. "I don't know exactly how," he said. "But I know you will. I've seen it." His dreams only rarely showed him the knight and his battle with the shadows—just often enough that Lukas didn't despair.

"Foreseen it?" Mei Ling clarified.

"Yes," Lukas said. "But it isn't clear."

"Prophesy is like that," Mei Ling said kindly.

"Will the shadows try to stop you?" Rudi asked, looking around the room, seeking their enemy.

"Yes," Lukas said, as certain of it as he was his hound soul. "And they'll attack the others who are part of the knight. You need to be careful. So will Sally, and Peter."

"They won't stop me," Mei Ling said, her smile brighter, her teeth suddenly larger.

"Or me," Rudi said, standing at attention, his ears and snout transforming him into a hound warrior.

"Good," Lukas said. Hamlin rose and he added his own snarling voice, "I've been wanting to go hunting shadows for a long while."

***

The flip-flops Albert found hurt Lukas' feet: He didn't remember ever wearing such things. The gray drawstring pants barely slid up past his hips, and he couldn't button the bright yellow-and-green shirt.

But at least he had enough clothes to be decent, to go outside.

Lukas sat in the backseat of Rudi's car. It was uncomfortably small. His head brushed up against the ceiling and his knees were pushed up against the front seat.

The air was no longer alive with scents. Lukas missed chasing and teasing apart all the smells he could catch. His human nose couldn't identify anywhere near as many as Hamlin's.

After they dropped Mei Ling off at a hotel (at her insistence), Lukas gratefully moved up front. However, even with the seat fully pushed back, he still couldn't stretch his legs all the way out.

"I'm going to have to get a new car, aren't I?" Rudi

asked as he watched Lukas squirming in the seat, trying to get comfortable.

"I'm going to have to learn to drive, aren't I?" Lukas groaned. Even as a hound, he hadn't liked cars that much.

"It's a handy skill, Prince."

Lukas twitched, but he wasn't sure why. Before Lukas could think more about it, however, Rudi asked, "Was it Lady Metzler, your grandmother, who cursed you?"

Lukas paused for only a moment before he said, "Yes." Then he took a deep breath. He didn't feel relief after letting go of that secret, not like he'd expected.

"I suspected she had, when I saw her last week," Rudi said. He added, "I'm sorry."

Lukas shook his head. Sorry wasn't right. She'd saved him, kept him safe from the shadows by forcing him to stay in the form of a hound, despite how she'd done it. His dreams had shown him, too many times, what would happen if he'd remained in human form.

It had still been such a terrible price. Why hadn't she found another way?

"I can't get us to Germany, to the court, for at least a day, maybe two," Rudi said. "I need to get papers for you, first."

There it was again, that uncomfortable twitch at something Rudi said, and not just about going home, seeing his family after all this time.

"Papers?" Lukas asked, pinpointing it after a moment. He didn't need to prove his hound heritage, did he?

"Passport. Birth certificate. Social Security number. Like that." Rudi paused, thinking. "When we get to Germany, we can replace them with real versions. A German passport, visas, like that."

"Okay," Lukas said. He'd misunderstood. He'd leave all that to Rudi.

"Do you want to tell them?" Rudi asked quietly. "Before we get there? Your family, the court?"

Lukas shook his head *no*. He didn't want them to know, not until he could tell them in person, could see them again.

To see Da, and Mama, and Greta—anytime Rudi had started talking about them, Lukas had left the room. He hadn't wanted to know. Not if he couldn't be there with them. Now—he didn't know how he felt about seeing them again. He knew he should want to, but he just wasn't sure.

Lukas followed Rudi into the house, trying to listen to his instructions on how to turn off the alarm system, but he couldn't pay attention.

This had been his home for over a year, and while it smelled the same, it was still so different.

First, everything was smaller. He hadn't realized the walls in the living room were a cheery yellow, or that the couch was a comforting brown. It seemed neater as well, or maybe that was because he could see around all the obstacles.

"Are you hungry?" Rudi asked, noticing Lukas' distraction.

Lukas paused. Was he? Was that what he felt? "Yes?" he replied, unsure.

Rudi laughed. "Come on," he said, walking into the kitchen. "I don't know a seventeen-year-old boy who isn't perpetually starving."

Rudi continued to lay out plans as he prepared thick cream-of-tomato soup, wheat-free garlic-cheese bread, and fatty sausages, "Comfort food," he proclaimed as he served them. He talked about buying clothes for Lukas, getting "barefoot shoes" (whatever those were), and luggage and certificates and on and on.

Lukas focused on the taste and feel of the food—so very different than what he'd been eating. While his nose wasn't as good, there were so many more flavors and textures in his mouth: Savory and sweet, salty and creamy, crunchy and juicy.

"And you should go talk to Sally and Peter," Rudi said as they finished. "I can loan you some sweats and a hoodie that I think will fit you."

Lukas nodded. He did need to talk to them, to tell Sally why he'd been guarding her, to make sure they both understood how important they were.

Rudi's clothes did fit better than what Lukas had on—long, comfortable, navy blue sweats, a soft, faded gray T-shirt, and a hoodie. Rudi even dragged out an old pair of sneakers that had belonged to his older brother.

"Thank you," Lukas said, still feeling as though he was settling into his own skin, decorating an outside that didn't belong with his insides.

"Of course, Prince," Rudi said casually.

"Don't call me that," Lukas said, then bit his lips, as if he could take back the words.

Rudi raised a single eyebrow and waited as the silence rolled between them.

"That's a dog's name," Lukas explained finally. It was what Rudi had always called his hound form.

"Ah," Rudi said, nodding. "But you are my prince. I may have called you that when you were in hound form, but it was to remind both of us of your royalty."

"Okay," Lukas said, looking down at his covered feet. He hadn't understood the human nuance. He suspected he was going to embarrass himself frequently as he learned.

He'd been living in the human world, but not as a human.

"I won't use just 'Prince' since that makes you uncomfortable," Rudi promised.

Luka nodded, the continued embarrassment turning the warm food in his stomach to a solid, uncomfortable ball. "I'm going to go visit Sally and Peter," he said, wanting to flee.

"I'll walk with you," Rudi said.

"I can walk myself," Lukas snapped. Then he shook his head. He kept stumbling over his tongue, inserting his newly human feet into his mouth.

"Yes, yes, you can," Rudi said, agreeing. "But I just got you back, Lukas. I'm afraid to let you out of my sight."

Lukas understood Rudi's fear all too well. He didn't want to change into hound form again, to call Hamlin too close, afraid the curse would return or that shadows would attack.

But he also had to learn to navigate this human world as a human, and he needed to do that on his own.

"Flank guard?" Lukas proposed, meaning that Rudi would walk behind him and to the side. That way, Rudi could keep him in sight, help him if he got into any trouble, but wouldn't be next to him, by his side.

"It would be an honor," Rudi said seriously.

Lukas walked over to where Rudi was standing. "I don't know how to do this," he said out loud, but he tried anyway, giving Rudi a hug, like how Da had hugged him when he'd been a boy. "Thank you," he said, his heart full of everything he couldn't say, of ten years of gratitude toward this man who had kept him safe.

"It was always my pleasure, my prince," Rudi said.

Lukas knew there wasn't anything horrible waiting for him outside the house, but even if there had been, he knew he would face it gladly with this man at his side.

L ukas stayed in human form on the walk to Sally's apartment, so he couldn't really sense Rudi behind him. However, the knowledge that Rudi was there made him walk with broader steps, secure and safe. The streets were full of people on their Saturday errands. One day, would he be able to walk so aimlessly, like he had as a dog? Right now the need to do more buzzed under his skin, pricking him sharper than the shadows.

Even without his hound nose, Lukas could still smell Sally's apartment building from half a block away, a unique mixture of old cat, older bricks, city dust, and the particular people living in the three-story building.

Lukas buzzed Sally's apartment number on the intercom, waiting until the crackling voice said, "Hello?"

"Hi," Lukas said. "It's Lukas." He paused, and though he knew no one was close by, he still very softly added, "Pixie."

"Oh. Oh! Let me buzz you in."

The hallway smelled more strongly of a cat's litter box. Lukas was surprised at how dingy it seemed. As a hound, he'd loved the old, red carpet; it held so many interesting scents. Now, he could see how threadbare it was, how the walls were all scuffed, and that two of the lights in the hallway were burned out. Thinking back, he realized it had been out for a while.

"Hi," Lukas said, awkwardly sticking out his hand to Sally when she opened the door. "I'm Lukas."

"Sally," she said with a cheery twinkle in her eye that made Lukas feel better. She wore a bright red–and-white plaid shirt with jeans, her hair pulled back into a high ponytail. "It's nice to finally meet you."

Peter came up and they shook hands as well. He was in

an old T-shirt advertising an even older band. They stared at each other in the dark vestibule.

Not only did Lukas' nose tell him that Peter was more than he seemed, Lukas' eyes did as well: Even though Peter was fully human, he still appeared to wear a large, long, feathered cloak.

Peter stared right back. "I don't see it." His eyes suddenly turned raven-black. After a moment, he said, "There's something there, but I don't know what it is."

Lukas nodded, fascinated that Peter couldn't tell just by looking at him that he was from the hound clan. It meant the old curse still worked.

When Peter came all the way back, he seemed chagrined. "Sorry. I shouldn't have made you wait like that."

Lukas shrugged. It hadn't bothered him.

"Come on in," Peter said, gesturing to the living room.

Like Rudi's place, this old home of Lukas' looked smaller. It also seemed a lot more run-down. The long olive green couch Lukas sat on was patched on the arms, the TV cabinet was badly scratched, and the coffee table needed to be refinished. It still felt happy and warm, a welcome refuge.

"Can I get you something?" Sally called from the kitchen. "Coke? Beer?"

"Just water, thanks," Lukas replied. He had yet to try alcohol, and he'd already learned that even unsweetened food tasted overly sweet to him.

"So you were cursed, huh?" Peter asked as Sally joined them.

Lukas nodded. "Thanks," he said, taking a sip of his water. "Ten years," he added.

Peter gave a long whistle. "It's been ten years since you've been in human form?"

"Yeah."

"Do you know who cursed you?" Sally asked.

"Oma, my grandmother," Lukas admitted. It was easier to say it out loud the second time—but admitting it still didn't bring any relief.

"Dude, that sucks," Peter said.

Lukas looked up, surprised at his sympathy. Was it possible that he could make friends now? He hadn't even considered it. "The curse did protect me from the shadows. Saved my life."

"The shadows?" Peter asked, growing dangerous and still.

Sally looked at Peter, then at Lukas, then said softly, "Tell us about the shadows."

"They don't—I don't think they come from here. They've been brought here, through magic. If they gain power, more power than they have, they'll move out into the world and destroy everything. Suck the life out of every living thing, boil the oceans, dissolve the mountains into heaps of dust." Lukas shivered, images from his childhood nightmares returning.

"Oma said they were connected to hound magic," Lukas continued. "However, that creature that attacked you—" he nodded toward Sally "—that was tiger magic, and it was infected with shadows. Which means either my grandmother was wrong, or they've already spread. Maybe tainting the magic of all the clans."

Peter got up and went digging in a green canvas backpack sitting near the door. He brought back a charm, made from twigs but tied with a strong, white thread. "How about this?" he asked, showing it to Lukas.

Hamlin rose and scent entered the world: The smell of the burgers that Sally and Peter had eaten the night before, the sex they'd had earlier, the car outside with the bad engine, the couple above them cleaning their camping gear, the squirrel in the tree near the window with the cat two branches away, and...

Lukas shook his head and focused back on the charm. The magic in it was surprisingly uniform, but not strong.

And not a hint of the shadows was attached to it.

Lukas shook his head and handed it back to Peter. "No shadows," he said.

"I made it," Peter admitted.

"Cool," Lukas said. He'd never had training in magic, making charms or casting simple spells. Maybe now he could learn. Then he paused.

There *was* the faintest trace of the shadows still in the air, that foul, wet-ash smell.

Lukas stalked over to the bag. It didn't hold any shadows, but it had been near them. Smeared with them. "This pack?" Lukas asked, turning and showing it to them.

"Was my friend's, Jesse's," Peter said. "He was killed by the same woman who cast that tiger shadow creature that attacked you two."

"She's strong," Lukas said, taking in her scent, the barest thread of it still intertwined with the bag. "And completely corrupted by the shadows."

Peter exchanged a glance with Sally. "She won't be walking for a while. We don't really have to worry about her."

"She can still do magic from her bed," Lukas pointed out, putting the pack back on the floor. "I wouldn't discount her."

Peter nodded grimly. "I understand."

Lukas sat back down. "There will be a battle, with the shadows," he said, hesitatingly. "You're essential to it," he added, addressing Sally. "Both of you are. I don't know exactly what will happen when we confront them. There's the knight. You," Lukas said, nodding toward Sally again, "you're the heart."

"That's why you came to stay with me?" Sally asked.

"Yes. I am a guardian hound. My breed is rare. We rise only when needed."

"Interesting," Peter said. "So your dad—"

"Is a scent hound, like most of the court."

"I—we know so little of the other clans," Peter confessed.

"We all know about the ravens," Lukas replied. He looked down at his hands, running them together. They were so big. "We were warned about them, actually."

"Why?" Peter asked sharply.

"Why?" Lukas asked, surprised. Didn't Peter know what they'd done?

"The raven elders, uhm, purged, I guess, a lot of our history. I didn't even know about the existence of the other clans until recently," Peter explained.

"Back in 1731, the raven clan betrayed all the other clans," Lukas said. "They told their secrets to the British, then worked with them to decimate every clan at their sacred temple."

Peter turned white under his normally dark skin. "I didn't know."

Lukas nodded. The recitation had started with the Roman meaning of "decimate," to kill one in ten. For some clans, though, the number had been higher. "In the end, the British turned against the raven clan. Your clan was decimated, too."

Peter stared off into the distance. Sally reached out and squeezed his hand. Then he turned and looked back at Lukas. "It won't happen again," he said softly. "I'll work to make sure it doesn't."

"It can't," Lukas pointed out. "The clans split as a

result. There's no longer a single temple or court where you could wipe us all out."

"Even the ravens?" Sally asked.

"Of course. There's an American branch and a northern one—Iceland, I think."

"Really?" Peter asked, surprised.

"Yeah. Why weren't you told?" Lukas asked.

"There's a bunch of things we weren't told," Peter said bitterly. "Many things were held back from the American branch by the current batch of elders. Your court's in Germany?"

"Yeah. And the second one's in Russia," Lukas said.

"There's so much to learn," Peter grumbled.

Lukas shrugged. "You should probably talk to Rudi. I missed out on most of those lessons." He paused, then said shyly, "Or maybe both of us could learn. Together."

"Deal," Peter said. "But in the meanwhile—what do we do about the shadows?"

"Be vigilant," Lukas said. "The shadows will try to confuse you. They'll also drain you, exhaust you. Peter— you're more susceptible, because of your raven soul. Sally, if he ever seems like he isn't himself, you'll have to snap him out of it. Bring him back to you."

What else had Oma said about fighting the shadows?

"If you find you're arguing for no reason, it might be the shadows. Or if you suddenly start acting irrational. You won't be able to smell them, Peter; you're not a scent hound. But maybe if you see them sometime, your raven soul can help you detect them."

"When will the battle start?" Sally asked, taking Peter's hand. "And what should we do to prepare?"

"I don't know," Lukas said, grimacing. "I have to go to Germany, tomorrow. I have to let the court know the curse has been broken. See my family."

Lukas paused. It still hadn't sunk in, that he'd be seeing Da and the others soon. He made himself continue. "You aren't the only ones who are essential to the battle with the shadows. There are others. I have to find them. Bring them together. Then we can fight, and have a chance of winning."

That was the other thing Lukas' dreams had always made clear: They might not win.

"We're getting married next week," Peter said. "And we were planning on going to Mexico for our honeymoon."

"I'll delay the war until you come back," Lukas said with a grin. "Congrats, you two."

"Thanks," Peter said. "When we come back, uhm, eventually, we'll be moving to Wyoming. To Ravens' Hall."

"We'll figure it out," Lukas assured him. He'd never had to organize something like this—he wasn't sure anyone had. Rudi probably had some sort of technology to keep everyone in touch. And he had no idea when the final battle would be—in a month, or a year, or even ten years.

"Hey," Sally said, reaching out and squeezing Lukas' knee. "It'll be okay. We'll be here when you need us."

"Thank you," Lukas said. It was all he could ask for, their help defeating the shadows and saving the world.

But when? And how?

Lukas wished he knew. He stood up to go, not sure what else they could do now. He'd warned them, and he'd guard them as best he could. Sally and Peter stood up as well. For some reason, Lukas was absurdly happy that he was taller than Peter. Not by much, but enough.

"So you've never had a beer, have you?" Peter asked as he followed Lukas to the door.

"I am only seventeen," Lukas pointed out.

"Not in dog years," Peter said with a cheeky grin.

Lukas stood with his mouth open for a moment, unsure what to say. Had Peter just said that? Was he teasing him?

Before Peter's face could fall all the way and he could apologize or something, Lukas finally replied. "Bug off."

Peter laughed. "Stay safe, man," he said, giving Lukas a final handshake, with a one-armed half hug.

Sally gave him a quick hug as well. "Take care."

"You too," Lukas said. "Both of you. Congratulations. And take care of each other. Watch out for each other. Guard yourselves against the shadows. I'll be in touch."

Walking down the hall, Lukas couldn't help his grin. The shadows might be devious and powerful, and he might not know exactly how to fight them, but he had found three of the six he needed to defeat them.

It was surely just a matter of time before he found the others.

INTERLUDE 11

THE TIGER'S SHADOW

India, 1947

Betty could never admit to Mother or Father how much she missed the English rain. Not just the way it patted softly against the roof of the gazebo in the garden, but the smell of it, green and fresh. Even when it was cold, and the sun had been hiding behind gray clouds for weeks, the rain still carried the scent of rich soil and new leaves slowly unfurling.

Calcutta never smelled that way. Instead, it smelled of hot bodies that never bathed, of the cow dung and dirt that made up the streets, of pasty dye used to dot the natives' foreheads and drizzled across women's palms in beautiful patterns.

Yes, it was exciting to live in such an exotic, foreign city, with the mad colors and the noise of the market, the women in their elegant saris, the men looking formal in their white tunics, long trousers, and funny hats.

Her friends back in England complained bitterly that since the London Victory celebrations heralding the end of the Second World War, there was nothing to do, and begged her for anecdotes of her travel.

However, Betty had no tales to tell them, not recently. The British were leaving, letting India rule herself. There was much unrest. Mother and Father didn't let her travel anymore, telling her that she was too young at only sixteen, and that it was too dangerous, even with an armed escort of soldiers.

Betty suspected they might be right, at least for now. Layered underneath the smell of rich spices and extreme poverty rolled a thick scent of fear.

Not the delicious, sizzling fear of prey, or the heady scent of a combatant certain to lose a challenge. No, a cloying scent that clogged the back of Betty's throat and made the air, already humid and moist, even stickier.

Betty wasn't sure why there was so much fear in the air. The natives were probably capable of ruling themselves. Even the council of the tiger clan had agreed to split, with two groups leading, one all Indian, and one all British. They were going to separate for a decade or more; Betty was sad she wouldn't be able to visit her cousins again for so long.

As independence day approached, Betty had seen her cousins walk taller, as if they were trying out their new freedom. Of course, they told her she wouldn't understand—that was their most common response to any of her questions. Her cousins still covered their heads like all the women did here and said the proper, polite things.

However, a restlessness boiled just underneath the placid surface.

Betty was on edge as well. Her skin seemed to shrink and mold onto her bones, as if there wasn't enough room for her inside her own body. Sparking electricity bubbled in her blood, as if even her usual limp brown hair was about to stand on end.

To Betty, it was similar to the transformation, like the time just before her tiger soul emerged.

Aunt Tanita had described the change like slipping into a stream of silk.

Betty had never felt that way. It was always a fight to let her tiger soul completely out, another to reign it in. She scoffed at the old recitations even as she carefully memorized and wrote out each one. *Find the balance. Be one.*

Her tiger soul meant power and control.

No one would ever be able to accuse Betty of being *wild*, the worst insult she and her cousins could hurl at one another—out of control, not tame, a mere beast; no longer human or tiger, but a creature that none could reason with.

Though in her secret heart of hearts, Betty wished she could let go and be as wild as her soul sometimes felt.

The summer heat pressed down on Fort Williams, making it too hot to sleep. Betty walked along the second floor veranda facing the formal gardens, breathing in the sweet night jasmine, the musky clematis, and the heady wild roses.

She never saw stars in London like she did here in Calcutta. Then again, except for during The Blitz, London had always had her own light.

Betty shivered in the hot, humid night, pulling her knitted shawl closer over her white cotton nightgown. She couldn't imagine living through such an attack. It made her want to growl just thinking about being closed in at night, every night, for weeks.

Even without the light, Betty, like the rest of the tiger clan, saw well in the dark, easily avoiding the pots near the railing filled with Mother's hopeless English Ivy, as well as the chairs that had been pulled from the nearby gallery.

Then she saw the shadow, a patch of night darker than the rest. Betty looked behind her, as well as above, but she didn't see a light source, nothing bright enough to cause such a dark spot.

The troubling cloud slid to the side as Betty approached, leaving a thin, black trail behind.

Betty reached out and tried to grasp the slight remains of the dark, but it was like catching at smoke: It left nothing behind but her slightly chilled fingers.

It was magic, though, something powerful.

Betty hesitated. Should she go get Mother? She knew much more about spells and charms than Betty did.

Then Betty's tiger soul rose. *They* could face anything together. She didn't need Mother, or Father, or her cousins.

She would prove that she was capable of handling this on her own, despite only being sixteen.

Claws emerged from the tips of Betty's fingernails. Her jaw grew heavy, stronger, and her mouth filled with razor sharp teeth.

The darkness before Betty intensified, spreading like oil across clear water. Fear spiked through her chest, but she shook her head, growling.

If her cousins could battle for independence against their own people, Betty, and her family, then she could be brave as well.

But she didn't have to be stupid.

Instead of wading into the blackening cloud, like her tiger soul urged, Betty reached out with one clawed hand and carved a bit of the shadow off, a long squiggling line, separating it from the rest, as easily as a knife cutting through silk.

For a brief moment the two remained separate, the cloud and its little tendril, then the shadow collected itself back together, and no trace of the tear remained.

Yet, something had happened.

Betty sensed the shadow's rising excitement, much like her own these days at the mere mention of leaving the fort, or of coming visitors.

The shadow pulled in on itself, slowly, leaking out of the world until nothing remained except Betty, the too-hot night air, and a lingering sense of promise.

***

"Let's go to the market," Betty proposed to her cousins Abhya and Shalini, visiting from the north. They weren't much older than Betty, but their mother had let them travel by themselves, coming by train with a male cousin.

The cousins had the same mother, but different fathers, as was traditional in the tiger clan. Abhya had dark skin—almost as dark as the little African boy the missionaries had brought back with them. Shalini was pale as milky tea. They shared the same deep brown eyes, thick black hair, and moon-shaped faces as their mother.

The three of them sat together in the morning room, leaning against pillows and drinking tea. The day was humid and still, no wind to carry away the hot stink of fear that had invaded the fort that week. Betty was desperate for something, anything, to distract her from the tingling anticipation and anxiousness that buzzed across her skin.

"Is it safe?" Abhya asked.

Betty always found it funny that though *Abhya* meant

fearless, her darker cousin was constantly concerned about potential risks.

"We'll take one of Father's soldiers," Betty assured her.

She didn't bother to tell them that Mother had deemed it safe; her cousins didn't think much of Betty's mother. Not many in tiger clan did. She'd not only married Father, but they'd raised Betty in the human fashion, with nannies and tutors, instead of sending her to the *shishu greeha* to be raised with the other tiger clan girls her age, sisters for life regardless of actual blood ties. Betty had still traveled to the commune every summer, so she'd at least met her sisters, but she'd never bonded with them—she was always an outsider, even to her own clan.

Betty suspected that the reason her parents sent her was so that they could have time by themselves, something they greatly desired. Her parents always looked at each other with such tenderness, as if Betty wasn't even there.

Shalini finally said, "Only if we go by car."

"Of course," Betty said.

She didn't tell them that the only car they could get was one of the Royal Force's Jeeps. It was a horrid beige color, like dried mud. The wide wheels took every bump hard, jostling Betty's bones, and the straw-stuffed seats didn't make the trip any smoother.

However, her cousins seemed happy to be riding in it, even if they couldn't drive fast enough to raise a decent wind.

Freddie, Betty's favorite guard, drove them to the edge of the market, then informed them he would stay with the car.

Abhya looked worried at that, but Betty told her again, "It's fine."

Though the stench of fear still rolled at their feet, at

least the market had enough other smells to mask it: the salty odor of fresh fish, lemons and oranges from the countryside, dusty tea from the plantations, and the spices —spicy ground peppers, sweet coriander, musty cumin, and comforting cinnamon and nutmeg.

Betty didn't need to buy anything—the cooks did all the proper shopping for the fort. All she wanted to find was another memento for her friends back in England.

Abhya and Shalini trailed behind Betty as they strolled through the crowded corridors of ramshackle stalls, whispering to each other and barely nodding when she held up a bracelet or oddly carved statue for their commentary.

"What are you two gossiping about?" Betty asked, exasperated.

"Nothing," Abhya said.

Betty smelled the fear, could practically see it rising like a dirty tide, flowing from their feet up to their waists. She looked around, but she didn't see any threat. Indian merchants stared at her as they always had, her fair coloring marking her as foreign in this land of dark natives.

"It's nothing you would understand," Shalini said dismissively. "Have you finished your shopping?"

"Why wouldn't I understand?" Betty asked sharply, tired of these digs.

Shalini took Abhya's hand into the crook of her own elbow, patting it. She whispered something to Abhya and took a step forward.

Betty didn't give, didn't move back. Instead, she stared at them in the most rude way possible.

Finally, Shalini looked over Betty's shoulder and pointed with her chin to a merchant standing there. "We should go."

Betty turned and stared at the man. His black hair shot was through with gray, while wide brown eyes and thin, disapproving lips filled the rest of his narrow face. He wore the usual local costume: cotton tunic over baggy trousers, with a vest on top, all in shades of gray and tan. He glared fully at them, his hands at his sides, clenching and unclenching.

There was nothing unusual about him, though. Many of the natives were upset with the British for one thing or another. Betty was used to it. She turned to tell her cousins that when she realized he wasn't even looking at her.

He glared at Abhya and Shalini, instead. In fact, so were many of the other merchants.

The scent in the market had changed as well. Anger began to overlay the constant scent of fear.

"Why are they mad at you?" Betty asked. She would have denied feeling a bit put out that the natives, for once, weren't paying attention to her.

"They think we're Muslim," Abhya said softly.

Betty shook her head, then turned and started walking back the way they'd come. Of course, her cousins worshipped Traya, goddess of the tigers, same as all the tiger clan. They just pretended to follow the local religion, just as Betty and her parents regularly went to Church of England services.

Fit in was one of the recitations Betty resented the most strongly, but still obeyed.

"Why would that matter?" Betty asked as she stopped, picking up a small leather purse and waving it at the wizened old woman sitting behind the counter, sucking on her three remaining teeth.

"Five rupee," she croaked out, holding up a wrinkled, frail hand, all fingers extended.

"You wouldn't understand," Shalini said.

"Of course I wouldn't," Betty muttered. Then she turned her attention back to the old trader. "Half a rupee," she said. "Look at how small this is! It will barely hold even that small a coin. Bah!"

The old woman heaved a tremendous sigh. "Feel how soft," she said. "Each stitch, prayed over," she added, folding her hands over her chest and bobbing her head. "Blessed," she said. "Three rupees."

Betty held the purse up, opening it and looking inside. "Any luck will fall out," she complained. "The stitches are too wide. Uneven. One rupee."

"One and one half, with blessings on my dear boy's head," the old woman said, dropping her hand to a picture of some Indian god blowing a flute, blue and smiling, with many arms.

Betty sniffed but gave in. She handed the purse to her cousins without looking back while she dug out her coins.

When Betty turned back to Abhya and Shalini, they both scowled at her.

More of the merchants were standing, drawing near, looking angry as well, but at least their anger wasn't directed at her for once.

"I am not your servant," Abhya hissed, drawing near. "I am not here to fetch and carry for you," she added as she pushed the purse back into Betty's hands.

"Of course not," Betty said, confused. What had she done wrong? She would have helped carry their things if they needed. Or was it one of those Indian things she'd never understand?

"We must go now," Shalini said.

"But—" Betty started. She really wanted to go get some lemonade from a shop near here.

"Now," Abhya said, looking over Betty's shoulder.

The merchants had gathered closer.

"Don't worry. I'll protect you," Betty said, reaching out for Abhya's other hand.

"Not for much longer, English," muttered one of the nearby merchants.

Before Betty could make any remark in return, Freddie was suddenly there. "We need to get home, Miss," was all he said.

No one looked away or sat back down. Betty suddenly realized that just as her cousins had started walking taller, so had the rest of their countrymen.

Betty nodded and followed Freddie out of the marketplace, letting him push through the crowds of staring Indians, clearing the way for all of them. She kept her head high, her expression, stern.

Yes, the British would be leaving India soon.

Good riddance.

* * *

A tendril of shadow followed Betty into her dreams that night. She stood in a cave dark enough that she needed a torch to see. The walls reflected back yellow and gray, with hidden water dripping behind her. The smell of dust and long-dried bones tickled her nose. Under her feet, the path was covered with fine dirt that puffed up as she walked and muffled all noise.

In the absolute darkness, Betty could follow the shadow more easily. Here, in her dream, she could tell just how different it was from the surrounding blackness. It moved like an eel, swimming upstream against the currents of air.

Betty followed it, further under the mountain. She knew (as one does in dreams) that she was the only person to have ever been there. No intrepid explorer had ever dug down into these depths. No other eye had beheld the graceful dripping of rock, like artful chandeliers hanging from the ceiling, or the subtle colors, layered like a sunset, red, yellow, and white.

The path led to a large, open cavern in the heart of the mountain. Shadows churned in the center of the wide open space, boiling up like a fountain, then falling back down again. The walls sweated with the effort of the shadows, smelling like sweet incense burned in sacrifice.

But this wasn't what the tendril of shadow wanted to show Betty.

It led her around the frantic clouds to a side corner, where a thick, still pool gathered at the foot of the rock. It looked like crude oil, midnight black and sticky.

The tendril of shadow urged Betty forward, wanting her to step into the pool.

For the first time, Betty resisted. The darkness of the pool seemed complete and overwhelming; if she stepped into it, she might never get clean again. The shadows here were angry and chaotic—they moved outside of human purpose, like a wild beast, unknowable and not moved by reason.

The little shadow reared up in front of her, changing form, its head flattening out like the snakes Betty had seen performing in the marketplace, fangs extending.

It was still just a wisp of a thing, not truly deadly. Still, Betty retreated, and her tiger soul pushed forward, taking over.

The cave grew brighter and the shadows lost form and density, becoming more like mist or fog.

However, the pool gained depth, as well as a telltale shimmer.

Magic, thick and potent, floated there.

Betty suddenly understood: Stepping into the pool

would meld her own meager magical abilities with those of the shadows. The further she submerged herself, the stronger she would grow magically.

Betty's tiger soul hissed, backing away from such a change. She didn't trust it. She leapt up, the shadowy mist unable to hold her, pushing her way higher and higher through the air until they flew out of the mountain.

The land below was no longer India, but Betty's beloved England. Sparkling green fields dotted with lazy sheep spread out in all directions below her, while hedges covered in fragrant pink roses divided the green into neat, orderly squares.

The brightness of the sun warmed not only Betty's back, but her soul. It made her tiger soul playful as it never was awake. They landed softly on a hill, pink petals floating up. Her tiger pounced on the petals, capturing them in gentle paws, then rolled in the sweet grass.

Something made Betty turn and look back.

The towering mountain loomed behind them, dark and powerful, its shadow growing.

Betty gave a loud, body-shaking roar, but it sounded like a kitten's squeak in the face of such might.

"Stay inside today," Father ordered, showing up as Betty ate her breakfast alone in the room adjacent to the kitchen; too lowly to call it a dining room, and too homely to be called a breakfast nook. The walls were painted a drab brown, the table in the center taking up most of the space.

Betty tried to convince herself that she was like the lady of the house, sitting alone and having her tea and toast, but she was actually lonely.

"Why?" Betty asked, not because she cared, but

because she hated the idea of being stuck anywhere, at anytime.

"The Muslim leadership is calling for a general strike — some sort of day of direct action."

"Abhya and Shalini left this morning," Betty told him. "They were heading back home, by train."

"Hmm," Father said, obviously worried. "I'll send some guards to the station, pick them up if the trains aren't running."

"Thank you," Betty said. "Where will you spend today?" she asked, just to keep him there a bit longer.

"I'll be in my office all day," Father said.

He looked so dashing in his uniform, with his finely trimmed mustache and twinkling green eyes. Betty had always thought he looked like the epitome of a British officer.

"Reports and paperwork are the most exciting things I have to look forward to." He paused, giving her a conspiratorial wink. "I think you should find your mother. She said something about making a tent…"

"Oh, yes!" Betty said eagerly. She would happily stay inside if Mother was in a playful mood.

Still…

"Be careful, Father," Betty said. The air continued to reek of sickening fear and blazing anger.

"Don't worry. I shan't be faced with anything more deadly than a paper cut, I promise." He leaned down to kiss her cheek. "You've grown," he said softly. "I forget sometimes how old you are now."

Betty sat up straighter, preening.

"Now, that's enough of that," Father said with mock sternness. "Go attend your mother. I'll try to have lunch with you later."

With that, Father strode from the room.

Betty hastily downed the rest of her tea, then went off in search of her mother. She found her in one of the long galleries that faced the garden, which had portraits of the King and other important leaders glaring down at them.

"Quick, quick!" Mother said, reaching for Betty's hand, then pulling her along.

Mother was in native garb that day, a pretty pajama tunic made from plain white cloth, though the placket in the front, as well as the cuffs and hem, were decorated in black and gold. She wore a traditional shawl over her auburn hair, and nothing on her feet.

They raced the length of the gallery, Betty giggling as her mother tugged at her hand and urged her to go faster. They barely slowed going around the corner, then Mother led Betty to the corner study.

Mother had decided to play "tent" that day. Carpets and pillows lay heaped across the floor, while the walls were hidden by long, billowing strips of cloth, making everything seem soft, hiding the hard lines. The room had changed from drab brown to rich red, orange, and pink. Sweet patchouli burned on a low altar against the far wall, and candles were lit everywhere, hanging from the ceiling and lining the floor.

It was also stifling hot.

Betty paused by the door. She saw the distraction charms twinkling in the cardinal points, while enchantment dots wove their way between the soft silks.

It was a trick. A distraction. Mother and Father must have planned it together.

Father had lied. Something bad must be happening.

"No, no, nothing bad," Mother reassured Betty, tugging on her hand.

Betty resisted, staying stubbornly on the threshold.

"It's just—I know how much you hate being cooped

up," Mother confessed. "This was an easy way for us to spend the time."

"I'm not a child," Betty said. "You could have just told me."

"Perhaps. But perhaps you wouldn't have listened, either," Mother said quietly. "And today, you needed to listen."

"What's going on?" Betty asked, risking a single foot inside the room.

The magical appeal of the room washed over Betty quickly, tempting her with unknown delights. It would be so easy to lose a day in there. But there was something she needed to do first, something she had to tell Mother.

"We don't know," Mother admitted. "There have been warnings. Not from the Indian government, of course. But others. We were supposed to have a visitor today, from the Americas. To bring us news. Of course, he was delayed. So we delay."

"But Mother—" Betty knew she must tell her mother something about her cousins. She'd told Father, but it wasn't enough, she knew it wasn't enough.

"So come," Mother said, drawing Betty all the way into the room. "I know you saw the distraction and enchantment charms, but what about this one?" she asked, pointing to the ceiling at a charm Betty hadn't seen.

What a pretty charm. She sensed that it was more about light than distraction, though. "What is it?" she asked, the little niggling fear in the back of her thoughts disappearing.

The door closed silently behind her, swung shut by no human hand.

And Betty was entertained for the entire day.

Betty and Mother came out of the room, laughing. Betty knew she wouldn't remember everything from that day—the distraction spells had been too strong. But she'd remember the magic Mother taught her: the protection spell, the light charm, and others.

The distraction spell had also lessened the hurt when Mother commented, yet again, on how meager Betty's own magic was.

A soldier waited for them in the corridor, directly opposite the door. "The commander would like to see you," he said stiffly, bowing.

Mother sniffed the air, then gripped Betty's hand again and set off quickly.

Betty could smell it, too: The stinking fear that had invaded the city was now mingled with an undercurrent of spilled blood.

Father sat behind his desk. Instead of the order Betty was used to, the top was littered with reports, maps hung off the edges, and books were open facedown with other books crushing their spines. The cabinet in the corner had its drawers pulled out, papers and folders strewn across them.

"Are Abhya and Shalini with you?" Father asked at once, standing, looking worried.

"No, of course not," Mother said. "I was training Betty all day."

"I sent soldiers to the train station after the general assembly," Father told Betty.

Mother looked at Betty.

"They decided to go back home this morning," Betty told her.

"You should have told me," Mother accused her, growing pale. "Why didn't you tell me?"

"How could I? You had me distracted from the moment I set foot in there," Betty spat back.

"Distracted! Not addlepated!" Mother shot back. "You should have been strong enough to resist. At least long enough to have told me that your cousins had left the fort. This is all your fault!"

"I told Father," Betty said.

"We couldn't find them," Father said. "And the leaders of the general assembly put forward a call for *direct action*. Many answered that call—now there's rioting and mayhem in the streets."

Betty could smell the small current of relief from Father—as least the mad bastards were only attacking each other, Muslim versus Hindu, not both of them against the British for once.

"Come," Mother said. She raced back to the corner study, plucking a wad of unspun cotton from the air, wrapping it in plaited twine. Then she spun the lure, muttering a seeking spell.

The lure flew in a direct path north, then abruptly stopped as if it had hit an invisible wall and fell to the floor.

Fear pounced on Betty, making her sway where she stood.

Someone else's spell blocked them from finding her cousins.

"We must go get them. Now," Mother growled, turning toward the door.

"No," Father said.

Betty turned to look at him, surprised that he'd followed them into the room. Mother must have let down the guard spells for him to come in.

Or maybe she never blocked Father.

"It's too dangerous," Father insisted. "Listen to the city."

Mother waved her hand and suddenly the far-off sounds were magnified.

Angry shouts filled the room, punctuated by the tinkling of broken glass. A terrified woman's scream was suddenly cut off, followed by the cracking of out-of-control fires.

"But—"

"I cannot lose you," Father said softly, moving forward to touch Mother's shoulder.

Betty knew what always came next, and turned away. When she turned back, Mother and Father were in each other's arms. At least they'd finished kissing.

"Those poor girls," Mother murmured.

"It's too dangerous," Father repeated. "Even for you. Especially for you, if there's another spell caster out there."

Betty bent her head and looked at the ground. No one would save her cousins. Mother might have been able to do it, to push past the other's magic, but Father wouldn't let her go.

And Betty couldn't do it. Her magic wasn't strong enough.

Mother was right.

If her cousins were dead, it was all Betty's fault.

That night, Betty kept vigil with her parents. Father sent a few scouts into the city, mapping out the worst of the fighting but not engaging.

His superiors had been very clear about that: The British forces weren't to engage. Not yet.

They sat on the veranda overlooking the gardens, the night wrapped around them, each wrapped in their own thoughts.

Betty told her parents of the incident in the market. Father directed his spies there, but they found nothing.

The sounds of fighting in the far distance died as the false dawn crept in. Smoke and tears joined the other scents, the jasmine mingled with fear, hot, coppery blood with the roses.

Mother tried her finding spell again as soon as it was light enough. The blocking spell was gone. The lure flew freely around the still-tented room.

However, it landed upside down.

The fear that had settled in Betty's gut rose up again, making her feel sick.

"Just past the market," Mother hissed, giving directions. "Quickly."

Then she took Betty's hand and returned to the veranda, waiting.

The normal sounds of soldiers returned: muttered conversations, the clank of boots on concrete, shifting sounds of metal and uniforms. Cook had fixed porridge for breakfast, but both Betty and Mother had let it sit, not even tasting it.

Dread clenched Betty's stomach. She told herself that the lure may have found clothing or bags belonging to her cousins. That was why it had landed upside down.

Not that it had found bodies.

Mother looked up when the Jeep returned. How she heard the single engine and identified it, Betty couldn't be sure. Her own magic wasn't strong enough. She could only follow Mother from the veranda.

One long wooden stretcher lay across the hood of the Jeep, while a second across the back. Even as they entered the courtyard Betty knew they were merely corpses, not her cousins.

Mother gave a great tiger howl. Betty joined in.

Other women in the compound—natives—joined in their cry of grief, shattering all the activity around them, the soldiers freezing as the sound undulated.

The girls hadn't been desecrated, at least not physically. No, it was much worse. They stank of putrid herbs and foul rites.

The damn native *dhayana* had stolen their tiger souls.

"Mother—" Betty said, horrified.

"We will deal with this," Mother said, her voice like iron.

The tiger clan would get revenge on the witch.

Hurt one, hurt all...a recitation Betty was truly grateful for.

That night, the shadows brought a different dream. Betty strolled through the rows at a country fair in a mythical England, bright and green with soft air filled with the scents of new grass, spring tulips, and daffodils. She wore an old-fashioned frock made from frilly white lace that swept down to the ground, with matching white gloves and a pillbox hat.

Crowds of people stood in the distance, but whenever Betty approached them, they moved to the next spot, so when Betty arrived where they'd been, it was deserted. She knew they'd been there, however, because of the debris they'd left behind: half-eaten candied apples, torn tickets and wrappers, nuts and dried fruits stepped on and pushed into the soft ground, even a lone, gray silk glove.

Betty walked slowly past the carnival stages. One had

a guessing game about the number of rusty horseshoe nails in a glass jar big enough to hold a person's head. Another had a hoop-throwing game, where customers paid to throw brightly colored bracelets over wooden pins and win silly stuffed toys.

Then Betty came to the row of freak shows: the ancient blond man who had wings instead of arms; the fat female boar who rode a tricycle in erratic circles on the small stage; the ugly tattooed man with a huge, flat head and the eyes and tongue of a snake; the pathetic dog boy; and a scary Asian woman with a long snout and scales instead of skin.

The last stage held a mighty tiger who struggled against the shadows that had pinned down all four of her paws as well as wrapped around her muzzle so she couldn't pace or roar.

Betty leaped up on the stage easily, despite her long skirt. She plucked the shadows from the tiger. They stretched like taffy, then snapped up, wrapping around her hands and wrists. However, they didn't weigh her down like they had the tiger. Instead, they seeped into her skin, down to her bones, spreading along them and making them like steel.

The shadows also wormed their way into the base of her spine, where her magic pooled, expanding it and thickening it, making it more like molasses than black wine.

Betty shook with the changes, surprised that her frock still fit as she felt her insides grow and expand, her skin growing tight.

The tiger gave a loud roar, startling Betty, making her look up and see that the tiger stared at her with the dead eyes of her cousins.

"I'm so sorry I couldn't save you," Betty said, reaching out and patting the stiff, matted fur. "I'm so sorry."

Next time, though, with the help of the shadows, she would be strong enough.

Betty was still tired from no sleep the night before. However, she perked up when one of the guard announced their American visitor had finally arrived.

Mother went to greet him and walk with him to the morning room, while Betty went to the kitchen to order tea. Then Betty followed the servant back up, pausing at the threshold.

The visitor looked quite plain, almost like a native. He wore a common cotton tunic and pants, but he wasn't an Indian; he wore his black hair long, to his shoulders, and his dark skin had a red tint to it. His face was broad and somehow familiar.

When he turned his black eyes to Betty, she hid her surprise.

He looked like the snake man from her dream.

Not only that, she could tell he was from the viper clan. A shadow creature imposed itself over his face, with scales, snake eyes, and a great golden hood. She was amazed at how clear the vision was. Before the shadows had merged with her magic, she wouldn't have seen so much, just a vague light making him seem brighter than other regular people even when he stood in the dark.

What could be so important that the clans would contact one another? After centuries of keeping apart, primarily so that no clan would ever betray a rival clan, either accidentally or on purpose like the raven clan had?

"Yes, the shadows," he was saying as he accepted the

cup of tea. "You haven't had any contact with them? You must avoid them at all costs."

Betty froze. What did he mean? Why was the viper clan afraid of the shadows?

"I know of no shadow creatures," Mother said. "Just the dark times we live in."

"They are coming," the young man insisted. "Here. We've foreseen it."

"Interesting," Mother said. "So your mystics still dream?"

The young man nodded.

Betty had heard tales of the viper clan living far away in their mountain villages where mystics spun out visions and dreams, but she'd never seen anyone from another clan. She wondered if the other tales were true: the horrible ravens and their black-hearted assassins, the stupid hounds who were so easily distracted, the chaotic boars that you never brought to a fight because you couldn't trust them not to turn against you mid-battle, the wealthy crocodiles and their hedonistic palaces.

"Oh, Betty, darling," Mother called, beckoning her to come further into the room. "This is Gezane, from the Americas. This is Betty, my daughter."

"Hello," Betty said, bowing her head so she wouldn't have to come closer, wouldn't have to take his hand.

"You haven't seen any shadow things, have you?" Mother asked.

Gezane caught Betty's eye. He stared hard at her, his flattened nostrils flaring.

"No, Mother, I haven't," Betty lied.

The shadows rose, much like her own tiger soul, giving her words weight and truth so Mother believed her.

However, Gezane knew she hadn't spoken the truth.

Betty lifted her chin in defiance. What could he

possibly do about it? The shadows weren't just in her anymore. They were connected to her magic, as well as all of the tiger clan's magic.

"I see," Gezane said softly.

"What do they do, these shadows?" Mother asked. "What should I look out for?"

"They're powerful and dangerous," Gezane said, still looking at Betty. "They confuse the mind, and make you say or do things you normally wouldn't. They can trick you into believing things that aren't true. Long association can also make a person callous and cruel. They'll also drain you of energy and life."

"Are they really that much of a threat?" Mother asked.

"Yes," Gezane replied, turning his gaze from Betty. "We've foreseen that if they're allowed to grow, they'll first take over all the clans, then the human races. They'll destroy our entire world. If you ever see them, you must contact the other clans immediately. You can reach the hounds the easiest, at their court in Germany."

Betty heard the warning he uttered: She must keep the shadows all to herself.

"Thank you," Gezane said, standing abruptly. He glanced once again at Betty, looking as sad and pathetic as his dream counterpart. "Goodbye. Good luck." He nodded to Mother, then walked past Betty as if he no longer saw her.

"What an odd man," Mother said. "He didn't even finish his tea. Do you have any idea what that was about? Did your cousins ever say anything to you about the shadows?"

"No, they didn't," Betty said easily as she sat down next to her mother.

Power worked in more than one way—and *dangerous* might only mean that the tiger clan grew stronger than all the other clans. Betty dismissed this Gezane's claims of the shadows taking over the world. They were just there to help her.

Betty talked with her mother of inconsequential things, distracting them both from the funeral later that day, the packing ahead of them, and the long trip back to England, where Betty would nurture the power she now carried inside of her, that was only a shadow of the greater power to come for the entire tiger clan.

GERMANY, PRESENT DAY

LUKAS

The castle was the first thing Lukas had seen that looked the same as when he'd been a boy: clean gray stone looming over him up to the toothy edge of the roof; pretty leaded-glass windows glinted in the afternoon sunlight; endless green grass and formal gardens spread before the building like the sea.

However, the whole place reeked of shadows.

Rudi stood beside Lukas as they paused on the perfectly maintained lawn, marveling at the manicured trees, taking in the scents of home: the sweet flowers, the many hounds all gathered together, the ancient stone.

Lukas did, but didn't, want to walk into the castle. It wasn't home, and hadn't been for a very long time. What would he say to Da, Mama, and Greta? Let alone how to confront Oma.

Before Lukas could walk forward, the wide wooden doors flung open and out rushed Da. His hair was still black like Lukas', with only the temples gone gray. His eyes were the same brilliant blue that Lukas saw in the mirror. Lukas recognized the dark business suit his father wore, as well as the ruby red tie.

Without a word, Da ran directly up to Lukas, throwing his arms around him in a tight hug.

"It's true," Da said, his voice breaking. "It's true. You're here. Human."

All Lukas could do was nod. He held on just as tightly. No words could make it through his crush of emotions, the shock of seeing his father alive but old—so much older, so much smaller.

Da pulled back a little, reaching up to cup Lukas' face. "You're here," he said, repeating himself, as if he didn't know what else to say.

Through his tears, Lukas was able to smile. "Yes. It's me. I'm here."

"What happened? Where have you been?" Da looked between Lukas and Rudi. "Did you find my son?"

"He helped me break the curse," Lukas said. They'd agreed to hide Rudi's part in the kidnapping. The consequences were too dire.

Rudi had never said there had been a huge search for Lukas. Rudi had always assumed that they knew Lukas was alive and well, just not exactly where he was. That's what Oma had told him.

However, given the way Da was acting, they hadn't known.

Lukas vowed to protect Rudi every way he could.

"Curse? You were cursed?" Da asked. He dropped his hands from Lukas' face and stepped back.

Lukas stopped himself from telling his father that he wasn't unclean or contagious. Instead, he merely said, "Yes. Cursed with shadows. That's why I couldn't change back."

"Shadows? Nonsense. Your grandmother's always talking about shadows."

Lukas rocked back on his heels, stung. "Really, Da?" he fumed. "I was stuck in hound form for ten years because of the shadows. They are not nonsense."

"Of course not," Da said. At least he had the grace to look embarrassed. "I didn't mean to imply—it's just, I can't see them," Da whined.

"I know. I don't think any sight hound can sense them. Just the scent hounds," Lukas said, nodding toward Rudi.

Da cocked his head to the side and stared at Lukas. "You're not a scent hound."

"No." Lukas took a deep breath, filling himself with the warm, sweet smell of his father. It was going to be all right. He wiggled his toes in his new, painful shoes and made himself continue.

The time for secrets was over.

"I'm a guardian hound, Da. Part scent, part sight, and part guard."

"I don't think I've heard of that breed before," Da said thoughtfully.

"We're rare," Lukas assured him with a smile. Maybe Da would at least believe that part of his story.

"But—cursed. You said you were cursed," Da said, circling back like a hound on a scent.

"Yes," Lukas said, what little comfort he'd had disappearing faster than a trail in the Seattle rain. "It was Oma. Grandma."

All the color drained out of Da's face. Lukas put a hand out toward him, ready to catch him.

"She went into a sudden coma. Three days ago," Da said softly. He still looked like he might be sick.

Lukas nodded. "When the curse was broken. It had sustained her. I want—I want to go see her."

"Of course." Da suddenly stepped forward and hugged Lukas again, as if he couldn't help himself. "But where have you been all these years?" Then he slipped his arm around Lukas' waist, turning them toward the castle.

More ministers stood in the doorway. Lukas knew they'd hear anything he said, so he was doubly glad he'd been careful with Rudi, who walked behind him, guarding him.

"In America," Lukas said, sliding his arm shyly around his father's waist. It all seemed so unreal.

"Were you alone? In a pack?" Da asked.

"Rudi found me and took care of me," Lukas admitted, preparing himself for the next blow.

"Didn't you know he was the prince?" Da asked, horrified. He stopped and stared at Rudi.

"I knew, Sire," Rudi admitted. "Lady Metzler asked me to find him and keep him safe, away from the court." He frowned, then stepped closer. "Sire, she told me that you knew Lukas was safe."

Da nodded slowly. "She told us frequently, at first. But then she started losing her wits, going on and on about the shadows and other crazy things—"

"The shadows are real," Lukas assured his father. He could scent them here. "They will attack. Soon."

But Da looked at him blankly, and Lukas knew his words fell on unhearing ears, like seeds scattered across solid rock, with no place to root or grow.

Oma still looked solid and strong, though she lay too still on her bed, and the skin around her eyes looked dark and bruised. Her gray hair curled neatly across the soft pink pillowcase, and her elegant hands lay above the white blankets, the right one attached to three machines. The room smelled like the vinegar cleaner Rudi used, with only the faintest trace of the lavender Lukas remembered.

The hospital was an old house that had been converted, with many rooms facing the gardens. Few in the hound clan got sick enough to need hospitalization, so most of the time the place stood empty or had only one or two patients. Instead of white sterile walls and cold tile floors, it was painted a warm cream color, with spotless hardwood floors and many comfortable nooks for sitting and resting.

"The doctors say she's—she's—non-responsive," Da stated. "There's very little brain activity, just enough that she's still living."

Lukas nodded, walking closer. Someone had put fresh yellow roses on the stand next to Oma's bed, and a book, *The Popcorn Thief*, that had a bookmark three-quarters of the way through.

If Oma hadn't been so still, Lukas might have thought she was just sleeping.

Though no shadows marred her rest, and they hadn't invaded this room, Lukas still smelled their influence. Either that, or the faint smell of decay and death came from Oma herself.

"Can I talk to her for a moment?" Lukas turned and asked. It took him a moment to realize he'd automatically asked Rudi, not his father. He turned all the way and added, "Alone, please." At least Da hadn't seemed to notice, even if Rudi had.

"Certainly," Da said, nodding. "We'll be right outside." He gave Rudi a strong look, and Lukas knew they'd be having words in the hall.

Before Lukas could tell them never mind, Rudi walked forward and pulled what looked like a black brick phone from his pocket. He set it on the end table, tapping a button on it once and saying, "For your privacy." He glanced up at the corner, where Lukas noticed a round black camera stuck to the ceiling.

"Thank you," Lukas told Rudi, though he wasn't sure it was completely necessary.

Da looked at the device suspiciously, then at Rudi, and turned to walk out.

Lukas knew he'd have to hurry. He needed to protect Rudi.

Standing next to the bed, Lukas took Oma's left hand. Her fingers were warm, her skin was soft, but there was no strength or life in it.

"Oma," Lukas started, his voice hollow in the almost empty room.

She'd saved him, taught him how to hold onto secrets, then cursed him so he couldn't grow up like a normal boy.

He wanted to howl at her.

Had it been worth it? He didn't know—wouldn't know unless they defeated the shadows, and possibly not even then.

And how many others were there? Now, seeing her, he realized that she hadn't trained just him and Rudi; no, there was probably a hidden army out there, ready to leap at her every command.

"Don't die," Lukas choked out, squeezing Oma's hand tightly. She had too many secrets to pass away so quickly. "You need to tell me more," Lukas added. More about being a guardian, more about the knight, more about how to defeat the shadows. "You can't die. Not yet. Not now. Please."

Lukas put her his grandmother's hand back on the bed, sniffing and wiping away the moisture gathered in his eyes with the back of his hand.

There was nothing else he could say, no plea that would make her do what he'd asked. He'd never been able to bend her to his will—she'd only ever bent him to hers.

She would decide whether to come back to him or not.

Even if it was just to say goodbye.

***

Lukas didn't have to put his ear to the door to hear his father talking with Rudi, questioning him about how Lukas had come under his protection, why Rudi hadn't returned the prince to the court. He stayed in his grandmother's sick room, waiting and listening, like Oma had taught him.

Da didn't believe Rudi, of course. No one from the court would ever trust Rudi or anyone in his family, or even from his line.

Lukas had wondered where Mama was, why he hadn't seen her. He wasn't surprised when Da had told him on the way to the hospital that she was out of the country, and it made his heart beat faster to know that she'd be there this afternoon. He had no idea what he'd say to her, either.

Then Da told Rudi that Rudi should leave after that.

Lukas realized that his father had assumed that since Lukas had returned, he was going to stay in Germany.

Yet another thing to try to clear up.

"I'm going with Rudi," Lukas informed them both, stepping out of his grandmother's sick room and into the hall. It was cheery like the rooms, with a beautiful antique table proudly displaying pink, purple, and white petunias.

"No, you're not," Da said firmly. "You're not going anywhere else with this man."

"Da, you don't understand," Lukas said softly. "It isn't because I want to go away with Rudi, or to leave you again. But there's a war coming, with the shadows. And I must gather the defenses together. Or the world will die."

From the way his father pressed his lips together, Lukas could tell he wanted to tell Lukas yet again that the shadows were nothing.

Magic must be hiding the shadows from the sight hounds, like some sort of curse.

"Do you remember the raven clan? How after the decimation, all the clans got together and cursed the ravens, so they could never find us again?" Lukas asked.

"Yes," Da said slowly.

"I think the shadows did the same thing to you, to the sight hounds," Lukas said eagerly. "Which is why you can't see them, can't believe in them."

Da looked away, thinking. Then he turned back to Lukas, his steely blue eyes blazing. "So your grandmother's been telling the truth all these years? That these shadows are here, they've infected us all?"

"Yes," Rudi said, stepping forward. He glanced at Lukas, then back at the king. "Sire, I think some of your ministers have been infected. They've grown cruel and are no longer themselves."

Da nodded, then said, "You know, after you left, your sister…. She changed. Grew, well, peculiar."

Lukas' heart dropped out of his chest and burrowed far under his feet, where not even a terrier could dig it out.

"Let's go see her," Lukas said grimly. Though he'd known home wouldn't be anything like he remembered, he'd foolishly hoped for better than this.

Lukas left Da and Rudi hovering in the hallway outside Greta's laboratory, trusting that they wouldn't kill each other and that Da wouldn't banish Rudi before Lukas came back.

It wasn't that Lukas wanted to go forward alone. The stench of shadows was so strong from beyond the door he expected to see them rolling through the air, amassed like a great cloud. He insisted that both Da and Rudi stay outside —Lukas had to minimize Rudi's exposure to them, as well as his father's.

He was supposed to be a guardian hound, after all.

The acrid smell of magic threaded through the death scent of the shadows. Plants lined the shelves on the walls, bathed in humming purple lights. Two long stainless-steel tables divided the space, front from back, side from side. Against the far wall on the counters sat microscopes, machines that spun a dozen test tubes, and other modern equipment that Lukas didn't recognize.

A tall blond woman in a white lab coat slowly rose as Lukas walked across the room, stopping at his side of the stainless steel tables.

"Greta?" he asked softly.

His oldest nightmares had come true: Not only had the shadows infected his sister, they'd turned her into a doll.

Blond curls perfectly ringed Greta's face. Her eyes were brown and expressionless, as if they'd been carved from glass. Bright red tinted her lips, forming a Cupid's bow that looked painted, not real.

"Lukas?" Greta asked, her voice as mechanical and contrived as the rest of her. She stayed on her side of the table, examining him like he was an unexpected result from an otherwise successful experiment. "Is that you?"

Lukas didn't dare touch her—he was afraid the

shadows would try to infect him again. He nodded and said, "Yes. It's me. I'm here. Human again."

Greta waited, impassively studying him. "You're taller than I think anyone expected," she finally said, showing some humor in her voice.

But again, she could have been talking about anyone, not her long-lost brother.

Lukas shrugged. "Finally grew into my paws. What are you doing?"

"I became a scientist, like I told you I would," Greta said. "You were stuck, as a hound. I wanted to free you. I searched for your cure."

"You dove too deeply into the shadows," Lukas told her.

"Shadows? Nonsense," Greta said, dismissing them.

Lukas was getting tired of hearing that word.

"Here, let me show you," Greta said. She started walking around the table.

Lukas stepped back, not wanting her to touch him.

"Please," Greta said. For a moment, something human broke through her glazed eyes.

Lukas shuddered, but made himself reach his hand out and take her cold fingers in his.

"Now, this," Greta said, leading him to a shelf where a row of string peas grew in clay pots. One third were stunted, skinny, as well as a sickly green. Two thirds looked healthy and hearty. "There's no growing magic, nothing to help crops, at least among the hounds," Greta said.

"Do the other clans have growing magic?" Lukas asked, despite himself.

"We don't know," Greta admitted. "It might just be a human type of magic."

"You have magic," Lukas said, suddenly realizing how

the shadows had gotten to her. She wasn't clan, and Oma had always said the shadows came through hound magic. Maybe it was all magic that attracted them.

"As a scientist, I tried to tell myself that there was no such thing as magic, at least in humans. But then—this happens."

Greta waved toward the withered plants, pointing at a charm that Lukas hadn't noticed before. It was a bundle of bound twigs wrapped in twine, with the shape of a barrel. It looked plump, full as an over-fed mosquito, and it reeked of shadows.

"That charm is supposed to help the plants grow," Greta said. "Strictly a human spell. However, this is what happens when I make it."

Lukas nodded. Greta's magic had been infected with the shadows.

"And that," she said, pointing to the middle group of healthier plants, "is what happens when a hound makes the same charm."

"Those two sets of plants look the same," Lukas commented, pointing to the middle group and the far group.

"Of course they do. Control group and magicked group," Greta said with a hint of older-sister derision in her voice.

"Your magic is tainted with shadows," Lukas said softly.

"No such thing," Greta said automatically.

Lukas shook his head. How could he free Greta? He'd never been able to do so in his dreams.

"How was this experiment supposed to help me?" he asked finally, looking between the healthy plants to the unhealthy ones. His palm itched to grab the bloated charm and crush it.

"This growing spell, this healthy charm, it seems to draw health to it instead. Life. Magic," Greta said, her voice dropping to a whisper. "Maybe it could have drawn your soul out, too."

Lukas nodded. It was a good idea, actually. Then he turned and looked at Greta. Could it help her as well? Draw her soul out from where it was hidden behind the shadows?

But the blank eyes that returned his look gave him no hint.

The real Greta was in there. He knew it. He just had to find a way to free her.

GERMANY, PRESENT DAY

RUDI

R udi walked behind Lukas and the king to the room where Oscar, the heir apparent, waited. Each walked silently, wrapped in their own thoughts or, in Rudi's case, guilt. Many of the people they passed stared at the prince, though just as many bowed their head in respect. A scurry of whispers swirled after them—hissed comments, gossip, and speculation.

What did the clan think of Rudi and how he'd kept the prince? Was he despised or admired? Could he ever come back to the court? Or should he start testing all his food, making sure no one had poisoned him?

From the main working areas, they turned down a darkened hall—one of the older parts of the castle—with cold stone floors and no rugs to soften them. The narrow passage smelled sterile and contained only traces of old dust and faraway deserts.

Ancient statues brought from the original hound temples lined the walls, with some partially hidden in climate-controlled boxes. Rudi slowed as he walked, fascinated. He'd only ever seen photos of these, not the actual stone deities.

The elongated snout of I'tiram still bore flecks of the original green paint, though most of the stone he was carved out of was bare. He was the one who guided faithful hounds to peaceful pastures after they died. Na-ya, the warrior god, stood with huge flexed arms and a chest piece carved with wings. According to the myths, he spoke with the birds just as the raven clan could. Kulka, Izcuintlia, all were there, in their various incarnations though the millennia.

Rudi wished he had time to study the figures, to spend time with the history of his clan, but it had never been a priority. At least no shadows tainted the air here.

Two of the hound guard waited outside the chamber where the heir apparent waited, standing in the usual blue uniform, with large automatic weapons at their sides and their hands transformed into claws.

A minister of the court waited with them, dressed in a fine navy blue suit, a white shirt with red pinstripes, and a gold-and-red tie. The king merely nodded at him as he and Lukas entered the room.

The minister stepped neatly in front of Rudi, licking his flabby lips and saying, "The heir apparent would like to speak with the king and Lukas alone."

Heir apparent? But wasn't the vote next summer? Lukas was no longer in the running at all?

Rudi glanced at Lukas, who stood rigid, his face betraying no emotion. Only the stiffness in which he held himself told Rudi the truth: that Lukas was also surprised, as well as possibly hurt.

"No," Rudi said, stepping forward. "I'll accompany him." Rudi had no intention of letting Lukas out of his sight. He'd never admit it, but on more than one night in

Seattle, he'd woken late and gone to check on the boy, making sure he was all right, that he was still human, still here.

Lukas turned back and looked at Rudi. "It'll be okay," he said.

"Are you sure?" Rudi had to ask. The political waters here were deep, and Lukas had never learned to swim in them.

Lukas looked at the door, then back at Rudi, and nodded. "Yes. Nothing here could hold me. Or harm me."

Rudi didn't bother pointing out that Lukas could be facing hurts other than physical. But at least the boy felt safe. Rudi wondered about Lukas' hound soul, why it felt comfortable making such declarations (because it was obvious to him, at least, that this pronouncement had come from Lukas' hound soul, and not from the gangly teenaged boy who stood in front of him.)

Then again, no one here at the court had seen Lukas transform to his natural hound shape now that he was fully grown. He'd been big as a boy, but Rudi would bet they had no idea that Lukas' hound form had grown so large. They wouldn't be prepared to defend against a hound the size of a small pony.

"Why don't you wait with Oma?" Lukas suggested.

"All right," Rudi said. He bowed his head to the prince and added, "I will wait for you there, Lukas." He said the name deliberately, to show the minister, the king, and the guard the closeness of their relationship, as well as to respect Lukas' wishes and not address him by his title.

"Thank you," Lukas said. He turned, visibly braced himself, then walked into the room.

Rudi waited for a few moments, listening hard, scenting the air, making sure that nothing had attacked

Lukas, that an ambush hadn't been laid. When Rudi didn't hear or smell anything, he turned to go.

"I hear we owe you a debt," the minister said.

Rudi turned back. "It was an honor," he said. And he meant it. He'd always been honored by Lady Metzler's trust and request. He still wished, though, that his actions hadn't caused Lukas' family so much pain.

"Yes," the minister said, his whippet-like snout pushing forward. "But is it a debt of honor? Or a debt of blood?"

Rudi stared at him passively, consciously not reacting. A debt of blood was usually decreed when a deed required revenge.

The minister sniffed the air, then transformed fully back to human. "You have little fear. That is good," he declared.

Rudi didn't roll his eyes at the pompous proclamation. The minister must have some sort of public-facing aspect to his ministry—it was the only thing that explained his glad-hand style.

"And you care about the boy."

"Of course," Rudi said, keeping his tone mild. "He's my charge." Rudi had always felt that way about Lukas, even when he'd been in hound form. In many ways, Lukas was the son Rudi would never have.

"Guard him well," the minister said as he strolled past Rudi, back down the hall. "The court needs him," he threw over his shoulder.

Rudi shook his head. The world needed Lukas more, if the threat of the shadows were real.

In the darkened hall, Rudi grew as stiff and still as one of the statues.

If the threat were real?

Where had that thought come from? Not from him. Rudi had seen the threat. He knew it was real.

The shadows were more insidious than he'd realized, getting inside his head that way. He would have to tell Lukas later, make him aware of the danger.

Rudi strode out from the castle into the late spring sunshine, breathing in the clean air. He passed into the kitchen gardens. Pumpkins and squashes decayed in one corner, spilling their guts and seeds across the bare ground, preparing and planting the patch for the fall. Spring shoots pushed thin blades out of the earth in strict rows. Rudi remembered fresh cabbages, green and wax beans, cucumbers, and tomatoes from these gardens.

No shadows tainted the modified house that held the hound infirmary. Their scent trailed after Lady Metzler, but that was just because she'd been infected with them for so long.

Was there something native to the building, either in the original architecture or one of the redesigns? Some sort of healing spell that held them at bay? Or was it in the nature of the place, where few people lived, and only those who were sick and dying?

Rudi stepped out of the bright sunlight into the darkened hallway, then stopped and let his eyes adjust. He encouraged his hound soul to rise, then he sniffed the air, trying to tease apart the scents, to see if there was something different here.

Beyond the normal warm fur smells of the hounds and the medicinal and chemical scents of modern medicine lay a thread of cool mint green. Rudi didn't recognize it; he'd never scented anything like it before. It seemed important, and his hound soul kept bringing him back to it after he'd moved on to the scents of the people there and the traces of things the wind carried through the cracks and crevices.

Finally, he understood: It was the opposite of the scent of the shadows.

Head held high, Rudi tracked the scent through the hospital, down the twisting halls, past Lady Metzler's room, around the two examination rooms, then finally, back to the kitchen.

White-and-green tile in an old-fashioned hexagon pattern made up the splashboards. The counters were white, and the cupboards, too. However, the kitchen didn't seem sterile, but homey—maybe it was the large butcher-block table supported by stout legs in the center of the room, the bright yellow daffodils in the center of it, or the copper-bottomed pots and pans that hung from a black iron oval above it.

A young woman from India sat on a stool near the sink, looking out the window. A plate with half a sandwich rested on the counter before her along with some pickled vegetables. Her long black hair was pulled back into a loose braid, highlighting her broad and friendly features. She beamed a large smile directly at Rudi. Her traditional sari was red and orange, worn over a gold blouse.

"Good day," she said in accent-less German.

"Good day," Rudi replied, just as formally. He walked over to where she was seated, still seeking that scent. He smelled finely baked bread, liverwurst, stone-ground mustard, vinegar, and dill.

"Is there something I can help with?"

She didn't seem put out by Rudi's inattention, how he sniffed the air around her. Though she was fully human, she obviously knew about the clans.

Finally, Rudi tracked the scent trail to the open jar of pickled vegetables next to the woman's plate. Below the strong smell of vinegar, sugar, and dill came that intriguing odor.

"Where did you get those?" Rudi asked. They weren't magic, not really, just soaked or blessed with something pure and green.

"My brother makes them," the woman replied happily. "Would you like some?"

"Please," Rudi said, already anticipating the fresh crunch of dill, the heady mint, and that trickle of something spring-like and alive.

"I'm Harita," she said as she got a plate and fork for Rudi. "I'm a medical student, doing shift work here."

That made sense, to bring in medical students for the quiet shifts. Rudi eagerly helped himself to small pearl onions, baby carrots, and baby cucumbers. "What are you majoring in?"

"Clan diseases and cures. For all the clans."

Rudi almost choked on the amazing baby carrot he'd been chewing. "Not just the hound clan?" he clarified.

"No, no. Not just the hound clan." Her voice dropped and Harita looked around the room, as if verifying they were alone. "My family isn't hound clan," she said softly.

"Really?" he asked, surprised. Though the court had regular interactions with other clans and other clan members, he was surprised that they'd hire someone from a different clan. Then again, that must mean she was doubly competent, probably some level of genius when it came to healing. "I'm glad they hired you, though," Rudi said. And he was. There was something about her, something calm and cool, that he'd welcome if he were ill.

Harita gave him her wide smile again. "I'm kind of the black sheep of the family," she explained.

"What, did you stay out past your curfew one time too often?" Rudi teased. This woman—girl, really—was far too good and pure. To label her as some kind of shamed family member was ridiculous.

"No, no, nothing like that," Harita said, laughing. Then the smile fled her face. "I'm from the tiger clan, you see. The power is supposed to pass from mother to daughter."

"I see," Rudi said. And he did. Still. "Not every child born to a clan family is supposed to inherit the clan form." If they did, there would be far too many of the clan.

The numbers of each clan stayed constant through the centuries. Philosophers had debated this for just as long, speculating on reincarnation, natural limits on the number of animal souls, as well as more outlandish theories, like moon cycles and battles between the gods keeping their numbers low.

"True," Harita said, pushing the open jar of pickled vegetables toward Rudi so he could have more. "But it was worse than that."

"I'm sorry," Rudi said. He didn't ask any more questions—Harita could tell him or not, if she chose. He recognized what she was doing, though: telling a story about her past to gain his trust. As an outsider, and a full human, it was a good strategy.

"You see, my brother inherited the power. Not me."

"Ah." A male tiger warrior would be as out of step with his clan as a female hound. "Were you raised here, in Germany, then?"

Harita shook her head. "My family is in England, and—"

Lukas barged in, heading straight for the pickles, picking up the jar and sniffing it. "Where did you get these?" he demanded.

Harita gave her brightest smile to the prince, making Rudi instantly uncomfortable.

Lukas hadn't shown any interest in girls yet—then again, he'd barely had time to be human.

Fortunately for Rudi's blood pressure, Lukas seemed oblivious to the charm being thrown his way.

"My brother makes them. He gets the freshest produce he can, then ages the brine," Harita replied, still with that sweet smile.

Lukas held the jar up to the light, as if he could see something through the liquid, see the secret of its delightful taste and power. Then he turned to Rudi and said one word.

"Knight."

———

Virmal, Harita's brother, was still in classes and wouldn't be back to their flat until after eight, so after getting the address and instructions, Lukas insisted that Rudi take them to a hotel.

"Are you sure?" Rudi asked, drawing Lukas outside into the cool evening. The spring air nipped at Rudi's bare neck and ruffled his hair, carrying a thousand interesting scents that he wanted to chase, a sure sign that he was tired and distracted.

"Yes," Lukas replied immediately. He wrapped his arms across his chest.

Was he tired? Or upset? Rudi didn't know.

Lukas stopped for a moment, taking a deep breath.

Rudi took in all the scents as well, letting the clean air fill his lungs and brush away the remaining stench of the shadows.

"I can't stay there," Lukas said, looking mournfully back at the castle. "Not until it's been cleaned. Purified."

"We'll go, then," Rudi said. The heady scent of the woods rolled over him, filled with the rich promises of scented earth and the mysteries hidden by the trees.

When Rudi pulled his awareness back, he found Lukas was staring at the trees, too. He waited until Lukas shook himself and looked forward again. "You could go for a run first," Rudi suggested.

Lukas shook his head violently. "No. I don't want to. I can't change. Not yet." Stark hunger filled his face.

It was obvious that Lukas wanted to transform, to run in the woods of his childhood. What was holding him back?

"It'll be okay," Rudi told him.

"You don't know that," Lukas snapped. He stopped himself, sighed heavily, and continued, addressing his shoes. "What happens if I get stuck again? If the curse comes back? What if I can't change back?"

"We'll just find Albert again," Rudi said lightly, though his heart was heavy and his cheeks enflamed. He should have realized Lukas didn't want to transform—would probably fight it until his hound soul forced it on him. Most of the hound clan only changed once a month—older recitations recommended following the cycle of the moon and transforming when it was full.

It must have been doubly hard on Lukas, though, since he'd spent so much life in his hound form.

"Let's get out of here," Lukas said, turning and walking toward the car.

"Don't we have to stay until your mother arrives?" Rudi asked, falling into step beside Lukas.

Another sigh. "I saw her."

After a long pause, Rudi finally had to ask, "And?"

"The good news is that she hasn't been infected by the shadows," Lukas said slowly. "But she's…different. Changed. I remember her being one of the strongest people in the world. Stronger than Da, really. She was the driving force in our family. But, something broke her. Losing me, losing Greta, maybe. She knows Greta's gone, too. It was probably worse, seeing Greta every day, knowing she was no longer there."

The boy's voice cracked, along with Rudi's heart. "Lukas," Rudi said, pausing. "I'm so sorry." He tentatively reached up and put his hand on the back of Lukas' neck, squeezing gently.

Lukas nodded, closing his eyes for a moment, then continuing. "She and Da are separated, I guess."

"There's no word of problems outside the court," Rudi told him.

"She can't stand to be in the castle." Lukas gave a harsh laugh. "Says it smells like death. She's the only one who believes me about the shadows, and she won't stay."

"What do you mean?" Rudi asked. How could he protect Lukas from such hurts? He was completely inadequate as a guardian.

"She wouldn't even stay for dinner. She did want to have breakfast with me, tomorrow, at her hotel."

"That's good," Rudi said as they started walking again, passing the side of the castle and out to the front yard.

Rudi hesitated. He had to say something. But what? He waited until they'd gotten into the car before he turned to Lukas and said, "Lukas, I'm sorry."

"What for?" Lukas asked, looking bewildered.

"Lady Metzler, your grandmother, assured me that she would tell your parents that you were alive and well."

"She did tell them," Lukas pointed out. "For a while, until the shadows grew too much."

"But I should have realized, I should have sent more reports, figured out how to let them know…I don't know. Something. I'm sorry I—"

"No," Lukas said adamantly. "Don't you dare regret what you've done. Don't you dare regret taking me in."

Rudi had never seen Lukas so angry. He responded with his own fierceness. "I don't regret it," he said with a snarl. "I'm glad I kept you safe from the shadows here. They're an abomination. I believe you when you say you wouldn't have survived. I just—"

Rudi deflated, his anger flowing away. "I just wish I could have done more." He'd never be rid of this guilt and regret, he was certain.

Lukas nodded. "There really wasn't anything more you could have done. Not until I met Sally. She was the first sign. Besides, no matter how hard you pushed, I wouldn't have told you anything."

Rudi shook his head. The strength of the boy, the secrets he'd had to carry. It just wasn't fair, that he'd been forced to grow up that way.

After they started driving, Rudi asked, "Have you found the tiger warrior you need?"

"Maybe. I'll know when I get close enough to really scent him," Lukas admitted. "But how will I get him back to Seattle? Do we all need to be in Seattle? Or do I need to bring the others here? I don't know where the final battle will be. Or when."

"We can figure it out," Rudi said.

Lukas gave a dejected sigh.

"Those are simply logistics," Rudi pointed out. "We live in a world connected by good transportation. Car, trains, planes—we'll make it work." He had money saved for emergencies—and flying an elite band of warriors to fight the shadows and save the world surely counted as a legitimate cause for dipping into his savings.

Lukas nodded, then added, "Thank you for today."

Rudi snorted. "What did I do?"

"You were there, always ready to support me, or protect me."

"You're my—" Rudi stopped, unsure if there was a term. "Charge. Ward, I suppose."

"Ward. Good. I like that," Lukas said. "I don't want to leave you," he added in a small voice.

"No, Lukas, my prince, I am bound to you. I will serve you and take care of you, as long as you desire," Rudi said fiercely. "Never doubt that."

Rudi looked over at the boy. The strain of the day was obvious in the dark circles under his eyes, the lines around his mouth.

"I'm here, and I'll stay by your side, as long as you'll have me. While you protect and guard the others, I'll guard you," he promised.

"Thank you," Lukas said, his eyes closing as if he finally felt safe.

Rudi drove them carefully down the hill and into the city. Though he still felt as though he'd failed the prince for most of his life, he really hoped he'd be able to keep at least one of his promises.

ENGLAND, FIFTEEN YEARS AGO

VIRMAL

Sun poured through the old-fashioned leaded-glass windows, baking Virmal and his twin sister, Harita, where they lay on their blankets for their afternoon nap. Gold painted-radiators with fancy scrolled tops hissed and clanked under the windows. The wood floor pushed up against Virmal, uncomfortable and not giving, under the soft fur blankets. Virmal liked burying his face into the fur, the musky smell comforting.

Harita, of course, had more of the sunshine. She always got more of everything.

Virmal grumbled and rolled closer to his sister so his right arm wouldn't be in the shadows. He pulled at his blue jumper, tugging down the sleeve. It was always too cold here in England, especially compared to his home in New Delhi. He never felt truly warm.

A cloud passed over the sun. Virmal opened his eyes and glared up at the gray cover.

It would probably start raining again or, because England was cruel, it would wait until it was time for them to go out to the park and play.

Virmal growled softly, deep in his throat. Grandma Irita had said he shouldn't growl like that, not out loud; it was disrespectful.

But sometimes the growls crowded his throat, forcing their way out.

It was like something else lived under his skin. Something fierce and wild and *glad* that he could make his grandmother shiver.

The sun peeked out from behind the clouds. Virmal stretched his hand up to it, wanting to capture every last drop of warmth.

Harita pushed at Virmal, shoving him away and out of the light.

Without thinking, Virmal slashed at her, growling loudly.

Harita grabbed hold of her bleeding arm, staring at Virmal with wide, scared eyes.

Everything was silent and still in the front room. Virmal scrambled up to his knees. What had he done?

Then Harita screamed. The sound ran claws up Virmal's back and he snarled in response. She needed to shut up, shut up, *shut up*.

If she wouldn't shut up, he would make her.

Virmal rocked closer and growled again, low and deep, a noise that rumbled wonderfully through his chest. Color fled the world, and the smell of blood, of small things wounded, of *prey*, took over everything else. He could taste it on his tongue, lap it up like cream.

A tiny voice in the back of Virmal's head said no, he shouldn't do this. She was his *sister*, his fraternal twin.

The other didn't care, and leaned closer still, filling itself on the complex scent of fear and family, blood and home.

At least the girl had stopped screaming. Her rabbit large eyes darted around the room, seeking escape.

Maybe they could let her run. At least toward the door. Then they'd trap her again.

They snarled and showed their teeth, big and sharp.

Before they could reach up their paw/hand and bat at the girl, a commanding voice ordered, "No. Don't. Virmal. Don't."

At the mention of his name, Virmal shook himself and blinked, the world returning to normal as if he'd just woken from a dream.

But Harita's fear was real, and so were her wounds.

"Grandma?" Virmal said, turning toward her, tears springing to his eyes. He'd been bad. He'd hurt Harita. And everyone always loved her more.

"Hush now," Grandmother Irita said, looking sternly from Virmal to Harita and back again. "Harita, can you growl back?"

Harita shook her head.

"Not even a little?" Grandmother asked.

"No!" Harita said, trembling despite her strong denial.

Grandmother Irita sighed and tugged on her blue and gold sari, pulling the material down. "Ah well. I'd hoped you'd share this, like you've shared everything. But it's not to be." She pressed her lips together and put her fists on her waist.

The clouds covered the sun again, making Grandmother Irita's sari suddenly look black, stealing all the light from the room. She looked like a terrible, angry goddess as she pronounced their fate.

"You will stay here, with me," she announced. "And not return to India."

Virmal turned from Grandmother to Harita. "I'm

sorry," he whispered. Sorry for hurting her. Sorry for trapping them both here in England.

That broke the spell that seemed to hold Harita. She wailed loudly, scrambling up from the floor and throwing herself at their grandmother.

Virmal twisted back to look at them. Grandmother Irita had bent down and was stroking Harita's head, but her eyes were full of sorrow as she stared at Virmal.

"Why does she have to be here?" Virmal whined when Harita stood in the doorway to their classroom, her notebook pressed hard against her chest by her crossed arms.

"She has to learn the recitations, too, in case she births a girl who comes to power," Grandmother Irita said dismissively as she walked to the front of the room. Beyond the tall window, red and orange leaves twirled in the autumn wind. Grandmother Irita laid her books down on the desk, then sat behind it, facing them.

Virmal sighed, but he didn't say anything more. He'd liked spending time alone with his grandmother, learning the stories and history of the tiger clan. It was so unfair that Harita got to be there. He was the one with the power. He was the tiger warrior, not her. He was the one with the tiger soul: She wandered near to his human soul, then away again, but always within reach.

But she still got everything.

Virmal planted his elbows on the hard wooden table that served as his desk, pressing his heels down on the worn rungs of the chair. Scents of *dahl* and sweet tea floated up from the kitchen along with the smell of rain that always rode the wind. He didn't look at his sister when she sat down, but he also didn't growl at her—Grandmother Irita had trained them both out of that.

"And more than that, she's family," Grandmother Irita added. "Maybe we'll start with that recitation today."

Virmal knew better than to groan. While some of the recitations were cool and had neat stories associated with them, too many of them listed all the things he couldn't do, like *don't show yourself to other people, don't transform in public, don't use your claws against an unarmed human*, and on and on.

Grandmother Irita put the recitation notebooks on their desks. Since they were here in England and not at any of the tiger temples, every page of the recitations that they wrote had to be destroyed at the end of their lessons.

Virmal liked putting the pages in the flames of the hearth downstairs in the parlor. But, knowing his luck, that would be something else Harita would get to do today.

The sound of Harita unzipping her pencil case made Virmal look over at her. It was pink with some kind of Japanese anime cat on it. If Grandmother Irita hadn't been there, he would have made retching sounds. How could she be from the tiger clan and still like such cute, girly things? Virmal would never understand his twin.

Then Harita grimaced as she reached up and put the pencil case at the top of the desk.

Was that a bruise on her arm?

Virmal got out his own pencil and tried to sniff the air without Grandmother or Harita noticing. His nose told him astonishing things.

There was the milky porridge they'd had for breakfast, and the thin trace of dirt from when Harita had gone outside to check the bird feeders, and just there, before she'd come down, underneath the kitchen smells, were salty tears.

What did Harita have to cry about?

Virmal wrote the first recitation as Grandmother Irita recited it: *The tiger clan comes first.*

First before family, though? Harita was family, but wasn't clan.

If you hurt one, you hurt all.

Many in the tiger clan were solitary in nature. Some of the recitations, like this one, were a way to bring them together. Virmal didn't like being with many other people, but he didn't mind being with his sister if she was quiet. She mostly didn't set his back up.

Temper revenge with wisdom.

Virmal didn't like the story that went with that one. It made him shiver, just thinking about how the tiger clan families had attacked and wiped each other out for generations.

It was one of the good things to come after the treachery of the ravens. The clan had stopped turning against each other and had united as one, instead.

Defend the others in the tiger clan, the ambush of tigers.

That one was harder, actually, for Virmal. He was never sure what was the right way to defend the ambush. Was it to be like Sree, and attack with claws and fangs? Or to be like Ansuya, and talk everyone into agreeing? He never saw himself like Soniya, who sacrificed herself, drawing away the hunters and their dogs so her family could escape.

Harita shifted in her seat, and Virmal could smell tears coming closer.

Was Harita defending the clan in some way? A way that was hurting her?

She'd never tell if she was in trouble. She might be a spoiled brat, but she kept secrets better than the goddess

Surina, who knew the end of everyone's life but carried the burden alone and would never tell the pilgrims who came to worship at her temples, no matter how much gold they left or how they pleaded.

Surina could be tricked into revealing what she knew, though.

Virmal wrote the next recitation without really hearing it. How could he trick his sister into telling him?

Though Grandmother Irita didn't say it, Virmal wrote the first recitation of their lesson again.

If you hurt one, you hurt all.

V irmal had never been so aware of his sister before. He kept track of Harita all the time, following her by scent when he couldn't be close enough for sight or sound.

It surprised Virmal how gentle Harita was. All his female cousins, tiger warrior or not, had a cruel side to them. They'd put their dolls into paper prisons, denying them food while they had tea parties sitting outside the gates, or they'd make up long, involved stories about their teddy bear generals and pony captains and the war they'd bring and how the farmers would suffer and curse them.

The stories Harita told with her dolls involved playing house and taking care of their children, or starring in a Bollywood movie, or even holding a pageant show.

In the corner of the playroom, Virmal drew pictures of spaceships exploding, ninja warriors with cat-like features, or creepy voodoo ravens with Xs for eyes, doodling as he always did, but also listening like never before.

On Tuesdays and Thursdays, Virmal and Harita went to the big school, with the other kids; they were homeschooled only on the other days. Virmal had friends he walked with from homeroom to history class, down the loud hallways filled with kids and lockers. That Tuesday, he finally noticed that Harita only had two friends, and all three of them looked and smelled wary, carrying their books tightly.

Harita always wrapped her arms across her chest, carrying her books. So did the other girls.

Virmal wasn't stupid. He knew what that meant.

Someone was bullying his sister, and she had her books pulled out of her arms on a regular enough basis for her to be defensive all the time.

His tiger soul growled at that. She didn't like it. Not one bit.

Hurt one, hurt us all.

"Sorry, I can't go," Virmal said as he shut his locker. Vijay, Sal, and Eric all complained. "Come on, you promised!"

"Look, just play three-person footie," Virmal suggested.

"Lame," Eric replied.

"I'll play next week," Virmal promised, hurrying out of the dim school hallway and into the autumn cold. God, he hated England. He quickly buttoned his heavy, blue wool peacoat up to his neck, then pulled his gray hat down more snugly over his ears. He took the stairs from the school two at a time, then raced up the block, trying to catch up with Harita.

Nasty wind pushed at him, blowing through the thick wool as well as the sweater Virmal wore underneath. Maybe he should switch to his winter down jacket; at least that resisted the wind. But the guys would make fun of him. Ornate metal fences enclosed the gardens to his left. Only a few brave, colorful leaves dangled from the trees. The smell of rain was in the air, but the wind *always* smelled like rain.

Ahead of Virmal, Harita walked alone. She walked quickly, like a rabbit scurrying across a field. Even from a block away, the wind carried the scent of her fear. She turned the corner, and Virmal hurried.

Three boys had surrounded Harita by the time Virmal caught sight of her again.

"Going home so fast, little mouse," the tall white boy in the dark green coat said.

"Did you bring us the money?" a dark Indian boy asked, in a black coat that looked very much like Virmal's.

Harita bared her teeth at them. "Never," she said.

At least she was standing up to them. But there were three of them and only one of her. Plus, they were all bigger than she was.

Why hadn't she told anyone, though?

"Leave me alone," Harita said loudly.

"Or you'll scream?" the last one sneered. He was short and white. He shoved Harita's shoulder. "You know what happened last time you did that."

The Indian boy pushed Harita next, hard enough that she almost stumbled and fell. Then he yanked on her backpack, trying to strip her of her books.

Virmal couldn't hold back. His tiger soul growled as he hurried forward. "Leave her alone," he ordered as he pushed through the boys to stand beside his sister.

"Oh, a big bad knight in shining armor," the tall white boy mocked.

"I can take care of this," Harita hissed at Virmal.

Virmal's tiger soul pushed at him. *Brave*, she purred.

Harita shoved Virmal back, behind her.

No wonder she hadn't told anyone. She thought she needed to deal with the boys all by herself, as a matter of honor.

"*An ambush is stronger than each warrior, alone,*" Virmal quoted to Harita in Hindi, one of the recitations.

"*Each warrior makes her own way,*" Harita quoted back.

"Bored now," the smaller white boy said. He reached beyond Harita and pushed at Virmal.

"Together?" Virmal suggested, for the first time happy that both of them had taken some warrior training, learning to fight. Harita hadn't taken as much, but he'd ask for her at every class, now.

They took off their backpacks and turned their backs to each other. Virmal spread his legs wider, one a little in front of the other, his weight on his toes, rooting himself in the earth, his hands up in loose claws. Though Virmal couldn't see her, he knew Harita did the same. Then Virmal let out a low growl. Harita echoed him: a human sound, but eerily accurate nonetheless.

The three boys seemed uncertain, suddenly. Then the tall white boy in the green coat sneered. "She can't really fight. I bet you can't either. They're bluffing." His voice gained strength.

"You're bigger than we are," Virmal told him calmly. "And there are three of you. But together, we're stronger."

"What, you and your girlfriend?"

"She's my sister," Virmal declared. A sudden pride filled him. "And we have greater heart than you do."

With a second snarl, both Virmal and Harita attacked.

Virmal exploded forward. He couldn't use his claws or teeth—Grandmother Irita would skin him alive for that.

However, he could still use the speed of a tiger warrior.

He drove the heel of his palm directly into the lower chest of the Indian boy, making him gasp and stagger back.

Down! cried his tiger soul.

Virmal ducked.

A wild swing of the tall white boy whizzed over Virmal's head.

Virmal grinned at the white boy, showing all his teeth. Then he *slammed* into the other boy, coming in low and extending up, driving his shoulder into the boy's chest and his elbow into the boy's stomach, pushing the him away.

The tall white boy recovered quickly and tackled Virmal, driving them both to the ground. Then he reared up and smashed Virmal in the face.

Virmal howled, wrapped his legs around the boy's waist, and flipped them so he was on top. Blood pounded in his skull and dripped from his nose. He didn't bite the boy's shoulder, even though he wanted to. Instead, he brought his knee up into the boy's groin, then, using both hands, slammed the boy's head against the ground, once, twice.

Stop, his tiger soul warned before he did it again.

Virmal lifted himself up and away. The boy groaned but didn't try to get up. Virmal quickly looked over to his sister.

Harita's opponent was also on the ground. She grinned at him, one eye already bruising, her hair pulled out of its neat braid, her knees as muddy as his.

The Indian boy had run away, deserting his companions.

Harita and Virmal silently picked up their backpacks and walked away. Virmal's face hurt, and he knew he'd have a shiner that matched Harita's. But his tiger soul was content. Honor and duty had both been served.

"Why didn't you tell me?" Virmal asked as they turned the next block.

"I could have handled it," Harita said hotly.

Careful, now, his tiger soul warned.

"I couldn't have fought all three, not by myself," Virmal told her. Of course, like his sister, he would have tried to at first.

"Why did you help me?" Harita asked.

The wind blew at Virmal. He was suddenly tired and cold. "You're my sister."

"But you hate me."

Virmal thought about it for a moment. Harita always got the best of everything. Even though he was the tiger warrior, Mama and Papa always asked about her first when they called, always talked with her first. She got better grades than he did both at school and at home. Grandmother Irita liked her better.

"You're my sister," Virmal finally said.

His tiger soul gave a comforting growl, as close to a purr as she could.

"But—"

"No. You're my sister. You're clan. You're family."

Nothing else mattered, not really.

"Those boys might be back," Virmal warned as they neared their flat. "With their friends."

"Grandmother Irita is going to ask about that," Harita pointed out, gesturing toward his throbbing eye.

"*The ambush takes care of its own*," Virmal quoted.

If more boys came, and Virmal and Harita couldn't handle them, they could get help.

Neither of them had to stand alone.

INTERLUDE III

THE VIPER IN TULUM

Mexico, Present Day

Zane woke to absolute blackness. He blinked his eyes, making sure they were open, but he couldn't see anything in the dark.

That didn't scare him as much as the stifling silence did.

Where was *el océano* and her comforting waves? Where were the little ones just on the other side of the crumbling plaster walls of his decrepit, one-room apartment, and their daily fight over who ate which cereal? Where was the ancient *señora* on the other side, and the whine of her equally ancient TV? The constant scent of burnt toast, peppers cooked in oil, and cheap perfume from the girls three doors down the hall were missing, too.

Zane reached up to feel his eyes, his eyelashes fluttering against his fingertips. Then he plugged and unplugged his ears with his fingers, but it made no difference.

The world still remained at a distance.

Panic jolted through Zane. He couldn't be dying. Not yet. He hadn't finished his mission. He still hadn't met.…

Ah.

Zane took a deep breath and calmed himself. He sat up slowly on his narrow cot, his old bones protesting, then swung his legs over.

His bare feet landed solidly on the cold concrete of his floor.

Zane pushed himself up, and after a shaky step, the world slammed back into him.

His tiny room still looked the same, with stained plaster walls painted a somber peach color—supposedly to brighten the place up but they looked dingy, instead. The corner held a sink with dishes piled high and too many empty *cerveza* and tequila bottles. A dresser stood in the other corner, with his few shabby and never completely clean shirts and jeans.

When Zane turned around, he saw that a shadow still lingered on his bed, like a lone cloud, unraveling and disappearing even as he watched.

"*Tsk, tsk.*" Zane shook his head.

Las Sombras were playing their tricks again.

The shadows knew Zane watched. They knew he waited. But after all this time, even with the tricks they played on his mind, they still didn't know for what.

Zane wasn't sure himself, some days. It had been so long since he'd been given this task. And the shadows confused him, as did the *cerveza*, the tequila, and time.

He took a deep breath and let his senses expand. The TV on one side played a light jingle, a happy couple in love with their washing machine. On the other, the little ones argued over who got the last of the orange juice. The *señora* had burnt her toast again, and over that, from outside, drifted the smoke from an untuned motorbike.

Two blocks away came the scent of wet concrete, new hotels for tourists. Under it all, *la mer* whispered her dreams to him.

Zane pulled in his senses and shambled over to his sink to splash water on his face. A tiny mirror hung over it, but Zane didn't like how it reminded him of his grizzled skin, the patches of gray whiskers, the dark, day-laborer's tan his hands and arms held; or how his hair grew only along the edges of his overly large skull, and was now more silver than black.

He'd never been handsome, not even as a young man. But he'd had a vitality—the opposite of the old-man exhaustion that hung on him now like a shroud.

He looked up, watching his eyes change from washed-out brown to burning yellow. His pupils elongated, turning into a slit that stole all the color from the world but let him observe even the tiniest movements. He almost didn't recognize himself; it had been so long since he'd transformed.

In a blink, his human eyes returned. However, his viper soul remained close, just under the surface of his skin.

Soon. The word hissed gently through his blood, as soothing as the morning prayers of his people that he'd forgone long ago.

Zane nodded. Yes. Soon. It was why the shadows had been so merciless in their tricks that week.

Soon it would happen.

His debt would be paid. And maybe his honor restored.

***

Zane perched himself high on a wall of the Tulum ruins, next to *El Castillo* overlooking the ocean. The water was calm and so blue that morning, as pretty as the postcards made it look. Below where he sat, gulls hopped from one rock to the next, certain to find some tidbit missed by the others. Off in the distance, tourist cruise boats sailed, free of care.

The sun soaked into Zane's skin, stupefying his viper soul. Or maybe that was also his disguise—the nearly empty bottle of cheap tequila in the brown paper bag beside him. He hadn't meant to drink so much, particularly this early in the morning. The park guards wouldn't approve if they saw him—a drunken day laborer might scare the tourists. From looking at him, they'd never know that he was actually an American and not some down-on-his-luck, back-country Mayan.

But Zane had been here in Tulum so long, gone so native, he forgot himself sometimes.

His friends, the shadows, helped hide him today—at least for now, before they decided to trick him again.

Maybe they weren't really his friends.

Ah, but that didn't matter. Nothing mattered today except looking out over the beautiful coast with its perfect white sand and blue-blue waters, and waiting.

Tourists scrambled up the steep pyramid steps behind Zane, but they mostly didn't see him. They remarked about the castle and the gorgeous location, their voices as raucous as the gulls. They snapped pictures like mad when an iguana strolled by.

It warmed Zane's cold heart that the creature recognized him as a threat and kept a safe distance from him, as if he would bother with such poor, unrelated cousins.

The sour smell of the liquor washed over Zane as he finished the bottle. He knew that to play the part of the drunken local, he should just toss the bottle over the side of the wall, but he couldn't make himself do it, couldn't bring himself to dirty the clean white sands beneath him.

Instead he stood, slowly stretching, swaying in the constant ocean wind. Maybe today wasn't the day. He could go back home and nap through the heat of the day, come back out looking that evening.

A squawking laugh echoed behind him.

Black rage clouded the bright day. Zane turned around.

A dark-skinned young man with light-colored, spiky hair raced up the steps. A young woman, pale-skinned with brown hair done up in a ponytail, ran beside him. Obviously tourists, wearing immodest T-shirts, shorts, and sandals.

Though the boy looked fully human, Zane saw what he was, and he couldn't contain his hiss.

One of the raven clan? Here?

Those damn birds had ruined everything, betrayed his clan and all the others.

What they'd done had been worse than his own misdeeds, when he'd been arrogant and young.

Shadows suddenly gathered at Zane's side, their cool wisps sliding across his skin.

Zane had never seen faces in the shadows—he didn't think they had any. They'd never spoken to him directly. They remained like clouds, even after all these years, unknowable.

For the first time, they thrummed with excitement, something Zane understood.

This boy. He meant something to them.

It was finally time.

Zane took one drunken step forward as the couple veered off—warned by some instinct to explore the other tower first.

Before Zane took two more steps, a tour group walked

around the corner of *El Castillo*, pooling around their guide at the bottom of the steps.

Zane shot a scathing look in the direction of the young couple, then he let himself shift, subtly, his nose flattening against his face, his cheekbones spreading out as his viper soul rose closer to the surface.

Yes, there was their scent: musty old feathers, the bright glass of armor, the sweet odor of youth and sex.

He had their scent signature now. He could follow them blindly through a crowd at an open market, over the smells of live chickens, fresh tomatoes, and heaps of chilies.

Zane slowly walked back down the stairs of *El Castillo*, the tourists sliding around him like river water around a rock.

It was good that Zane could track the raven warrior and his mate, but honestly, it didn't matter that much.

Damn tourist was a bird. He'd always seek the highest ground, no matter where they went.

And the next time they met, it wouldn't be in so public a place.

The day continued bright and sunny, with sea winds to keep it from getting too hot. Zane still felt as if a storm were brewing, could almost see it in the heat haze on the horizon, over the miles of ocean blue. Far below the high stone shelf where he sat, the white sand sparkled. An old iguana the length of his leg warily baked on the warm rocks a few feet away. The wind carried the foreign scents of the tourists on the beach, their perfumed oils and plastic toys.

It also brought the scent of his prey, playing in the water.

His viper soul counseled patience, as always. He listened to it better now than he had as a young man, impetuous and full of his own grand schemes.

Soon, he'd be able to right his wrongs.

A few feet down the trail, just beyond the last sharp turn in the trail up the hill, Zane had dragged a large tumbleweed, deliberately blocking the path so no one would accidentally stumble on him and chase him away from his ambush. The path above was blocked as well. He was confident his trap would work.

The warm sun made Zane sleepy, but he kept his watch through slitted eyes. Fear also kept him awake. If after all these years, these *décadas*, he failed to....

But he was right. The scent of feathers was suddenly closer.

Zane slipped off his rock and removed the artificial barrier below him, his hands stinging as the thorns pricked him. The raven boy would be too drawn to the highest point to resist, his laughing mate by his side.

Zane had no mate. None would take him after what he did. He would die alone and friendless.

Hopefully, though, he would die satisfied.

The mate led the way up the trail—foolish or selfish on the part of the boy, Zane couldn't decide. They paused just below the last hairpin turn, looking back the way they'd come, admiring the view.

"It is beautiful from up here, Peter," she murmured.

"Yeah, Sally, the best view is always from up high," he replied.

Still, Zane held his breath until they came around that last turn, then he stepped out from where he'd hidden behind a boulder, blocking their way down, their easy escape. They stopped at the far side, on a short incline, where the trail was also blocked, with a rock wall on one side and a long, long tumble down the hill to the other.

"You have come, finally, haven't you?" Zane proclaimed, feeling his head go broad, his skin hardening and growing scaly, the color draining out of the world.

At least the boy stepped in front of his mate, his fingers already lost to the knife-like feather-blades of a true raven warrior.

"What do you want?" he squawked. His eyes stared, bird-black, oblivious to the shadows about to take him.

"Your kind betrayed us all, didn't you?" Zane accused him. The pressure along his sinuses increased as his venom sacs filled.

"Centuries ago," the raven warrior said. "And our young still pay the price."

"We've never recovered, have we?" Zane hissed. Only a trickle of pilgrims came to the mountain monasteries, so few to hear the mystic messages and carry the word down into the valleys.

"I'm sorry," the birdman said. He sounded truly sorry, as well, not at all like the boastful bird he surely was.

"And you will be more sorry, won't you?" Zane promised as he took a step closer to the boy. His fangs had started to distend, still hidden inside his mouth but pressing against the bottom of it, longing to come out and sink into something, anything.

Shadows boiled beside Zane, eager for this new sacrifice, beyond the endless ones he'd already made—his family, his life, his true face, and his name.

Though the raven was fast, Zane was faster still. He rushed at the boy, but then brushed past him and grabbed his mate, her pulse a fluttering thing under his palms.

Time slowed. Zane raised one claw-tipped hand, nails

dripping with poison. The anguish on the boy's face was a marvel.

Zane almost felt pity.

But this time, he'd chosen the right target.

With a sweeping motion, Zane lightly scratched down the girl's left side, careful not to break the skin, hooking the tendrils of a shadow that curled around her waist and yanking it. With his other hand, he pulled the girl away, separating her from the shadow. He flung her to the side, heard her muffled cry and fall.

He hoped she wasn't hurt, but it didn't matter. He finally had his prey in hand, a shadow. It was unlike the ones that lived with him: This one had come in a direct line from the first tiger warrior who'd been corrupted by the shadows, the one he hadn't stopped.

A shadow made whole around the indents of his poisoned talons.

Before the raven or his mate could do or say anything else, Zane struck the shadow thing, sinking his fangs into it.

Finally, one of the damn shadows was solid enough for him to strike it, though its texture was more like biting into rancid oil, not flesh.

The shadow struck back the only way it knew how: cold upon cold upon cold. Ice seared into Zane's bones, lacing his viper soul with frost. Age dropped on his shoulders like an avalanche, making it difficult to even hold himself up.

Zane hung on, biting deep into the shadow, pumping his venom into its soul, taking away its life as a shadow, forcing his toxin into what served as veins in the creature.

Forcing the shadow to become corporeal, and walk in the light.

After wringing the last drop of poison out, Zane stepped back, letting the thing drop at his feet.

"Do you see?" Zane intoned, the syllables sliding one into another.

"Yes." The raven and his mate stared at the ground, at the nightmare Zane had made real.

"You will bear witness," Zane said, knowing that through his proclamation, he would make it come true. "You will tell the hound prince. This is the new form the shadows will take. This is what comes," he added, his words ringing like a clear bell across the hill, over the water, and through time.

"We will," they said, falling into the *geas* laid before them.

The weight of the task laid on Zane so long ago dropped from him, like he'd shed a skin made of stone. He'd finally made things right. The hound prince would know it was time.

Zane—no, he could take his full name again, so Gezane—felt himself grow taller, stronger, as the years fell from him and he reclaimed himself. He was still old, yes, but finally just his own age. The whispering need for liquor disappeared from the back of his mind, and instead, his viper soul circled closer than ever before. The edges of the rocks and the nearby cactus grew sharper, clearer, and the wind blew across him fresh and new, smelling sweetly of hidden flowers.

Gezane had worn his own face as a mask for so long, he couldn't even imagine how he must appear now.

The raven before Gezane was still fully armed, but he also stood straighter, like a soldier, ready to be commanded.

But the mate—ah—she shone brighter still. Just a

worm of a shadow had burrowed into her side and now that it was gone, she was like a beacon.

With a blink of surprise, Gezane realized that it was *she* the shadows had been after, not the boy. She was the arch stone, the only one strong enough to support them all.

"Thank you," Gezane said with a deep bow, both to the young couple on whose untested shoulders so much now depended, as well as to the gods who had let him do his duty at last.

They bowed in return. Before they could speak, Gezane told them, "Go now. Enjoy your last day in my beautiful Tulum, won't you?"

The time to fight would come soon enough for them.

They nodded and left, heading back down the path they'd come up, with many backward glances.

Gezane folded his arms over his chest and looked out over the beautiful ocean, her sweet and salty breezes playing with what remained of his hair. Pride filled him. He'd finally done what he'd been instructed to do, so many years ago.

He'd made the shadows real.

Then he glanced down at the rotting corpulence at his feet, the darkness slipping away in the wind. He knew it wasn't dead, that it would return in the new shape he'd forced on it.

Was it enough to clear his debt? It didn't feel like enough for what he'd done.

He'd purposefully delayed the chosen messenger from his people, the one who was supposed to warn of the encroaching shadows. In Gezane's pride and arrogance, as well as the confusion brought by the shadows, he'd thought he could take the other's place, gaining the glory for himself and his family.

Instead, he'd missed the meeting, the one chance when

the tiger clan would have been open to the message. He'd arrived a day late, and therefore had imperiled the world, the shadows growing stronger in the intervening years.

He'd hurt so many: all in his family were scorned; so many more people the shadows had corrupted because they'd been able to gain strength; the poor hound prince and the burden he'd had to carry.

No, giving his life as he had wouldn't repay his debt. But at least now, if the raven's mate proved strong enough, there was a chance the world wouldn't end in darkness.

Gezane spent the rest of the afternoon wandering, seeing Tulum with fond, fresh eyes. The markets amazed him, heaping piles of flowers, sharp spices, and racks of cheap clothes. People smiled at him as he slipped around them, *of* but not *in* the world. The sea called to him, and he dipped his hand in her, tasting her salt.

He didn't visit his rundown apartment—though he doubted anyone would recognize him, they might mistake him for a younger cousin or brother of the old drunk who had lived there, and he didn't want to accidentally endanger anyone who might be friendly to him.

The shadows would never let Gezane live after his decades-long treachery.

Still, Gezane walked down a crossroad two blocks away, letting his senses flare for only a moment. The young ones laughed as they watched secondhand cartoons given to them by the Americans. The *señora* was gone, but the scent of her burnt toast remained. The concrete from the new hotel no longer smelled wet, and underneath it lay the sweet ocean tainting the air with her salt.

As darkness stole the brilliant orange and red from the

sunset, Gezane headed out of town along one of the old roads, going toward the interior. Not the new road the tourist buses drove carelessly along, no; instead, an original *sak beh*, a white road long abandoned by the people who'd once lived there, distant relatives of Gezane's clan.

Even in the dark of the jungle night, Gezane could see the glittering stones of the road, reflecting the brilliant Milky Way as the humans naïvely called it.

Gezane preferred his people's name for it—the Unending Dagger—a promise not just of quick death, but peace on the other side.

The shadows formed quickly once Gezane stepped out from under the trees and into a clearing. They brushed against him, pushing him forward until a solid shape rose out of the ground.

The hissing tones reminded Gezane of the council who'd proclaimed his fate and the task they'd set him. The death-like stench rolled out from the shadow, reminding Gezane of the stinking heaps of garbage hidden from tourists south of town.

"I think you forgot to kill me," the shadow stated, swaying and undulating before him, like silk hanging from a window.

"Can you die?" Gezane asked.

The council hadn't been sure if the shadows could be killed in their natural state.

"Of course not," the shadow scoffed. "Still, you tried."

"Did I?" Gezane asked, surprised at how little bitterness flowed through his veins. Like his poison, it had been drained away.

"Do not play games with me, mystic," the shadow growled.

"Am I a mystic?" Gezane couldn't help but ask,

grinning. He'd never had a vision, just cheated the one who had, tried to steal it from him.

The cold struck with the force of a blow, though all the shadow had done was tap him on the chest with a curling tendril. Sudden exhaustion made him hunch over.

"Answer true," the shadow admonished.

Gezane caught his breath in the humid night as the touch withdrew, and drew himself upright again. He resisted reaching up to rub at the spot, but instead stayed in the game. "You don't know my clan well, do you?"

Never answer an outsider's question, except with another question, was one of the oldest recitations of his kind.

"Why haven't you ever spoken to me like this before?" Gezane asked after the shadow had touched him again, and the clarity of the night had returned with its uncaring stars burning brilliantly above his head.

"I only now have form. Form that you gave me," the shadow explained. "I don't believe that was your intent."

Gezane tilted his head to one side as if considering. He waited, enjoying the loud song of the cicadas in the surrounding jungle, the warm humid air, the rotting smell of jungle mulch mingling with the wet smells of rotting corpses from the shadows, as patient as his viper soul had always wanted him to be.

He would never, ever, admit that it had always been the council's intent to give the shadows form.

"You have made me much more powerful," the shadow claimed, finally ending the silence. It billowed out like a dust storm, filling the clearing, casting its dark form between Gezane and the stars, turning their light thin and tinny.

"Did I?" Gezane asked through rote, his features

shifting, his nose flattening and his skull widening as his venom sacks filled.

The shadow laughed, sending icy shivers down Gezane's spine.

"I will take the light from you," the shadow promised. "You will tell me everything, even as you forget your own name."

"Surely you understand my nature by now?" Gezane asked, the words slithering out as his mouth made further adjustments.

"That you are false, even unto the secret smiles you give your young, never to be trusted or believed? Yes, that much we have learned." The shadow paused, then added, "You robbed the bird's mate from us."

"Did you really have her?" Gezane asked as he swayed, undulating like the shadow before him, as if he couldn't help himself.

"No," the shadow admitted. "But we would have, eventually. Just as we'll have you."

"You know what they say about the viper clan, yes?" Gezane asked, the words hard to form now with his full snake mouth, fangs extending.

"No, I don't think I've ever—"

"Beware," Gezane interrupted, striking out lightning fast.

Nothing on earth could catch one of the viper clan, stop one of them from latching on. They moved the quickest of all the clans.

Yet, the shadow did.

"I do know you," the shadow said as Gezane stood, stretched forward, frozen, unable to move, barely able to blink in the shadow's iron grasp. "I know I can never be prepared enough for your treachery. But such a simple attack? Really? You should know better."

And Gezane did. He truly did. He knew how the shadows clouded his mind.

How fast had he been actually moving before he struck?

"Now we will milk you, relieve you of your poison until you are dry. Then again, and again. You will make all my followers as powerful, as corporeal, as I."

No! screamed Gezane, deep in his head, unable to move or make a sound.

Patience. A calm overtook Gezane as his viper soul rose closer to the surface.

The hound prince, the ravens, they will think I helped the shadows, that I worked with them, creating more of them, Gezane said, shuddering as the cold violated him, stroking his extended fangs, safely extracting his toxin.

Only enough, his viper soul assured him. *There are plans within plans. Now rest. You have earned it. It is the others' time to fight.*

But only because I put them in harm's way. Now the bitterness came back, flooding Gezane again. So much time wasted. So many lives.

You were part of the problem, yes. Now, you are part of the solution. So rest.

But—

Rest.

And the world faded into endless blackness.

GERMANY, PRESENT DAY

LUKAS

Harita and Virmal's apartment was in the old city, but wasn't old itself. It looked like it had been built in the 1960s, flat-faced, with red brick and symmetrical windows. It smelled like fake wood and glue, as well as long-boiled potatoes and fresh mud from the garden out front.

Lukas sniffed, but he couldn't find a trace of that cool green scent he'd been expecting. Maybe they had the wrong place.

Harita let them in after they buzzed. The dim and narrow hallway made Lukas hunch in on himself. He could touch the roughly textured ceiling without fully stretching his arm out. Cheap brown carpet muffled their steps to the door of the flat.

The door opened before they could knock. The parquet floor in the vestibule bore evidence of claws as well as fresh dirt. They hung their coats next to the thick parkas and heavy jackets already hanging there.

"Would you like some chai?" Harita asked, leading them into the living room. Strings of white Christmas-tree lights hung across the front window, complementing the two lamps and giving the room a warm glow. A sleek beige couch with wooden arms stretched along one wall. Brightly colored pillows were scattered across the floor.

"No, thank you," Rudi declined.

Lukas did the same. He kept sniffing, turning the corner of the room. Just off the long, galley kitchen sat a nook. A round wooden table with four chairs took up most of it.

A young Indian man waited there, in a dark burgundy shirt and jeans. He rose gracefully and strode out to greet them. His brown eyes filled up much of his face, with only a small, upturned nose and mouth. His hair was short, just over the edge of his collar.

Lukas held out his hand first. Only when he drew closer could he scent what he was looking for, that cool hint of power, spiced with mint and cardamom.

"Virmal," the man said, his voice deeper than his slight frame would indicate.

"Lukas," he replied, taking another step closer.

He couldn't get over how Virmal's scent complemented the others, a sweet harmony of the glass and warm feathers from Peter, the wild-beating heart of Sally, the rich earth and strong scales of Mei Ling, and now, this strength and calm, the opposite of the chaotic shadows.

If only Lukas knew what to do when he got them all together.

"Ah, sorry," Lukas said, shaking himself and coming back to the present day and finally dropping Virmal's warm, comforting hand.

Virmal looked suspiciously at him. Lukas immediately backed away. Damn it. He'd wanted to make a good first impression.

Rudi introduced himself, and Harita invited them to all sit around the table.

"Does your clan know anything about the shadows?" Lukas asked, seated directly across from Virmal, with Rudi on his right and Harita on his left.

"No, sorry," Virmal replied with an educated English accent.

Harita said, "There is one old story about them."

Virmal looked at his sister, puzzled.

"A man from the viper clan sought out one of our ancestors, warning of the shadows," she replied.

"'I've never heard that story," Virmal said.

"Grandmother Irita told it to me, long ago," Harita explained.

"So the viper clan knows about the shadows?" Lukas asked. Maybe he had more allies than he realized.

"They'd foreseen them, I guess? The mystics? Doesn't mean their vision ever came to true, though," Harita pointed out.

Lukas grimaced. "It's true. The shadows are here. They'll take over the clans, then move on to the human races. They'll suck all the life out of the world. I've foreseen it as well."

"Why are you telling us?" Virmal asked. He had drawn back in his seat.

Lukas wondered how close Virmal's tiger soul was. Hamlin pressed up against his own skin, ready to defend him if necessary. "You're part of the solution," Lukas replied softly. "I'm starting to believe that there needs to be someone from every clan: hound, tiger, raven, boar, viper, and crocodile."

Virmal shook his head. "Sorry, but I don't want to be part of your solution. Find someone else."

"But—but, you have to!" Lukas replied. "It has to be you. You're part of it."

"Nope. Wrong chap," Virmal said.

Rudi held up his hand to stop Lukas before he said something more. "We had those marvelous pickles of yours. They're taste like the opposite of the shadows," he said. "When did you start making those?"

"The summer I returned to New Delhi. My last year of university," Virmal said, wariness in his voice. He turned to Harita and asked a question in a language Lukas didn't know.

Harita seemed to be trying to convince Virmal of something. Finally, he nodded, turned back toward Lukas, and continued.

"I have a cousin, Niyati, who wasn't the most kind," Virmal said.

"That's an understatement," Harita interjected.

Virmal glared at his sister. "I was young, well, younger. I'd been raised primarily in England, and I was eager to impress my relatives. So I started following Niyati, emulating her, even."

Harita sighed and shook her head.

"After a long and rather extracted argument with my sister here, I finally agreed to at least cook with her on a regular basis. That's when I discovered my love of preserving things." Virmal looked down at his hands, rubbing the palm of his left with his right thumb. "Harita urged me to follow certain recipes, more than others, and I noticed that not only did Niyati leave me alone when I did, so did some of my other cousins. It was a relief, to be honest, by that point. I was tired of the challenges. It was like they no longer saw me."

Lukas caught a glimpse of the scar that Virmal rubbed. It ran from the base of his palm almost to the first finger.

He could almost scent the old tears still salting the long-healed wound.

"We suspect that some of the tiger clan is already infected with the shadows," Lukas said softly. "That it's tied to their magic."

At that, both Virmal and Harita looked up. "We noticed something like that as well," Harita admitted. "When Virmal came back from any of his charms or spells classes, I force fed him his pickles until he came all the way back to me."

"The shadows are real," Rudi said softly. "We need your help defeating them. Freeing your clan."

Virmal stood and strode from the table to the middle of the living room, where he paced. His right hand was clasped strongly around his left wrist, and his eyes watched his feet.

Was Virmal fighting with his tiger soul? Were they snarling at each other?

Harita spoke softly. "I'm sorry, you must go now."

"But—" Lukas sighed. Virmal just *had* to see that he was important. Essential! Lukas needed him.

"We'll go," Rudi said, standing.

Virmal continued to pace, not even glancing at them as they walked through the long galley kitchen and back out to the vestibule.

"You must convince him that he needs to work with us," Lukas whispered urgently to Harita after she handed him his coat. "Please."

Harita shrugged. "He's my brother," she said softly. "Family, clan, always comes first."

"And saving the world comes after that?" Lukas asked as he shrugged on his coat.

"We'll be in touch," Harita promised as she opened the door.

Out in the hallway, Lukas wanted to howl. He was so close! Hamlin pressed against his side, but it didn't help. Rudi started walking toward the exit, but Lukas wanted to stay right there, to hound Virmal until he agreed.

With a huge sigh, Lukas followed Rudi out into the cold night. The air here smelled so different than from the States. He wasn't sure what it was—maybe it was the closed-in spaces, or the age, or maybe it was just the earth speaking to him of his aborted childhood.

Lukas still wanted to just run.

"You could, you know," Rudi said softly.

Lukas shook his head. Not yet. He couldn't, wouldn't, go back into his hound form until he absolutely had to.

Safe, Hamlin said softly. *Trust*.

Lukas bared his teeth and sucked in the cool air. He wanted to run. He wanted to fight. He wanted to do…something.

"I have an idea," Rudi said. He ran a calming hand down Lukas' back, then started back to their car.

"What is it?" Lukas barked at him, chasing after him.

"Patience," Rudi said with a grin.

Lukas tried to take a deep breath, to relax, but he was too on edge. Ants were crawling over his skin like miniature shadows. He couldn't pay attention to where they were going; the lights were too bright outside the dark of the car, and the traffic made them slow down too often.

Finally, Rudi pulled up in front of a modern, one-story building that had only one light in the front and a small sign that Lukas couldn't read until they were closer: *Sportshalle*.

"A gym?" Lukas said. Why would Rudi bring him here?

"Want to go punch things?" Rudi asked with a toothy grin. "Learn how to fight?"

Lukas barked a laugh. He'd never had formal warrior training, but he'd watched Rudi go through the exercises twice a week.

"Yes," Lukas replied. Though his skin felt too tight, and the world was too dark, he still couldn't help but be grateful to this man, who continued to be more of a father than Da.

L ukas woke up to the blaring sound of the alarm on his phone. He groaned, stabbed at it, then curled back under the warm duvet. He took a deep breath, his limbs loose. The darkness of the hotel room lulled him to close his eyes. He scented warm water in the air—Rudi was probably already up, showered, and working on something on his computer.

Today, Lukas would have breakfast with Mama. It would be good to see her again. If only she would stay. But she'd be gone by that afternoon. She was too broken to remain.

Then, he'd go find Virmal and make him understand just how important he was. Maybe if Lukas transformed? Mei Ling had seemed impressed with his true hound nature.

Lukas relaxed, feeling more settled into his skin than he had since the curse had been broken. Learning how to fight the previous night had been epic. While Lukas had known joy in his hound form, blocking a solid hit, or landing one, had its own vicious joy as well.

A knock on the door startled Lukas back awake. "I'm up!" he called.

"We have a visitor," Rudi said. He smelled…worried.

That wasn't good.

Lukas was up and fumbling into clothes in a flash. That had been something Rudi had commented on: What Lukas didn't know in proper warrior forms, he could sometimes make up for in speed. His reflexes were faster than anyone Rudi had ever sparred with, and Rudi had been trained by the best of the hound guard.

It was only then Lukas smelled Virmal. Why was his scent so contained? Why hadn't it preceded Rudi? Lukas raked at his hair with his fingers, trying to get his wild curls to lay flat. He didn't want Virmal to see him like this.

But Lukas would have to pass through the living room of their suite to get to the bathroom. He tugged on a T-shirt and sweats. He didn't have time to fiddle with his clothes, change into something else.

Maybe Virmal had decided to join them, though. Even if he hadn't, Lukas could convince him. He was sure of it.

Lukas bounded out into the living room. "Hi," he said. It was good to see Virmal. He was wearing the coolest blue shirt that set off his dark skin, as well as black trousers and finely made, black leather shoes.

"Good morning," Virmal said, not smiling back. "I'm afraid I have bad news. I won't be joining your battle."

"You must," Lukas said, gently. "The fate of the world depends on it." He could do this; he could convince Virmal.

Virmal shrugged. "That's what you've foreseen. But not every vision comes true."

"I am a guardian hound," Lukas told him. "My breed is rare, and only comes when there's great need." He didn't want to transform, but he would if he must.

"Again, legends, myths," Virmal said dismissively.

Lukas wasn't sure what to say.

"Do you think the shadows don't exist?" Rudi asked from the kitchen alcove where he was making coffee.

Virmal hesitated. "Something exists. I don't know if it's the shadows or not. Harita believes in them."

"They're real," Lukas said. He didn't want to be cursed again, but he wished he had some way of showing them.

"That's what I'm afraid of," Virmal admitted. "It will be dangerous, this battle of yours, yes?"

Lukas couldn't lie about that, not to one who was to be part of the knight. "Yes." His dreams had more than once shown the knight slain.

"Then I can't," Virmal said firmly.

"Harita would want you to," Rudi said quickly, stepping around the breakfast bar and coming further into the room.

"And that's exactly why I can't," Virmal said vehemently. "I won't take her near battle, draw her into harm's way."

"But if we don't destroy the shadows, she'll be in harm's way. You won't be able to protect her," Lukas said.

Virmal snarled. "You're wrong. I will defend her and keep her safe."

Hamlin pushed up hard against Lukas. He was there, ready, if Lukas needed to fight.

A knock on the door startled them all.

Virmal's scent expanded as Harita walked into the room. Somehow, they were connected.

"You're already here," Harita said, looking at Virmal and sounding disappointed. She wore a bright red-and-gold sari today. "I'd planned on getting here before you."

"Sorry," Virmal said, sounding not sorry at all.

"Hmph," Harita said. "Well, it doesn't matter. I'm here to tell you that I will join your battle."

"What?" Virmal asked.

Harita turned on him. "I've seen the cruelty of the clan.

It isn't natural. They're infested, Virmal. This is our chance to help them all."

"No," Virmal said. "I forbid it."

Harita's merry laughter filled the room. "Has that ever worked? You saying that?"

"No," Virmal said, begrudgingly. "But it's dangerous."

"And more dangerous if we don't fight—am I right, Prince Lukas?" Harita said, looking at Lukas.

"Yes," Lukas said. She wasn't part of the knight. There was nothing in her scent that was part of that vision. But Virmal needed her. He wasn't complete without her.

"Don't worry. I'll protect you from the vicious shadows," Harita promised Virmal.

"How?" Rudi asked. "I know the shadows exist. I've *seen* them. I can scent them, even just a trace of them. And yet, too much exposure to the shadows had even me questioning if Lukas was right." He turned and looked at Lukas. "I'm sorry, I forgot to tell you about that yesterday. At the castle."

Lukas nodded. "It's all right." But it worried him that even Rudi with his natural protection against magic had been affected.

Harita shook her head. "Even at the tiger temple, they weren't able to affect my mind or my behavior."

"That's because you're too good," Virmal said, teasing. "Miss Innocent and Pure."

Harita rolled her eyes.

Lukas, however, knew what Virmal meant. Harita *was* good, and there *was* something pure about her.

"So you'll join us, when the time for the battle draws near?" Lukas asked Virmal. Then he added, "Both of you."

"We will," Harita said, stepping forward.

Virmal grudgingly nodded and stood beside his sister.

"Thank you," Lukas said.

Virmal finally smiled at him. "One thing you need to learn about Indians: When they say *no*, it's actually just the start of the negotiations."

"Hopefully you won't say no to our next request," Rudi said, drawing closer.

Virmal just looked at him, coolly.

"We'd like more of your pickled vegetables. And anything else that you've used to help keep you safe against the shadows," Rudi said. He turned to Lukas and simply said, "Greta."

"My sister is infected with the shadows," Lukas said, the words tumbling out.

"Of course," Virmal said, instantly.

Harita nodded. "Anything you need." She glanced at her brother and they shared a smile that was all about family and clan.

"Thank you," Lukas added. "For everything."

He didn't know if he could save Greta, but at least now he felt like he had something he could try.

***

Lukas marched directly into Greta's lab. Harita followed, carrying over a dozen jar of pickles, Virmal's entire supply. He promised more the following week.

The stench of shadows overwhelmed the fresh earth and plant smells, the bitter chemical smells of magic, and the modern chemicals themselves. Lukas carried an open jar of pickles. The clean mint couldn't overcome the sludge of the shadows, but still, Lukas was hopeful.

Greta still sat in her lab, still in her white coat, her curls still perfect and her eyes still glazed. She stood and walked to her side of the dividing tables. "What's that?" she asked, wrinkling her nose.

"Try one," Lukas said, pushing the open jar across the table toward her.

"No, thank you. I don't like pickles," Greta said primly.

"These will help your experiments," Lukas promised. He reached into the jar and pulled out a carrot, then ate it himself while Greta watched with large, blank eyes. "You should try one."

"What is she doing?" Greta said, finally tearing her eyes away from Lukas to watch Harita. The young Indian woman walked from shelf to the next, placing open jars of pickles, then shuddering as she removed the tainted charms, dropping them into jars with just brine.

"Harita, this is my sister, Greta," Lukas said.

"Hello," Harita said, her accent pure and her German flawless. "I'm a medical student, here to take care of your grandmother." She continued her work, first down one side of the room, then up the other.

"Nice to meet you." Greta turned to Lukas. "Are you going to tell me what you're doing?"

"You really should try one of these," Lukas said. He fished out a baby cucumber from the open jar between them.

Greta wrinkled her nose, but finally took it. "Pickles?"

"Preservative," Harita explained. "You're doing growing experiments, right?"

"Yes," Greta said. She seemed to relax. "And you're a healer? You understand these things?"

"I try," Harita said modestly. "Growing and preserving, and healing, are all related."

Lukas watched with interest as Greta finally took a bite. The loud crunching filled the quiet lab. Greta seemed puzzled, her head twisting to one side, then the other. "What are these?" she asked again.

"They're preserved vegetables," Harita said, coming over to stand next to Lukas. "Extending the life of fresh, growing things," she added.

Lukas handed Greta another pickle. "They're good, aren't they?"

Greta nodded, still puzzled. But she ate it, as well as the rest of the jar.

The shadows didn't suddenly flow away from his sister, and her scent didn't suddenly change. However, she did look more human, her eyes growing softer, less doll-like.

"I think that you should experiment with preserving, not just growing," Harita said. "I could help you, while I'm here."

"I could use the help in the lab," Greta said grudgingly. "None of the lab attendants ever want to stay," she complained.

"Maybe you'll be able to preserve some now," Lukas told her.

Greta nodded, and blinked, straightening up again, her voice growing more harsh and chipped. "It is good to see you, brother," she said.

"And you," Lukas said. He wondered if her soul wandered like his had when Oma had first cursed him, returning only for a few moments at a time.

With Harita's help, hopefully Greta's soul could come all the way back, like his had.

"How soon can you get us to Seattle?" Lukas asked as soon as he said goodbye to Peter and Sally on Skype. He got up out of the hotel desk chair and strode to the kitchenette in the suite. Rudi had coffee going, of course, though he complained about how it wasn't as good as Seattle coffee.

Rudi was already working his magic on his phone, the only real magic Lukas knew he had. "Noon, tomorrow," Rudi said distracted.

Lukas nodded, though he knew Rudi didn't see him. It was so great about the mystics. Most clans had some foresight ability, but the vipers were best known for it. And they knew about him! The hound prince. That meant he allies among the viper warriors.

Surely it was time for the great battle.

"We'll have to bring Virmal and Harita," Lukas warned. He regretted having to take Harita away from Oma, but he needed her more.

Rudi nodded. "Already on it."

"And then…" Lukas sighed. He didn't know what to do next, what they would do, this disparate collection that made up his knight.

Sally and Peter hadn't been able to find the viper warrior again before they left Tulum and returned to Wyoming. Lukas hoped they didn't need him, that he'd already paid his part by making the shadows physical.

Physical! That had always been Lukas' problem, in his nightmares, fighting mere clouds. Now that the viper warrior had made the shadows corporeal, Lukas and the other warriors would surely be able to destroy the shadows for good.

When Rudi looked up from his phone, Lukas continued his thoughts out loud. "We have a raven, tiger, and crocodile warrior," he said, then paused. "I need to get them together, to see if that's all we need." He'd recognize the knight by their combined scents. "Hopefully that's everyone, and I don't need to find a warrior from every clan, like a viper, a boar, and a hound."

Rudi frowned, his gray eyes troubled. "What do you mean, maybe find a hound warrior? You're a hound warrior."

Lukas shook his head, the old disappointment pressing against his chest like a solid fist. "I'm not part of the knight. Oma was always clear on that. I just gather the warriors together." He looked down at his hands, laced together and squeezing tightly, one against the other. It was all right. The knight destroying the shadows was enough. It had to be enough.

"My prince," Rudi said softly.

Lukas reluctantly looked up.

"You talk about the knight. And his sword. And occasionally about his battles. But how do you know?"

"I watch," Lukas said.

"But how?" Rudi insisted.

Hope flooded through Lukas, like the sun breaking through a cloudy Seattle day. "I watch as the knight's hound."

"So maybe Oma was right. You aren't part of the knight. You play a more important role. His faithful companion. His hound."

Lukas nodded. He couldn't help himself—he reached out and gave Rudi a quick hug.

He'd been so certain his role was almost over.

But maybe, maybe, he could play a part still.

Lukas stepped across the threshold of their Seattle house, then paused and took a deep breath, taking in the scents of home.

This was home, really. Not the cold stone and delightful grasses of the castle in Germany. He knew he should feel more sad about leaving Da and Greta, but he just felt relieved. The acidic metallic scent of all of Rudi's computer equipment; the rich, wet dirt of Seattle's spring; the comforting, lingering smell of the bacon that Rudi cooked every morning: These were home.

So many scents of home involved the man standing next to him. Lukas didn't know what he'd do when Rudi decided it was time to move again. Lukas desperately wanted to stay, to settle here, in this city and into his human life. Sally and Peter wouldn't always be here, but they'd come back. They'd help him, even if Rudi left.

"Good to be home, eh?" Rudi asked, his smile echoing the joy Lukas felt. "You hungry?" he asked, shedding his coat and hanging up Lukas' as well.

"Always," Lukas said truthfully. And he was. He didn't know human boys ate so much. It was like his legs were hollow in addition to his stomach. There was no place else for all that food to disappear into.

"It won't last forever," Rudi assured Lukas, leading him into the kitchen. "You'll stop growing eventually, and it won't feel as though you're starving all the time."

"But when?" Lukas whined as his stomach growled again. Just the mention or promise of food set him on edge.

"Soon," Rudi said with a grin. "So what do we do next?" he asked quietly as he got frozen hamburger patties out, then chucked an apple toward Lukas.

"First, this afternoon, we meet with everyone," Lukas

said. He bit greedily into the apple, the sweet juice trickling down his throat. "Then tonight, we'll gather. Outside. At Miller's Park."

"Why there?" Rudi asked as he started grilling the patties.

"It's wide open," Lukas explained. "There are houses near by, but not too close. The sports lights on the field will keep it bright, make it easier to see the shadows. You can hack those, right?"

"I'll figure something out," Rudi said dryly.

"Good," Lukas said, devouring the rest of the apple, core and all. "Thanks," he added. He could never thank Rudi enough, for everything.

"Will the shadows come?" Rudi asked as he flipped the patties.

"They'll come," Lukas said grimly. They had to come. It had to be time.

UNITED STATES, PRESENT DAY

ARIEL

Ariel followed her nose through the forest. She stopped to root mushrooms out of springy moss at the base of a granddaddy oak, then a second time for sweet sage hidden in a raft of mint.

Back at the campsite, she quickly cleaned and prepared her finds. She made a simple dinner of dried eggs with the mushrooms and spices, bacon, and campfire biscuits fried in the leftover grease.

If there had been campers on either side of her, Ariel would have shared her bounty. She got awful lonesome sometimes, particularly since she was living cheap this ride. But it was mid-week in the middle-of-nowhere Nevada, and still early enough in the spring that the wind cut straight through her dreadlocks, sending goose pimples all across her skull. Her bike leathers kept her from the worst of it, though.

Passing trucks on the nearby interstate kept Ariel company as she wiped down her cast iron and cleaned up her dishes. The fire burned down, but she didn't need no light; she could see just fine in the dark, like all the boar clan.

Except—it was darker some places than others.

Ariel sniffed the air, but didn't smell any smoke besides what was coming from her fire.

When the wind gusted, the dark patches didn't shred or blow away, but waved through the breeze like scum on a pond.

Ariel picked up one of the burning logs from the fire and, using the business end of it, poked at one of the shadows. When it didn't react, she slashed through it.

Shadows burst out around her. They stank of weeds rotting in long-dead swamps. They bore down on her, pressing in on all sides of her, like a dirt tunnel collapsing in on her, burying her in darkness.

Ariel struggled to breathe without taking their stink into her soul. She flung out her arms, trying to strike at the shadows, but they had no form, nothing she could punch or fight against.

Stupid bastards. Ariel forced herself to swirl, drawing the burning log closer, hoping to burn them away.

Still the shadows attacked. Ariel called on Gret, her boar soul, and transformed into a warrior. Wicked tusks shot out of her elongated jaw, her fingers grew into strong, knife-sharp hooves, and a thick hairy coat of armor covered her forehead, arms, and chest. She roared her displeasure, taking her enemy's scent in fully, seeking weaknesses.

There. Where two of the shadows were loosely joined. Something agitated them about that connection, like a graft spot where two trees grew together.

Ariel stampeded to the spot, slashing wildly with her impromptu sword, the log flaring as she slashed through the air.

Only Gret's quick reflexes saved her leathers from the acid that spilled out from the shadow on her left.

What the hell?

It sped away and the other shadows attacked, flinging their filth into her face, pressing so hard against her chest it was difficult to breathe.

Ariel fought with all the fierceness of her kind, wild with rage and war.

The shadows changed tactics, and tried to distract Ariel, showing her an escape into the darkest part of the woods where she knew more acid-spitting shadows lay. Then they whispered that she needed another weapon and must draw closer to the fire.

A quick look told Ariel that the damn shadows had blurred the edges of her fire. If she'd followed their suggestion blindly, she would have walked directly into the flames.

Ariel snorted and laughed at the shadows. Their tricks might work with those who was weak-minded, but she was of the earth. They couldn't fool *her*.

The shadows drew back after that. Ariel sensed their surprise. She pushed her attack, sticking her burning log through every stinking patch of darkness. They huddled in a single sickening mass, no longer striking back. Finally, they fell in on themselves, disappearing like the Cheshire cat, a little bit at a time, 'til only their stench remained.

Ariel slashed through the air where they'd been, but there was nothing left to burn. Then she rushed to her fire and built it up, sending the flames high into the night. It wouldn't help with the shadows who'd attacked her, but it made both her and Gret feel better.

Then she sat, huddled in her leathers and blankets, awake and waiting for the dawn, while she wondered what the hell had just happened.

Ariel opened up the throttle on her bike until she crested a nice 70 miles per hour as she cruised down the interstate. The sunshine and brilliantly clear skies made her happy, even if it was still too damn cold.

The Wyoming landscape looked as abandoned as the moon, wide open and flat, with mainly gray rock. A hill sloped before her, the highway like a white ribbon curling up its side.

A black patch lay in wait on the side of the road. At first, Ariel thought it was some kind of burn mark, maybe from a car explosion or truck fire.

As she drew closer, though, she realized it wasn't on the ground. No, it was a cloud that rose several feet in the air.

Damn shadows were getting ready to attack her again.

There wasn't anything Ariel could do to get away—she wasn't about to drive into oncoming traffic, and hell if she was going to do a U-turn and run away.

Instead, she gunned it, swinging into the far lane, torquing her wrist as she pushed forward on the accelerator.

Ariel slammed through the edges of the black cloud. They tore at her, like a sticky web, spreading across her visor as if she'd driven through a spray of rancid oil. Where the shadows wrapped around her torso and arms, they wiggled like giant worms, trying to find a way through her leathers to pollute her skin.

The stench of mold and decay wafted up under her helmet, making Ariel gag. She shuddered, but didn't dare reach up to wipe the shadows away. Instead, she rode faster, trying to whip the shadows off with the wind.

She cheered when a glob flew off her chest and struck

a green sedan as she passed. Only a few shadows remained on her, distracting, casting illusions across the road, like cracks in the concrete and cars that weren't there. Ariel refused to slow down. Hell if she was going to let them confuse her, or make her crash.

A roaring beside Ariel made her start. The car she'd passed, the green sedan, was suddenly edging closer.

The interior of the car boiled with shadows. The driver clawed at his face, his mouth open, howling silent screams. He wasn't paying attention to where he was going; the shadows were probably confusing him, and the idiot was about to drive her off the road.

Ariel gunned it again, cursing her hog of a bike: It wasn't a racer, wasn't built for speed.

The car bumper kissed her wheel guard, and Ariel's bike wobbled hard. She made herself breathe as everything slowed down and she fought to keep the bike upright.

But then the car clipped her again, and Ariel felt herself going down. She held on as long as she could, keeping the bike upright before it started sliding, then she let go, tumbling like a rock rolling down a cliff. The bike skittered away, twirling as it scraped across the road.

Finally, Ariel came to a halt. At least she'd rolled the right way, off the edge of the highway and not into oncoming traffic.

Stupid shadows. She was going to kill them all, if she could get her hands on them.

The car came to a screeching halt behind her, and the driver flew out of the window.

Literally. Flew.

Driver had been a damn raven.

Figured it was the stupid birds who'd be confused by the shadows. Never trust a raven, that's what her ma had always said.

Ariel grunted as she pushed herself to sitting. God, she was going to be bruised everywhere. At least her leathers had saved her from most of the road rash. They were torn up and abraded, but better them than her skin.

The act of reaching up to remove her helmet told Ariel that she was even more hurt than she'd realized. Shit. Still, she made herself reach up, lift her helmet off.

The faceplate was cracked, and the helmet itself had taken quite a beating. No wonder her head hurt like it had been pounded on the pavement: It had been.

The smart thing would have been to stay laying on the side of the road until help came.

But no help had ever come for Ariel in the past. She'd been on her own for too damn long to count on anything or anyone.

Stiffly, Ariel forced herself up to her feet. She swayed, and the bright landscaped dimmed for a moment. Then Ariel made herself stand up taller and take small, shuffling steps to her bike.

She knew the food in her panniers was toast, squished beyond recognition. But she was suddenly so thirsty. She needed water, now. She paused, making sure it was what *she* wanted, that the shadows weren't trying to trick her. But they'd blown away, or maybe flown away with the damn bird.

Every single muscle along Ariel's sides screamed at her as she walked. She stubbornly kept at it, though, pulling off her gloves as she finally reached her poor fallen hog. She tried to squat down, but instead, fell awkwardly on her knees, crying out at the pain. Luckily, she found her water bottle intact, and ended up only spilling a little of it as she guzzled it.

Ariel sat for a moment after she finally quenched her thirst, wondering what she should do next. She didn't know how far the nearest town was. And she had to get going, she knew. That damn raven was sure to return soon, probably still confused, and would attack her again.

And speak of the devil—a black jeep was slowly crossing the median, then across the near lanes, coming straight for the wreck.

Ariel pulled herself upright, drawing Gret closer. She'd fight if she had to, tear the damn birds to pieces with claws and tusks.

A tall young man with light-colored hair artfully messed and wearing a padded plaid red-and-white jacket, hat, jeans, and hiking boots sprang from the jeep.

Just behind him stood another man, almost like a second person, wearing a great cloak made of raven feathers.

Another damn bird.

"Are you all right?" he asked as he came running over.

"Stay away from me," Ariel commanded.

The young man stopped immediately. "I'm not going to hurt you," he said.

Ariel snorted. "Yeah, you and your partner who was driving the car want to be my best buddies, right?" she asked. "Damn ravens."

"You're from the clans," the man said, looking shocked.

"That's right. Y'all can't see us anymore, can you?" Ariel said, feeling a little better.

The man shook his head. "No. And I'm sorry, for what it's worth."

"Not worth a damn lot," Ariel muttered. Exhaustion slammed into her, and though she held herself stiffly, she knew she still swayed.

"Please, let me help you. I won't hurt you," the man said earnestly. "My name is Peter."

"You won't mean to hurt me. But you will," Ariel said. She hadn't meant to tell the truth, but she was so tired. "And my name's Ariel." She wasn't about to give him her birth name, she wasn't that loopy.

"What do you mean?" Peter asked.

"What do you think happened here?" Ariel asked, indicating her fallen bike, the green sedan resting peacefully just up the road.

Peter raised his nose and sniffed the air, his eyes growing raven black. "Shadows," he squawked. "Attacked. Both you and the car."

Ariel blinked, surprised. "You know about those damn shadows?"

Peter shook his head, coming all the way back to human. "Yes," he said. "But why did they attack Kyle that way?"

"They weren't attacking Kyle. Or rather, they were trying to get Kyle to drive over me," Ariel said. "They first attacked me last night," she admitted. She shivered, swaying again. Damn it, she was tired.

Peter stared at her hard, as if trying to see all the way through her. "You need to come with me," he said slowly. "Back to Seattle. There's a battle coming. Us versus the shadows."

"Why would I want to be part of your battle, birdman?" Ariel asked. She didn't want to be involved in anything like this. She expected him to point out that she was already part of it, that she didn't have a choice.

Instead, Peter gave a cawing laugh and said, "Revenge. Don't you want a chance to destroy the shadows?"

Ariel wanted to be angry, but instead, she had to laugh.

Damn raven was right. She'd join him just for that.

WYOMING AND SEATTLE, PRESENT DAY

P eter sat on the side of the road with Ariel, waiting for the tow truck to take her motorcycle away. The flat Wyoming landscape went on and on, high alpine desert covered in scraggly bushes and tough grass. The sky went on and on as well, clean blue with only a few clouds to play hide-and-seek with the sun. Wind pushed at them, first from one direction, then the other, carrying scents of spring leaves and newly ploughed fields.

Ariel moved slowly, raising her water bottle for a drink. Peter was certain her dark brown skin hid the bruises on her face. Given the wrecked condition of her bike, Peter was surprised she'd refused all medical attention from the ambulance that had finally come by, despite Peter's insistence that the raven clan would cover any medical bills.

"We can get you to a healer back at the hall," Peter told her as she winced, putting the bottle back on the ground.

"I'll be fine," Ariel said dismissively.

"I bet you can't even take a deep breath right now — your ribs are either broken or bruised."

Ariel glared at Peter. "And if they are, there's nothing no one can do about it."

"Could give you something for the pain," Peter pointed out.

"We'll see," Ariel said with a shrug. "So how did you learn about the shadows?"

Peter eagerly told Ariel about Lukas, how he'd been cursed, and how he was bringing together a group of people who would battle the shadows.

"Sally, my girl—my wife," Peter said, a spike of happiness rushing through him. "According to Lukas, she's the heart of this knight who will appear when we all come together. Mei Ling—she's ferocious, and her scales do something with the armor. Virmal, he's developed some magic that works against the shadows."

"The shadow try to confuse you, fool your eyes," Ariel added. "But they can't fool me."

"Huh," Peter said. "You really need to come with us." Lukas was going to be so excited that Peter had found another member of their team.

"What about you?" Ariel asked as she slowly, carefully, pushed herself up.

Peter looked over his shoulder. The bright yellow flashing lights of the tow truck approached.

"What do you mean?" Peter asked, standing. He knew better than to ask Ariel if she needed help, or to offer, but he did take a step closer, ready to give her a hand if it looked as if she was going to fall.

"So I bring sight, and your wife brings this great heart. What do you bring, birdman?"

Peter opened his mouth and shut it again. He knew Lukas needed him for something, that there must be some sort of special ability that only he had.

But he had no idea what it could be.

Dozens of ravens cawed greetings to them from the numerous balconies and ledges of Raven Hall. The white brick glittered in the high noon light, jutting out from the white cliff behind it, looking as if it had sprung from it. Peter looked up and smiled, his raven soul tempted to caw back—this was home now, a school he could reform, a place where he and Sally could do good work.

Ariel stood with her fists on her waist, staring intently at the building.

"Pretty cool, huh?" Peter asked.

Ariel looked askance at him. "Yeah. That's one way of putting it."

Kyle came rushing out of the tall wooden doors before Peter could ask Ariel what she meant.

"Prefect Peter! I am *so* sorry. I just—" Kyle cut himself off when he saw Ariel. "Oh, geez. Look. Miss. I'm sorry. I don't know what happened. There was just—"

"It's okay," Ariel said grudgingly.

Kyle tumbled on. "Are y'all hurt? I could—"

"Yes," Peter interrupted. "Go get Prefect Kitridge. And make sure Dr. Elrah's in the infirmary."

"But—" Kyle hesitated.

"Go," Peter directed. Though he was only in his mid-twenties, Kyle made him feel like a wise old bird. "Sorry about that," Peter said, turning to Ariel after Kyle had dashed off. "He's just, uhm, excitable, I guess."

Ariel gave a brief chuckle that she cut off abruptly.

How badly hurt was she?

"Naw, I get it," Ariel said, dismissing his apology with a wave of her hand.

"Please, let us help you," Peter said insistently as they approached the building.

"Why do you care?" Ariel asked bluntly. "I mean, I ain't about to sue your ass or anything. Plus, you're a raven."

"It's the right thing to do," Peter insisted. Though not all the training he'd received at Ravens' Hall had been good, and despite Prefect Aaron's flawed ideas about discipline, he'd still been raised to be a gentleman and to do the right thing.

Prefect Kitridge met them at the door. She wore her usual white tank top to show off the muscles in her arms as well as the vibrant red-and-blue tattoos that went from her shoulders to mid-forearms. Her hair was still short and spiked, the tips bright green. She'd replaced the plain metal balls of her nose and lip piercings with dark green stones.

"What's up, boss?" Kitridge asked.

"Don't call me that," Peter sighed. Kitridge was at least ten years older than he was, and had been one of his teachers. It made him uncomfortable to suddenly be in a position of authority above her.

"Anything you say, boss," Kitridge said with a grin and a broad wink.

Not like she recognized his authority.

"Prefect Kitridge, this is Ariel," Peter said. "She's been in an accident."

"Bike?" Kitridge asked, taking in Ariel's leathers.

"Harley Fatboy," Ariel replied.

"Sweet ride. Bit of a hog, though," Kitridge said. "Let's go do what we can to patch you up. Give you something for the bruises."

"You're raven clan," Ariel said after she looked at Kitridge for a moment.

"Yep. One of the two female prefects here."

"Doesn't it drive you crazy?" Ariel asked as she turned

to follow Kitridge.

"You do what you can. Boys. I teach 'em how to fight," Kitridge explained.

Peter rolled his eyes. At least he'd made the right decision, asking for Kitridge to meet them. She was one of the few prefects he trusted.

"Uhm, Prefect Peter?" came Kyle's voice from behind him.

Peter made himself maintain his smile as he turned around. "Yes?"

"Is she gonna be okay? Miss Ariel?" Kyle asked, still nervous.

A laugh from the two women echoed down the hall. "I think so," Peter said.

Kyle stood there, nervously biting his lips, staring over Peter's shoulder.

"Did you need something else?" Peter quietly prompted.

"Oh! Yes! Your wife, Miss Sally, would like to see you."

"Good. I was just going to find her," Peter said, brushing past Kyle and heading to the southern wing of Ravens' Hall, where the prefects were housed.

As a student, Peter had never been in this part of the building. Wood paneling—some of it very old, brought from the ancient halls in Wales; some of it cheap 1950s knockoffs—dominated the common areas. Was all that wood supposed to make their raven souls more comfortable? It felt like an exclusive club for rich white men. Peter planned on replacing the heavy, carved chairs and couches with something more modern, as well as replacing the dark green wallpaper with something brighter and softer.

Peter's raven soul, Cai, didn't care much for human

spaces. But he didn't seem to mind these rooms, particularly after all the charms and cameras had been removed.

Why had the elders felt they needed to watch and control all of the raven clan who lived here to such a degree? Peter still hadn't gotten a good answer to that. Had it been an unconscious response to the shadows? But he hadn't found any lurking here, and Cai hadn't seen any, either.

Then again, Lukas has warned that their sight could be fooled. Peter mainly detected the shadows by scent, and only with Cai's help, when there were a lot of them. He didn't have as good a nose as the members of the hound clan, and so he'd never detected the one that had attached itself to Sally.

After Peter had vanquished Prefect Aaron, the elders had assumed Peter would take Aaron's quarters—the spoils of war. But Aaron's rooms had creeped Peter out, so he and Sally had moved another prefect there, taking a smaller suite on the far southern edge of the building.

No matter how cold the temperature was outside, the sunshine made their apartment warm. Floor-to-ceiling windows overlooked their own private garden. Brown brick made up the floor just in front of the windows and acted as passive solar: Once the sun warmed the bricks, they kept the rest of the rooms warm, too.

Much of the furniture had been scrounged from empty prefect apartments or the big storage locker the clan kept in town. It was a soothing mismatch of overstuffed 1980s couches done in dark purple velvet; ultra sleek, Danish-modern wooden tables; and two sturdy antique red-painted rocking chairs with brand new cushions that were surprisingly comfortable.

Sally sat in one next to the bright sunlight, her legs

tucked in under her and an ancient book in her lap. Peter had overridden the objections of the prefects and pulled out all the old books, wanting to learn not just about the other clans and the actual history of his own, but also to see if there was some mention of the shadows.

"Hey, you," Sally said with a bright smile. She wore a soft green hoodie over jeans.

"Hey," Peter said, his heart full to bursting with so many emotions at seeing her: Love, devotion, fierce protection, and joy. His raven soul sent the image of a fully lined nest, set high on a tree branch, an image of home. Peter leaned over and collected a soft kiss. "What's up?"

"I think I found something," Sally said, excited. "Here, look at this."

The pages of the book were onion-skin thin and had gone brown with age. The text was handwritten in black ink, the letters harshly upright, looking stenciled in.

Sally pointed to an ancient recitation. According to tradition since the time of Adwar the betrayer, who sold out the clan to save his family, all recitations were given orally. Yet, some books had survived the various strictures and purges.

Do not suffer the half-breed—they bring the shadows.

Peter shivered. The recitation lesson about half-breeds had been brutal. The prefect had killed a bird in front of the class to prove his point. A half-breed wasn't fully human or raven—half here, half there, and never truly whole or aligned.

Cai stirred, uneasy.

"I would bet that there's more than one reason behind the prohibition of the half-breeds," Peter said slowly. There was always more than a single cause for every recitation, more than one story. "But this is really interesting. When's it from?"

Sally gently took the book back and put it down on the table. "The book's about four hundred years old," she said. "This section is all the things you can't do." She paused and looked up at Peter. "Was this what you had to learn as a boy?"

Peter couldn't lie to her, as much as he knew he should. "Yes," he croaked, surprised at how close Cai had drawn near.

"Then it's good we can change some of this for the other boys," Sally said firmly. She reached out and took Peter's hands in hers. "Have you had lunch?"

"No, there was an accident." Peter quickly filled her in. He'd have to go and check on Ariel soon.

"You should call Lukas," Sally told him.

Peter nodded, then paused, squeezing their intertwined fingers. "Ariel…she asked me something. And, well, I feel really stupid asking you."

"But you're going to anyway because there are no secrets between us," Sally said, quietly encouraging him.

"Right." Peter took a deep breath. "So you're the heart of the knight. And Mei Ling's the scale or armor or something like that. Virmal has some magic that works against the shadows, and I think Ariel's naturally immune —she said the shadows couldn't confuse her."

"Yes," Sally said, nodding.

"So what am I?" Peter asked, trying not to whine. He wasn't some twelve-year-old boy, lost and alone.

Sally disengaged their hands and took Peter's head, her warm palms against his cheeks, her fingers wrapping around the base of his skull. Then she pulled him forward for a soft kiss. "Thank you for trusting me to answer," she said.

"When Lukas says I'm the heart, he really means more

like grit. Determination. I'll make sure we all make it through."

"You're the stubborn one," Peter said, teasing.

"Damn straight," Sally said. "But you, you're the real heart. You care about Lukas, and Ariel, and even Mei Ling, though she scares you. I'll bring us through, but you'll make us a team, as well as help us heal, afterward."

Peter wanted to shake his head and deny Sally's words. Everyone else who made up the knight was more special than he was. They didn't really need him.

But Lukas had insisted, along with the strange viper in Tulum.

Maybe Peter did have a part to play, as important as the others.

P eter had never been to the hotel in Seattle where Mei Ling was staying. It was on the far side of Pike's Place Market. She had a fantastic view of the Sound. Gauze curtains filtered the bright sunlight, and the glass door leading onto the outdoor patio was open just a few inches, bringing in the fresh smells of baking bread from the market.

Mei Ling had rented an entire suite. The living room was as large as Peter's old apartment, the walls painted a cool green with a fireplace mantel painted white and a gas fire. She'd provided a tray of vegetables on one of the fine wooden tables, alone with another tray of meats and cheeses, all beautifully displayed.

Peter led Sally to one of the off-white couches, setting his plate carefully on the glass-covered coffee table in front of him. He suddenly missed the wood-paneled rooms of Ravens' Hall.

Virmal and Harita looked perfectly comfortable in the rich surroundings. They were both dressed in fine red silk. She wore a fancy sari, while he wore a tunic and trousers. They laughed with Mei Ling, who wore a sleek black dress that draped to the floor. Ariel wore jeans, a black-and-white Harley Davidson T-shirt, and a new black leather jacket that Peter (and the raven clan) had bought her.

Lukas seemed too nervous to pay any attention to the surroundings. He sat down, stood up and looked outside next to Ariel, then stood next to Mei Ling before circling the couch as if he was herding them all together before he went and sat back down again.

Rudi sat down next to Lukas and put a hand on his arm before Lukas jumped back up again. "Should we get started?" Rudi asked quietly.

"Yes! Yes," Lukas said.

Peter cringed. Had he ever been that excitable as a boy?

Cai showed him the pair of them tumbling and cawing, high in the air above the hills west of Seattle.

All right, so maybe sometimes he had been.

"Let's get started. Can everyone sit down?" Lukas asked.

The twins sat down on the other couch while Mei Ling and Ariel perched on chairs.

What would he see if the raven clan hadn't been cursed? How would Mei Ling show signs of her crocodile soul? A long snout, or maybe golden eyes? Would he be able to see the shadows of Ariel's tusks?

Peter hadn't found an account from the raven's perspective of their great betrayal. He hoped that one of the old books would have a clue. Not what had happened —but why.

Lukas stood and moved behind the couch he'd been

sitting on. He stood taller as he looked at them. "I started having nightmares, premonitions, about the end of the world when I was five. So believe me when I tell you, I know the horrors we face."

Was Lukas' hound soul close to him? It was the only reason Peter could think of for the change in Lukas—how he'd suddenly gone from puppyish excitement to calm leadership.

"The consequences, however—the complete annihilation of this world and possibly others—is worth the risk.

"You are all here because you're special. There's something in you, native to you, that we can use in the coming battle.

"Sally, you're the brave heart, while Peter, you're the healing one. Virmal, your magic and calm are the opposite of the shadows'. Mei Ling, your ferocity and strong scales are the armor we need. And Ariel, you can see through the shadows' lies.

"Together, we can defeat them."

"How?" Virmal asked. "What are we supposed to do tonight?"

"I—I don't know," Lukas admitted. "I just know that together, all of you form the knight."

"Is it a literal knight?" Mei Ling asked. "Or metaphysical?"

"Do we transform somehow, into this knight?" Ariel asked. "'Cause, I'm sure y'all are nice, but I don't want to get that close."

"When I was a boy, I thought there was a knight. Now, I don't know. You all make up his scent. From you comes his essence," Lukas explained.

"Foretellings are not always clear," Mei Ling said.

"Even the best—and I have known many—cannot tell you directly what will be."

Why did Mei Ling have such regret in her voice? Just listening to her made Peter sad. Who had she lost recently?

"Will the shadows come?" Harita asked. "Once we're assembled?"

"I believe so, yes. In all my dreams, the knight is the only one who can defeat them. If the shadows can destroy him, nothing will stand in their way. So they will come. They'll be drawn irresistibly to our gathering. And then, we will fight."

"Then why aren't they here now?" Ariel asked. "It ain't because it's day out—they attacked me in broad daylight that second time."

"I've encircled the room with my special brine," Virmal explained. "It won't defeat the shadows, but it makes them uninterested."

Peter sniffed, finally detecting the faint smell of vinegar and mint.

"You'll each get a jar before you go," Lukas told them. "The shadows may attack us individually, before we gather."

"Great," Ariel muttered. "That's all I need. Another damn attack."

Peter squeezed Sally's hand. They'd walked downtown from her place and had planned on walking back up the hill. They'd both been alert and watching the traffic, just in case the shadows tried to confuse a driver and send him or her careening onto the sidewalk and after them.

"We know how important this is," Virmal said. "But if Harita and I are hurt…well, the tiger clan may seek retribution from the hound clan."

"Yeah, the boars may come riding for your ass," Ariel added.

"The raven clan…" Peter stopped, considering. "I don't know if they'd be more pissed or relieved if I'm gone. Sorry. I've upset them recently." More than upset them, really. One of the elders would probably challenge him in the next couple of weeks.

"I doubt the crocodile clan will care about my death," Mei Ling stated bluntly. "I was born outside the families."

Peter blinked. He'd never heard of such a thing.

Of course, under Prefect Aaron's rule, if the raven clan discovered someone born out of the families, they probably would have declared him a half-breed and killed him.

Rudi sat up abruptly. "You're a wild one?" he asked.

Mei Ling gave a toothy smile. "I am. I believe, in some way, we are all outcasts from our clan—different, yes?"

"I'm not," Ariel declared. "But the boar clan families ain't as closely knit together as y'all to start with."

Peter slowly nodded. He hadn't started out different, but somewhere along the line, he'd changed. Maybe that had been Jesse's influence—the closest thing he'd had to a best friend growing up.

"If we get through tonight, what happens then?" Peter asked.

Lukas shrugged. "Go back to your lives?"

Cai shook himself at that. No, there would need to be more. More healing.

Maybe Sally and Lukas were right about Peter. The battle would leave scars—both externally and ones that didn't show, he knew.

"I say, brunch tomorrow afternoon, here," Sally declared cheerily.

"Yes, eat and celebrate," Harita exclaimed.

Peter wanted to join in their optimism and good cheer, but he didn't trust what the night would bring.

SEATTLE, PRESENT DAY

LUKAS

Lukas blinked hard and tried to clear his vision when Rudi flicked on the large spotlights over the field. The green grass sparkled in the bright, false daylight. The ground, saturated from the spring rain, squished under his new hiking boots.

A tennis court sat between the field and the apartments to the west. The two-story, brick community center and annex buildings blocked the north, and the east was partially blocked by a group of tall pines. There was only a street and a hill separating the south from the field, and Lukas intended to stay well away from there.

The shadows couldn't hide anywhere on the field.

Mei Ling crossed the field with Rudi, both dressed all in black, looking determined.

Harita strode across next, now wearing a blood-red sari, while Virmal followed, in a traditional tunic and trousers, in black. They stepped in perfect unison, as if they listened to lilting dance music.

Peter and Sally came last, in typical Seattle-flannel

hoodies. Ariel walked with them, in black motorcycle leathers.

Lukas took in a deep breath, taking in the scent of the assembled warriors.

His knight. It was a more complex scent than he'd remembered, with threads of ripe wheat fields and fertile Seattle mud in addition to the cool glass, fierce heart, hard scales, and calm mint. The sharp bite of the knight's sword was missing, but Lukas felt sure that would come.

But all the warriors he needed to assemble were here.

"Now, we wait?" Mei Ling asked.

Lukas looked at the assembled warriors, each so strong, standing with nothing to do in the middle of an empty field.

"Yes?" Lukas said. He looked at Rudi, who shrugged.

"They'll come," Rudi assured Lukas.

Lukas shook himself. His neck hairs pricked up. "It shouldn't be too long." Embarrassment crept in. What if he was wrong?

The warriors shuffled from foot to foot, looking around.

Lukas raised his head and sniffed. Something had shifted, like a wind that suddenly puffed from a different direction, changing course.

He turned his head, seeking the change.

There. At the south end of the field, where the lights were the weakest.

The scent of the shadows rolled out, foul in the clear night. Lukas squinted; the bright lights overhead made it difficult to see past the edges of the park.

From the thin row of trees and bushes, shadows stirred through the dead leaves, rustling in the quiet night, slithering like great snakes.

Hamlin pushed at Lukas.

Lukas pushed back. *No*. He couldn't change. Not here. Not with the shadows so close. What would happen if they trapped him?

The other warriors started transforming. Peter's fingers had already changed to great feather-like blades ending in talons, a beak forming on his face. Virmal's skin grew orange, white, and black fur, while his hands grew into long, sharp claws. Ariel had tusks that curled up from her bottom jaw, along with hard eyes and wicked, knife-sharp hooves. Mei Ling's face had pushed out into a snout with glittering teeth.

"Sally, Harita, Rudi, in the center," Lukas panted.

Hamlin kept pressing against him. He couldn't change. Not until the knight formed.

"No," Sally said. "That's—that's not right."

"You're not a warrior," Peter squawked.

"You're the heart," Lukas said. Shouldn't the heart stay at the center?

Reluctantly, Sally stood in the center of the circle of warriors.

Hamlin pushed images at Lukas, of strong teeth and great claws. Not hound form, no, but at least a hound warrior, so they could defend themselves.

Lukas had never taken this form before. But he trusted Hamlin to show him.

Quick as his other changes, Lukas' snout pushed out, his nails grew into sharp, black claws, and hair pricked out of his face and chest. It settled on him like mist, comfortable and familiar, as natural as his hound form, or perhaps even more so: A true amalgamation of his human and hound souls, forming a warrior. Like the others, he didn't wear armor—it rose from within; the strongest silver lined his bones and protected his flesh.

A tall Douglas pine swayed in the southeast corner of

the field, moved by a wind that didn't ruffle Lukas' fur. Then it shuddered and split into two.

A towering shadow lumbered forward.

Fear ran down Lukas' back, his hackles rising further, like sharp blades ripping through his shirt but protecting his back and neck.

The chaotic, boiling clouds rose up and up. Lukas had to crane his head back just to see the top of it. The thing had no face, no eyes, no hands or mouth. Nothing for Lukas' eye to rest on, nothing to address. Foul scents of moldering corpses and bitter acid rolled over him.

"Ready," Mei Ling hissed.

A quick glance around showed Lukas that a wall of darkness and thick shadows had formed around them. They were surrounded by shadows. The bright field lights bounced off the dark clouds.

The thing in front of Lukas rolled to a halt. "Little one," it said, its tone jolly. "Is this all you can bring against me?"

Lukas stiffened, a growl reverberating in his chest.

The shadows had never talked to him before. They'd never communicated directly.

"We've been seeking you for so long," the thing continued. "The viper, he was seeking you, too."

"Where is the viper warrior?" Lukas asked. There was a trace of the viper clan in the awful scent, but it was thin and corrupted.

"We left him behind, resting, recovering from his great deeds," the thing said. "He has provided us with so much, giving us form. It will be so much easier, now, to live here."

"No," Lukas said, shuddering. "You cannot stay. You can't stop consuming. You'll destroy this world like you destroyed your own."

"If that happens, we will simply move on," the shadow replied.

"You will be stopped here. Now," Lukas said, growling.

"By you, little one? Or the puny birdman, or the kitten? I think not."

Shadows suddenly flew through the air, thudding solidly into Lukas' chest.

Lukas eagerly clawed at the shadows pushing against his chest. Finally! They were physical and he could really fight them.

He howled when acid bit into his hand.

The things were solid, and full of deadly acid.

Lukas fought frantically, tearing the things off and flinging them away, growling. He tried biting into them, but the acid ate into his tongue and he couldn't spit— his warrior mouth wasn't designed for that.

Mei Ling, beside him, whirled and had some success beating shadows on the ground with her tail. The smell of burnt fur rose from Virmal and Ariel, while Peter howled as he sliced through shadows with his knife-like fingers.

Why wasn't the knight assembling? Why weren't the warriors fighting together? And where was the knight's sword?

Rudi fought the shadows as best he could as well, trying to keep them away from Harita and Sally. But Rudi couldn't protect them. Acid burned his snout and paws as well.

Something wasn't right. Sally smelled scared, not like the wild, beating heart.

It was worse than any of Lukas' nightmares.

Lukas backed up as the shadows pressed in. The others pressed back as well. They were running out of room, out of time.

Where was his knight?

Dark, Hamlin said. *Dark now.*

"Rudi! Cut the lights!" Lukas called out as he clawed off another shadow threatening to drill into him, to corrupt his soul.

With a snarl, Rudi bounced up, leaping over the assembled group and racing toward the shed that contained the switches, shadows streaming after him.

Lukas desperately fought on, trying to keep the shadows back, fighting to keep the humans safe. But Sally cried when a spray of acid flew through the air and bit into her cheek.

How could they defeat these things? They weren't pure shadow. Peter had said the viper had put his poison into them, making them corporeal.

And unfortunately, even more deadly.

The humming lights fell silent and darkness overcame them.

The shadows paused their attack. They were almost impossible to see in the dark, at least until their eyes adjusted.

Hamlin propelled Lukas forward. Lukas bit into the large, towering thing, pulling off a hunk, worrying it and then dropping it.

His mouth didn't burn.

The shadows flowed together around the leader, then dissipated like morning fog, growing thinner and lighter until they disappeared.

Lukas turned around, panting. His eyes adjusted and he examined his warriors, all changed back to human.

Mei Ling's perfect hair was pulled to the side, her mouth and chin torn and bloody. Peter cradled his bleeding hand to his chest, and even in the dark, Lukas could tell his normally dark skin was pale. Virmal had burns all down his right arm. Arial sat on the ground, crooning, holding her arms tightly across her chest.

Even Sally and Harita were hurt. Rudi, too.

"I'm sorry," Lukas whispered, though he wanted to howl.

Why hadn't bringing these people together, with the threat of the shadows, assembled the knight? Where was the knight's sword? Was Lukas still missing someone? Was there something else wrong?

How was Lukas going to defeat the shadows if the one thing his dreams had foretold wasn't true?

UNITED STATES, TWENTY-TWO YEARS AGO TO PRESENT

SALLY

O ne of Sally's earliest memories was of trying to save the world.

She couldn't have been more than four or five at the time. They had traveled to La Jolla, California, to visit Dad's mom and dad.

Salt tinged the skin around Sally's lips and the warm sun kissed the top of her head. Grandma had tied her black-and-white-checked dishtowel under Sally's chin, so it flapped against her blindingly pink one-piece suit as she charged across the wet sand toward the waves. In her memory, she always shrieked as she dashed into the water, though she knew her mom wouldn't have stood that for long.

With her arms spread wide, Sally commanded the ocean to stop threatening her sand castle village. She raced back out of the water, to her masterpiece, scolding every encroaching wave.

It never worked. The water always won.

But that didn't stop Sally from trying even harder the next time.

S ally missed her dad after he moved out. She missed his funny stories about wild bands of alligators saving the high school or the teddy bear pirates rescuing the princess. She missed his carefully crafted, blobby pancakes and the outrageous lies he'd tell about how they resembled dinosaurs or castles.

She didn't miss the fights between Mom and Dad. Though they'd yelled at each other in whispers in their room, they didn't realize the vent above their bed went straight into Sally's room and she heard every hissed word and curse.

Liz and Mary, Sally's two older sisters, didn't like going to Dad's house on his weekend. Mom quickly claimed they were old enough to make their own decision, so it was generally only Sally who raced up the cracked and weed-covered sidewalk to where her dad stood on the porch with open arms and a sad smile.

Mom called Dad's house a shack. It stank like dog pee, the green plastic tiles on the kitchen floor were cracked and broken, it boiled in the Minnesota summer, and the cold winter winds pushed through the gaps around the windows.

Sally still loved it. The front room had floor to ceiling bookcases along two walls, as well as wide windows overlooking the porch and the yard. The tiny room Sally slept in was crammed full of brightly colored, half-finished canvases and always smelled like mineral oil. She loved the statue Dad had made that stood guard over her bed, created out of "found art": branches blown down during last summer's storm made up his arms, bottle caps formed his eyes and crooked smile, and bubble gum wrappers outlined his vest and tie.

More fascinating pieces filled Dad's room, such as the copper-wire-and-bolt men that floated on the ends of the mobile above his bed, the fantasy garden painting that he used to block one of his windows, and the window shade made of soft bearskin, leather, yarn, and cotton.

The weekend they celebrated Sally's eighth birthday, after presents and chocolate-chip-ice-cream cake, Dad asked Sally to sit down in the front room to talk.

Sally sat heavily, the cold from the ice cream still rolling around her belly. She knew it was going to be bad: Dad's art had changed again. Before he'd moved out, the usual happy faces he painted were suddenly tinged with blue, and the city he'd painted, with the broken walls and blank windows, had scared her. He'd started painting bright yellow sunflowers and cities filled with trees after he'd moved out, but now his art was filled with desert scenes in cool oranges, and sunsets over ancient gray and black stones.

"You know I love you, darling," Dad started. He knelt next to the old beige couch, his ginger-colored hair graying along the temples, wearing his blue denim painting shirt covered in splotches of all colors.

The books towered over them, and normally Sally felt most safe here, curled up on this couch, escaping into new worlds and faraway places.

"But?" Sally asked when Dad didn't continue right away, knowing the worst was yet to come. It had been too special of a birthday for everything to work out right.

"I need to go back home. To California."

Sally's chest suddenly hurt, as if Dad had stabbed her with his big tin shears. "But why?"

"I need to be back near the ocean. It's where my heart is," Dad said. "You can come visit."

"No, I can't," Sally said, tears hitching up, out of her

eyes, and down her cheeks. "Since you and Mom split, there hasn't been a single trip to California. Mom says it's too expensive, and you can't afford it."

Dad rocked back on his heels. "Where did you hear that? From your mother?"

Sally indicated the room. "You live here. We had to move, too, and I have to share a room, now, with Mary," she said softly. "There just isn't enough money."

Dad opened his mouth, then closed it again. "If there isn't a trip, it isn't because I don't love you or don't want you to be there. But you may be right. How did you get so wise?"

"Wasn't from you," Sally teased through her tears.

Dad chuckled. "Nope. Your mom was always the smart, sensible one. But baby girl, sometimes you've got to follow your heart. It isn't easy. But if you listen, and listen well, it will always tell you the truth."

"I don't believe you," Sally said. "You can't just follow your heart. Not if it means you're leaving." Mom had said Dad was always leaving—not finishing college, not sticking with jobs, now, not staying with them in Minnesota.

"You have a strong heart, too," Dad told her. "Stronger than your sisters. I know. I can see it. If you don't follow it, you'll regret it."

"There has to be more," Sally insisted.

"Oh, honey," Dad said, reaching out and squeezing her hand. "There so much for you to learn. It isn't about being wild or free. It's about being true to who you are."

"But why can't you do that here?" Sally asked, her own heart breaking.

"I would if I could, darling," Dad replied.

Though Sally let Dad hold her as she cried, she was

also determined to prove him wrong. She would figure out how to follow her heart *and* stay.

Sally followed her dad's advice and let her heart lead her into non-profit work—focusing on feeding families when they fell into bad circumstances, like her family had—then to Seattle.

When Peter came dancing into her life, Sally nearly called her dad that night. He'd been right: Her heart had always been strong. However, he'd never told her that there might be more pieces of her heart out there, waiting for her to find them.

Sally's heart told her to stay when Peter lied to her. She knew he was holding back about the tiger thing that had attacked her, the thing that Pixie had defended her from.

For the first time, Sally truly understood that staying wasn't always enough—that the brave thing to do was to walk away. She needed to have all her heart if she was going to live, and staying when Peter wouldn't let her in would only hurt her in the long run.

Of course, Sally had never imagined that Peter was hiding a raven soul.

After Sally learned about Ravens' Hall and the way they'd tortured the boys there, she understood just how brave Peter had been to tell her as much as he had.

It convinced her that she'd always been right: The will of her heart always had to be tempered with courage.

Sally had always known Pixie was special. She'd been as drawn to him as he had been to her when she first saw him at the shelter.

After the attack by the tiger creature, she suspected there was more, much more, to Pixie.

Sally wasn't surprised when the awkward, tall boy with the raven black hair who was Pixie's human form—Lukas—named her the heart of his knight.

Nor was she surprised when Peter tried to immediately talk her out of fighting the instant Lukas left.

"I don't like the idea of you in a battle," Peter started out, taking Sally's hand and drawing her to the couch. "I can't lose you."

Sally sighed, wrapped her arms around Peter, and held his head to her chest. "I couldn't lose you, either," she said. "Which is what I'd do if I insisted that you always stay safe. You had to fight that tiger warrior, Tamara. I would have lost you if you hadn't, as surely as if she'd killed you with her bare hands."

The man in her arms shuddered. "She did try to kill me."

"I know. And you had to fight her. Just as I have to fight with you, beside you."

"What if Lukas is wrong?"

"Do you think he's wrong?" Sally asked. "It's an awful long time to be cursed in the form of a hound and have it not be true."

Peter grunted. "I know. I just—I don't like these shadows. They're awful. I still don't want it to be you fighting them."

"We'll be careful." Sally suspected she'd be more on edge for a while, ever since the attack the previous night. "How about this? If I notice you not behaving, or being weird, like how Lukas said you might, I'll just smack you. Like this." She playfully slapped his arm.

Peter sighed and looked up at her. "The shadows are real," he said. His eyes grew dark, and Sally knew he was talking with his raven soul.

"And you will be in danger," he added after a moment.

"The whole world will be in danger," Sally pointed out. "It's up to us to save it."

After all, she'd always wanted to save the world.

W hen Lukas ordered Sally and Harita and Rudi to the center of the warriors, Sally knew he was wrong.

She wasn't there to be protected.

The clan warriors transformed around her, showing their true natures: fierce claws and sharp teeth. She doubted her heart, then. She couldn't fight as they could. Maybe it was better for her to be inside the circle.

At the first cry of pain, though, Sally knew she'd been right. The heart wasn't supposed to be protected—she was supposed to inspire the warriors and lead them.

But how?

Early the next morning, Sally lay on top of the bed while Peter still lay under the covers. His normally dark skin was still pale. The white bandage covering his burned hand lay outside the blanket, stark against her navy blue sheets. She lay on her left side—the bandage covering the burn on her right cheek hurt too much when she lay on it.

"I need to go talk to Lukas," Sally told Peter as she pushed her tired body up. She hadn't fought, but she found she was just as exhausted as everyone else. The shadows had drained all of them, sucked out their life.

"All right," Peter said with a sigh, lifting one corner of the sheets.

Sally pressed his hand down. "No. You're staying here."

"But—"

"Peter. I know." Sally tried to shove her own fear to the side, though it still hung like a tight ball in the middle of her chest. "Those shadow things are awful. But I need to talk to Lukas. Alone. And…" Sally paused, then made herself sit all the way up, forcing herself away from the comfort and warmth of her mate. "I need to go by myself. I need to not be scared of everything outside or of being away from you."

"You don't have to do this alone," Peter protested.

"Yes, I do, and you know it," Sally said as she finally stood up. "I'll text you when I get there. And when I'm on my way back."

"I don't like it," Peter said stubbornly. "You shouldn't go. Not alone."

"I love you," Sally told him, warmth bubbling up where there had only been fear and anxiety before. "And I won't ever do everything you want me to do."

"I know," Peter said, still sulking.

Sally took his good hand in hers, squeezing the fingers. "I promise to be back as soon as I can. But I have to go alone."

"I don't have to like it," Peter said. "But we trust you."

Sally fetched Peter's phone, gave him a last kiss, then stepped out into the brilliant Seattle spring sunlight. She shoved her hands deeper into the pockets of her hoodie and breathed deeply. It was too beautiful a day, particularly after the horror of the night before, to be stuck inside.

Still, Sally didn't dawdle on her way to house Lukas and Rudi shared.

Lukas opened the door before Sally even knocked.

"What is it?" he asked, his black hair mussed, his face young and vulnerable, as if he'd just woken up. "What's wrong?"

"What, you mean Peter didn't call to tell you I was coming?" Sally asked, amused.

Lukas looked down, sheepishly, at his long bare toes. "He did. But he couldn't explain what was wrong."

"It's okay," Sally said. "We need to talk about what happened last night."

Lukas looked up, worried. "You're not quitting, are you? You'll stay? You'll come and fight again tonight?"

"I'm not quitting," Sally said hurriedly. "But we have to figure out what went wrong."

"I know," Lukas said, slumping more. "Come on in."

The smell of bacon and morning coffee still lingered in the air. The bright yellow walls of the living room surprised Sally—it seemed more modern than what she expected Rudi would choose. She liked the big comfortable couches and the white-painted mantel with the portraits on it.

"Here. Sit," Lukas said, flopping down. He immediately stood up again. "Should I get you anything?"

"It's fine," Sally said, sitting down and patting the couch next to her. "It's polite to ask, but we're also friends. We're fine."

"Good," Lukas said, sitting beside her but not looking at her. "I don't know what happened last night. What went wrong."

"Have you ever fought the shadows before? By yourself?" Sally asked.

Lukas shook his head. "Only in my nightmares. I've never seen them before, like they were last night. I thought

—I thought it would help, you know, that they were physical. That we'd be able to fight them, finally."

"What about when you were cursed?" Sally asked. "Didn't you fight the shadows then? Didn't they attack you if you transformed into your human form?"

Lukas shivered, and Sally bit her lip. Maybe she shouldn't have asked that.

"They did attack. Trying to get inside me. To control me. Even when…" Lukas paused, his gaze distant. "I did fight the shadows one other time," he said softly after a long moment. "When I broke the curse. I couldn't really fight them, though. I had to let them roll over me. I had to endure them before I could break free."

"So you didn't fight?" Sally asked.

Lukas shook his head. "I've never fought and won. Not on my own. Only the knight has been able to do that."

"You've brought together a brave group of warriors, from all the different clans," Sally pointed out. "Of course they all want to fight the shadows. But maybe that isn't what they need to do."

"It's too much," Lukas protested. "To ask them to accept, to endure the shadows. It's too hard."

"But that's why I'm here," Sally pointed out gently. "I'll bring them through. That's what the heart is supposed to do, isn't it?"

Lukas sighed and looked at his hands, rubbing the left over the bandage wrapped around his right. "Peter won't like it. You, in danger. In the fight."

"You don't like it, either," Sally pointed out.

Lukas shook his head *no*.

"You can't really guard me, though, unless I do," Sally said, trying to reassure him. "You're the guardian hound. That's your job. To protect us while we endure."

"That makes sense. But—" Lukas sighed. "I don't

want to change. To…transform into my hound soul. I'm afraid I won't be able to change back."

"I understand," Sally said, nodding. "But you're going to have to," she added gently. "The knight needs his hound." She remembered reading about knights and their hounds in history class, going off to battle together.

"I know," Lukas said. "I will guard you as best I can," he promised.

"And we will endure," Sally promised in return.

She not only had a heart that beat wild and true, but the courage to stay—what her dad had always lacked.

SEATTLE, PRESENT DAY

LUKAS

A much more subdued group gathered in Mei Ling's expensive suite late that afternoon. Lukas winced at every bandage and scar that he saw. The sunken eyes and pained expressions hurt him greatly. His own wounds were nothing compared to what he'd put the others through.

"It'll be all right," Rudi assured Lukas quietly, standing beside him.

Lukas shook his head *no*, but didn't say anything.

All of the clan members that he'd found were warriors, trained to fight like how Rudi was training Lukas. He knew how strong the urge was to use tooth and claw against your enemy.

To stay still, strong, and endure in human form…how could he ask them to do that?

But Sally was right. He must.

Lukas waited while everyone got settled. Mei Ling draped herself over one of the chairs, her makeup hiding her injuries, but her dark eyes still showed how much pain she was in. Ariel sat more stiffly in the other, her face deliberately blank. Virmal sat even closer to Harita, looking as though he wanted to tear something—anything —apart. Peter and Sally looked pale and drawn.

Hamel pressed closer as Lukas cleared his throat. "Last night didn't go how I'd hoped," he said.

"You don't say," Ariel said dryly.

Lukas nodded, feeling his cheeks grow enflamed. "I'm sorry. I made more than one mistake, and I put you all in danger."

"You hurt my brother," Harita hissed.

Virmal gave a deep growl.

All the hackles stood up on the back of Lukas' neck. He didn't want to fight Virmal, not just because he was supposed to be working together with him, but because there was some odd attraction he didn't understand that made him want to bite and not tear.

"Hush, you," Ariel said dismissively.

Virmal turned to glare at her, still growling.

"Y'all don't scare me," she drawled. "So just put it back in your pants."

Part of Lukas was indignant at how Ariel talked to Virmal, yet part of him snickered at the putdown.

"We're not here to fight each other," Peter interjected.

"No, we're here to fight the shadows. And we lost," Mei Ling said pointedly. "I don't like to lose."

"I know," Lukas said. "And I'm sorry. But next time, it will be different."

It had to be different. Or they'd all be dead.

"So what are we supposed to do?" Peter asked. "What do you want us to do differently?"

"The only time I've ever really successfully fought the shadows on my own...I didn't fight," Lukas admitted.

Mei Ling raised one cool eyebrow at him. The rest of the warriors just stared at him.

God, he was such an idiot. He still pushed on. "I've

always just had to, uhm, endure, I guess. Not fight. Let the shadows do their worst, spend themselves, finish their attack. Only then could I break away."

"Not fight?" Virmal asked. "We're sitting ducks."

"If we give up, we'll die," Mei Ling said. "That's what you've said. The whole world. Dead."

"No, no, you're not supposed to give up. But just, hold on. As warriors, you're all strong, and different. Unique. But in human form—"

"We're weak," Ariel interjected.

"You may be able to combine, to transform, and be greater than you are individually," Lukas finished.

"Is that what your visions tell you?" Mei Ling asked.

"My visions aren't as clear as that. But somehow, you must form the knight. If you don't..." Lukas didn't have to finish that.

"But how will we protect ourselves, if we can't fight?" Virmal asked. "Who will protect my sister?"

Harita rolled her eyes at him. Lukas knew she didn't think she was the one who needed protecting.

"I will protect you," Lukas assured them. Hamlin pressed close, and Lukas' voice grew rough. "We are the guardian hound. And that was my second mistake."

"What do you mean?" Ariel asked sourly.

"I didn't take my true hound form, last night. I—I was afraid. I was cursed and forced to stay in hound form for ten years. I didn't transform, not as I should have," Lukas admitted.

Virmal snorted. "A hound? Protecting us? You have no claws, no armor."

"He is the size of small horse. You might be surprised," Peter replied.

"So we meet again tonight, to not fight?" Mei Ling asked. "I don't like it."

The rest of the warriors nodded.

"But you'll be there?" Lukas asked.

"The birdman promised me a fight," Ariel said. "But I ain't got a better suggestion. The first time I fought those damn shadows, I couldn't do anything, either."

"We'll be there," Harita said quietly.

"And the shadows won't be the only thing hunting you if we don't survive," Virmal promised.

A large drop of water plopped onto Lukas' nose as he stepped out of the house. He shook his head and looked up. Solid clouds blocked the night sky, reflecting back orange from the streetlights.

Of course it would rain tonight. The clear spring weather wouldn't hold.

Lukas sighed and brought up the hood on his jacket, shoving his hands into the front pockets. All his clothes—his sweatpants, T-shirt, jacket, and even his boots—were loose, so he could slip out of them easily when he transformed.

The wind blew cold and clean, carrying scents of cherry blossoms, crocuses, and new grass. Lukas shivered, and Rudi placed a hand on his shoulder, urging him forward into the wet night. Rudi left his hand there, giving Lukas a solid weight to ground him.

Hamlin bounded up to Lukas, then sank back down again.

Lukas didn't share the excitement of his hound soul: Dread marched with him, lining his stomach, making his chest leaden.

They didn't bother turning on the lights at Miller's Park this time. The ground squished under Lukas' feet, the tops of his boots already soaked through. The rain had turned into a mist, fine and persistently wetting everything it touched.

"Thanks for coming back tonight," Lukas told the assembled group. They all looked bedraggled by the rain, tired, and everyone bore wounds from the night before, bandages gleaming in the dark.

"So what do we do?" Peter asked.

Lukas looked to Sally.

"Let's try standing in a circle, holding hands," Sally suggested, taking Peter's hand in hers, then reaching for Virmal's.

"I don't do this Kumbaya shit," Ariel muttered, staring at the group, her arms crossed over her chest.

Harita took Virmal's hand, then reached out to Ariel with the other, while Rudi on the far side did the same.

"Fine," Ariel said, swinging out her arms and grabbing the offered hands.

As soon as the circle closed, shadows sprang into the night. They rushed at the group, speeding like snakes, rustling darkness across the wet grass.

"Closer!" Sally urged. She threw an arm around Peter's shoulders, drawing them in.

Rudi looked up from the group. "It's time," he told Lukas.

Fear struck Lukas. He didn't want to do this. His friends—the knight—they would stay human. Why did he have to change?

With a whining growl, Lukas stripped his hoodie and T-shirt over his head and toed off his wet boots. The ground was freezing against his bare feet and his skin was already wet.

Lukas spread his arms out and raised his face to the cloud-covered sky.

Come, he told Hamlin.

Let go, Hamlin replied.

Shadows slid past Lukas' feet, heading toward his friends. The tall tree in the corner of the field shook. It was only moments before the tall shadow thing was back.

How could Lukas let go? He wanted to fight. He *needed* to fight.

Fight, yes. And survive, Hamlin assured him.

But he couldn't fight. He'd never been enough, just by himself, to fight and win.

Endure. It was all Lukas was good at.

Lukas dropped his head down to his chest, his arms falling, then he let go, leaning against his hound soul, trusting that Hamlin would catch him.

Quicker than a blink, Lukas found he'd transformed. He growled, fighting back his panic. He wanted to change back to human, to see if he could, but there was no time.

Shadows slammed into the exposed backs of the huddled humans. Sally, Virmal, and Ariel all cried out in pain. Then Sally yelled, "Stay! Stay here!"

Lukas didn't know which warrior fought not to transform. He knew all of them wanted to. But Sally kept the group together, held them there, helped them endure.

With careful teeth, Lukas tore one long skinny shadow, then another, away from the group, flinging them across the field.

But there were too many for him to grab, and they came too fast.

"Closer," Sally called.

The group of humans burrowed into one another, their sides and heads touching.

Suddenly, a light sprang up above the group. Up it grew, fleshing out, taking shape and form.

The scent of the group flourished, overcoming the

stench of the shadows: cool glass and fresh mint, strong blood and warm silk.

Above Lukas, finally, stood his knight. He wore a full peaked helmet, with just a slit for the eyes. A solid chest plate covered his torso, while fine chain protected his arms. Broad gauntlets and leg greaves were buckled around his hands and shins. None of his armor looked new: It had all seen battle before, a dull silver with dents and patches.

Hamlin barked, greeting the knight happily. But the knight stayed frozen, floating above the group of humans, unmoving.

Where was the knight's sword?

Lukas turned and raced off to where the towering shadow beast had pulled itself out of the trees.

Another being strode beside it: a tall, dark man. A single sniff told Lukas it was a viper warrior; the acrid smell of clan poison mingled with his blood.

Was it the one from Tulum? Lukas wanted to howl. The viper warrior been thoroughly corrupted by the shadows.

"Good puppy," the thing called to Lukas. "Go fetch." It threw a ball of shadows at the knight. It hit the knight solidly in his chest, staining the metal further. But the knight didn't move, and stayed frozen above the field.

Lukas growled in frustration. What else was he missing? Why wasn't the knight acting, moving? The other warriors were going to kill him, if the shadows didn't, if they failed again.

Hamlin pushed them forward, diving toward the tall shadow thing, hoping to tear into it again as they had the night before.

The viper warrior was faster, however. He slashed out

at Lukas. Only Hamlin's quick reflexes skidded them to the side, narrowly avoiding the claws.

The viper warrior snarled, his fangs exposed and dripping. His eyes were as black as the shadows.

What did he see? What did he think he was attacking?

Then the viper warrior struck out at Lukas again.

"Play nice, boys," the shadow thing said as it rumbled across the field, heading toward the assembled group of humans and the nascent knight.

Lukas had to stop it.

However, the viper warrior was quicker than either Lukas or Hamlin expected. He attacked again, snarling and racing toward them.

Hamlin rose now, pushing Lukas further back. He leaped at the viper warrior, raising up on his hind legs, then crashing down, striking the man with his chest, forcing him to the ground.

The viper slashed up with his hands, tearing apart Hamlin's sides.

Hamlin struck out, and set his teeth around the viper warrior's throat.

The viper warrior stilled.

No! Lukas screamed. He'd only ever fought shadows. He didn't want to kill a man.

"Please," the viper warrior whispered. "Do it."

Hamlin snapped down their jaws, biting through the man's jugular. Then he shook the body, getting a better hold, tearing out the man's throat.

The viper warrior gave a peaceful sigh as he settled into the ground, death bringing a smile to his face.

Lukas backed up. Horror tripped through his veins.

He'd just murdered a man. What would Rudi say?

Shadows fled out of the man's body, making it suddenly lighter. The body started to glow. The light grew longer, brighter, sharper, until it flew up, out of the man's body, like an arrow, straight for the knight.

Stop! Lukas howled.

The knight suddenly moved. He held up his hand, and the light flew into it, growing steady and strong, changing into the knight's sword.

Lukas' sides ached where he'd been clawed, and his mouth burned from the poison he'd swallowed. But joy flooded through him as he watched the knight stride away from the group of humans, marching directly to the shadow beast, hacking and slicing into it.

The shadow fought back. Great sizzling filled the quiet night when the shadow's acid bit into the knight's armor. It used thin pieces of shadow like whips, smacking into the knight, scoring his arms, chest, and legs.

Lukas raced back across the field to the now-kneeling group. Shadows covered them, attacking every part they could reach. Sally hummed a quiet song, the melody jerking every time the shadows hit her.

Carefully, Lukas and Hamlin pulled the larger shadows away from the group, trying to give them some breathing room. Then he hurried back to the knight, harrying the shadow beast, not letting it retreat when the knight attacked.

Slowly, the shadow creature shrank. The knight continued to hack pieces of it off, pieces that flowed onto the ground and stayed there instead of rejoining the shadow creature.

Lukas again returned to the group of warriors. Fewer shadows attacked them. He tore around the group, circling quickly and flinging away as many shadows as he could before he rejoined the knight.

Just as Lukas reached the knight's side, the knight

swung his sword over his head, then down, biting into the shadow, slicing it in two.

Both halves quivered for a moment. Would they rejoin? But no, both halves tumbled to the ground, like a sand castle melting under a great wave. A spring wind skirted across the field, tossing the remaining shadows away like dry ash.

The knight paused, taking a deep breath and lowering his sword to the ground. He didn't remove his helmet, but now Lukas remembered the knight. They rushed forward, and the knight leaned down to pat their head.

Golden fields and a village made of clay. Older times before the rise of industrial machines. Hamlin and the knight had saved each other in battle so many times, then died together, protecting elders from the hound clan and promising to always do so.

Hamlin gave one last happy bark, seeing his true master again, before the knight faded away, dissolving into the mist.

Lukas shook himself, finding himself suddenly standing on two feet. He wrapped his soul around Hamlin's, feeling the weight of his sorrow. No matter how close Lukas and Hamlin were, his old master still had a special place in Hamlin's heart.

Then Lukas hurried over to his wet clothes, drew on his pants and top, and stepped into his boots before approaching the others.

They all stood, now. They looked as grim as they had the night before. Sally hid her face in Peter's chest, Virmal had his arm around Harita, while Rudi supported both Mei Ling and Ariel.

"You did it," Lukas told them breathlessly. "You defeated the shadows."

Rudi raised his head and nodded. "We did." He sighed, exhausted. "Are you all right? Is that blood?"

Lukas turned away guiltily, wiping at his mouth. He looked over where the body of the viper warrior had been.

The spot was empty now, but like Rudi, Lukas could still smell the blood.

"We all fought demons tonight," Mei Ling said. "The cost is always high."

Lukas wondered what price the others had paid, because the group shuddered as one.

"Thank you," Lukas said. "This couldn't have happened without you. And your sacrifice."

"Are they gone?" Ariel asked, sounding weary. "I mean, really gone?"

Lukas asked Hamlin, but he didn't know. "I think so," Lukas finally said. That had been how his dreams had always foretold it. The knight defeated the shadows, and the world was safe.

"But we'll see."

EPILOGUES

SEATTLE AND ELSEWHERE,
PRESENT DAY

SALLY

The nightmare started small. Sally was trying to clean her dad's old place—the shack back in Minnesota. Heavy clouds gathered across the sky, and the building shook from the strength of the wind. Grit filtered through the gaps around the windows until a fine layer of black dust caked over the bright sunflower paintings hanging on the opposite wall.

Plugging the gaps didn't stop the dirt. For every hole Sally filled, two more opened.

The filth covered the couch where Dad had read her stories, then crept up along the books until nothing clean remained. Sally stood paralyzed in the center of the room while the black dirt swirled around her, taking the shape of a nameless shadow that would swallow her soul alive.

Sally woke up sweating, her heart beating out of her chest, her stomach rolling with nausea. She yanked back the soft and suddenly claustrophobic sheets. The streetlight outside shone against the window shade. No cars drove by, and no one stirred in the apartment above hers. She did hear the kitchen tap turn on and off.

Peter came into their bedroom as Sally pushed herself up, her head light while her skin felt scratchy and sweaty. He carried a glass of water. "Was it a nightmare?" he asked, sitting down and handing her the glass.

Sally nodded. She took the heavy glass in both hands and sipped the cool water, clearing away the memory of the dust from her mouth.

"I wasn't sure. You just grew…still," Peter said. "I'll wake you, next time," he assured her, sliding his arm over her shoulder and drawing her closer.

Sally let her weight rest against him, the glass heavy and cold in her hands while Peter was warm and solid at her side.

"It will happen again," Sally warned.

Peter kissed the top of her head. "And I'll be here."

Sally nodded, taking another sip of water. "I'll be here for your nightmares, too," she said.

Peter laughed silently, his chest moving against her shoulder. "Think we'll ever sleep through the night?"

"Just wait 'til we have kids," Sally said. "Then the night terrors will really begin."

"Kids?" Peter asked softly after a long pause.

Sally took a last sip of water and placed it on the night table before curling back up in Peter's arms. "I know we've had such a whirlwind romance we haven't really talked about it—but yeah. Kids. I'd like to have a couple, at least. You?" Sally kept her tone casual, but her stomach was unsettled by more than just the nightmare now.

"You want to have kids. Though you know one of them may turn out like me?" Peter asked.

Sally pushed herself up so she could look Peter in the face. "Of course I'd love to have a kid who's clan. A raven warrior, brave and true like his father. Who will save the world the next time it needs saving."

Peter leaned forward and rested his forehead against Sally's. "If our kid is even half as strong as you are, the world will never be in serious danger."

Sally nodded and yawned.

"Think you can get back to sleep?" Peter asked, kissing her softly.

Sally kissed him back, a little more intently. "Or we could practice. The kid-making part. Give me better memories of tonight." The nightmare had already faded, but Sally knew it would return eventually, if not that night, then some other time.

"As you wish, my love," Peter said, drawing her closer.

For the rest of the night, any shadows that remained were soft and kind to the young couple.

ARIEL

Ariel dreamed she was back on the sodden field, the stupid Seattle rain turning her dreads into heavy, wet ropes. Even through her bike leathers, her knees were cold and wet, and ached after pressing into the hard ground.

The beings Ariel held onto on both sides wavered, like a campfire in a strong wind, transforming into a snarling dog on one side and a vicious tiger on the other.

"Go to Hell," Ariel told the shadows. "You ain't real."

The cold was real. As was the wet, and the rain, and the solid press of Sally's head against her own, the shivering warmth of the tiger kin pressed along one side, the hound who smelled yummy and was oh-so-single on the other.

Ariel loaned her sight as best she could to the others. While Sally sang, hummed, and kept them together, kept them human, Ariel fought the illusions the shadows cast: the shifting forms, the rising tide of filth, the constant barrage of *not good enough, not smart enough, not strong enough, too poor, too black, too female, too Southern.*

Those last few were the hardest. Ariel reminded herself

that she was there, kneeling on that hard ground, chosen by destiny, and she was enough.

They were enough.

But the nightmare continued, and one by one, Ariel's companions fell.

Alone, she wasn't enough.

Morning brought more of that damn Seattle rain. But it was real, and Ariel was not trapped in some nightmare of filth.

Maybe she'd stay. She knew some of the boar clan lived in eastern Washington, out toward Yakima—vineyard workers, of course. Her people were good with the earth. And food and wine, which Seattle had in abundance.

Maybe she could stay for a while.

Better than going it alone, at least for now.

VÍRMAL

"What do you mean, with everyone so sick?" Virmal asked his mother over Skype. The hotel Wi-Fi had been awful before Rudi had loaned him a booster, as well as installed some encryption software on his computer. However, his mother's expression kept freezing, the video connection lagging badly.

"This morning, early, at least half the temple fell ill," Mama continued. Her black hair was pulled back into a bun, her jewelry was the best quality, and her sari was finely made out of blue silk. However, her perfect makeup couldn't hide how pale she looked, and her mouth kept pulling into a thin, disapproving line.

"What is it, you think?" Virmal asked.

Harita stood behind him and reached out to squeeze his shoulder, loaning him her strength, as always.

"No one knows." Mama's face froze again, her eyes wide and scared. "At least half the protection charms for the temple burned out last night as well. And everyone's complaining that their magic feels…weak."

"We will come as soon as we can," Harita assured their

mother.

Virmal looked up at his sister, surprised. Why were they going to India? He had to get back to Germany, to school. And Harita was due back at the hound court.

"We've both been studying medicine, for all the clans," Harita reminded him. "Maybe we can help."

They said their goodbyes quickly, then Virmal turned to face Harita. "You think it's the shadows, don't you? Or the absence of them. That's suddenly made half the court sick and weak."

"Of course!" Harita said, her eyes sparkling as brightly as the rhinestones in her bright orange sari. "We need to go. To help them recover. Show them another way."

"It won't be safe," Virmal felt obligated to point out. "They'll be upset. Angry. More likely to challenge anyone new. They might choose fights with you because they think they can." He flexed his left hand, fire burning along the old scar he'd received defending Harita when they'd first returned to India. Had the wound been infected with shadows, all those years ago? Was that why it had never completely healed?

Harita sobered. "You're right." She paused, then shook her head. "But we have to. If we have the chance, we have to help them rebuild, learn how to be strong without the shadows."

"Then we'll go," Virmal said, though part of him wanted to run the opposite direction. Not because there was trouble for him, no—but because he didn't know how he was going to protect Harita.

But being a tiger warrior had never been about being safe.

And anyone who hurt his sister would have to answer to him.

Hurt one, hurt us all.

RUDI

Rudi shut down his email, turned off his monitor, and pushed back from his desk. He was going to have to arrange a Skype call for Lukas, or another trip to Germany.

Lady Metzler had woken up and wanted to talk to Lukas.

Rudi paced his office agitated. Lady Metzler had played such a huge role throughout his life, directing him, giving him purpose.

She'd trusted him with her grandson, something he would forever be grateful for.

However, she'd also cursed Lukas, forced him to stay in hound form for ten years.

No matter how Rudi tried, he couldn't forgive her for that.

Rudi's hound soul pressed closer. The familiar scent of Lukas' disguise, Pixie, rose up, the tiny black dog with such a huge heart, brave beyond knowing, with large, soulful eyes.

Pack, his hound soul reminded him. *Play?*

Rudi had only changed when he'd absolutely needed to

during the decade he'd taken care of the prince. He'd always needed to be able to plan, to be human.

But now—Lukas could make his own decisions. He was no longer trapped and cursed.

Rudi would have to let Lukas go, now, back to Germany, though his hound soul identified Lukas as not only pack, but home.

Soft sun filtered through the spring clouds, shadows of leaves dappling his floor. Rudi would miss this place when they left. It had been more of a home than anywhere else they'd stayed.

Still. Lukas needed to be told about his grandmother and given the choice about what he wanted to do, where he wanted to go, how he wanted to live. The choice had been taken from him before, and Rudi was determined to give it back to him.

Rudi opened the door to his study and found Lukas there, hovering.

"What's wrong?" Lukas blurted out.

The boy's face was still pale from the fight the previous night. He needed a haircut, too—his black curls fell regularly into his eyes, hiding the searing blue.

"Nothing's wrong," Rudi said firmly. He made himself smile. "There's good news, actually."

"Then why do you smell so worried?" Lukas asked, letting Rudi lead him to the living room.

Rudi sat down on the old, comfortable couch, leaning forward, pressing his palms together. "Lady Metzler, your grandmother, is awake. She's asking for you."

Lukas gave a whole body shudder. "We should go see her," he said, sounding as enthusiastic as if announcing he should go to his own funeral.

"You don't have to," Rudi said. How could he help

Lukas through this? "We could just set up a phone call. Or Skype."

Lukas nodded. "And Greta?"

Now Rudi gave a real smile. "She's better as well."

"Maybe we'll go visit this summer," Lukas finally said.

Relief settled over Rudi. "You want to stay? Here? In Seattle?"

"Duh," Lukas said, sounding every bit the teenager he was. "I like it here. I want to settle for a while. Everything else is new."

"Good, good," Rudi said, nodding. "I like it here, too."

Lukas cocked his head to the side and looked at Rudi for a long moment. "You know what else we're going to do? Become a two-dog family."

"Huh?" Rudi asked, not understanding.

"I know you rarely changed when you were looking after me," Lukas hurriedly explained. "So now, let me take care of you. I'd like to meet your hound soul," he added shyly.

Rudi's hound soul pressed hard against him, sending images and scents and roots to chase along and the wind to race against blowing through his fur and even more scents to follow.

"I'd like that, too," Rudi said, standing.

It was yet another way Rudi could pay back the joy the prince had always brought to him. Plus, it was yet another way to push the battles from the previous days into the past. Lukas' smile had returned that morning, but sorrow still tugged at the ends of it.

And no one could express the pure joy of being with the boy like a hound.

LUKAS

Lukas leaned back on the hard wooden bench, his arms spread wide and his eyes slitted against the sun. Gauner, the name Rudi had given his hound form, a gray-and-white fox terrier with curly hair, raced from one end of the open dog park to the other with his three pals, other dogs who they'd just met, also here to play.

The sun soaked into Lukas' bones, filling him with light, pushing into those places where there'd only been shadows before. When they went home, Lukas knew the light would dribble out, but maybe a little would remain, a tiny bit more than what he'd started with that day. Maybe, day by day, he'd fill up, slowly, until all the black was gone.

Hamlin pressed against Lukas, as if he were stretched out all along his side. Hamlin soaked up the sun as well, both of them resting, recovering from their battle.

Tomorrow, Lukas might talk to Oma. Or he might not. Rudi would never pressure him about it. He'd already helped Lukas set up filters for his email and his phone, so he wouldn't get pressured about it from anyone else either.

Rudi also wouldn't make any decisions for Lukas. Not anymore.

Gauner gave a happy yip and bounded over to where Lukas sat, putting his front paws on the bench, his little pink tongue out and panting.

Lukas lazily reached over and scratched Gauner's neck, getting a strong tail wag in response.

Yes, there was joy in being a hound. Changing still scared him, but Hamlin was there, and Rudi as well.

"You ready?" Lukas asked.

The hound looked at Lukas, then over his shoulder. He leaped back into the park, racing to greet the newest dog just coming in.

"Guess not." Lukas settled back against the bench. The spring winds played with his hair, pushing against his jacket, carrying the first scents of cherry blossoms.

Later that night, Lukas would cook with Rudi again, gaining more of that purely human skill. Eventually, he'd have to call Oma. He wanted to learn more about the other guardian hounds, the shadows, maybe even Hamlin's knight.

But he was done with secrets. He'd carried too many, for too long.

A young man walked toward the bench, carrying a mini pinscher puppy in his arms. He had soft brown hair and eyes, which kind of matched his dog.

When the young man sat down on the bench next to Lukas, Lukas' heart gave a sudden lurch at the friendly smile.

He suddenly remembered his reaction to Virmal—and now, this very cute man.

Maybe Lukas still had one secret that he wasn't willing to share…but just for now.

MEI LING

Though Mei Ling's plane landed after midnight, she was still up by five in the morning to walk to the market. Comforting Asian faces moved along the sidewalk with her. The wind carried the smell of thick chicken *congee*, rice, and fried pork. Waves of workers on black, sturdy bicycles rang their bells as they rode past her.

When Mei Ling turned the corner to the market, she was surprised to see the fortune-teller sitting there, as if she hadn't moved, still dressed in a plain white, Western-style shirt and jeans.

However, her eyes held white cataracts now, instead of being blindly black, or even like the last time Mei Ling had seen her, with the illusion of being sewn shut.

The fortune-teller usually felt Mei Ling's presence. But she didn't even look up when Mei Ling stopped in front of her and said, "Good morning."

Before Mei Ling could say anything more, a strong presence brushed up against her.

A tall Asian man stood on her left, his skin healthy and tan, his eyes dark, while a little bit of white flecked his sideburns. He wore an expensive, gray-mustard colored suit, with an appropriate navy blue power tie.

Mei Ling smiled at him. Everything about the man screamed power, money, and Other.

Though most of the crocodile clan were women, Mei Ling would bet this man was just like her. He wasn't like the other clans she'd met; she knew he had very sharp teeth.

"She can't see anymore," the man said, his voice like black velvet.

"She never could," Mei Ling pointed out. "She's blind."

"You know what I mean," the man chided. "With her other senses."

"What happened to her?" Mei Ling asked. Should she kill the girl? Would she thank Mei Ling for taking her away from this half-existence?

"The shadows took her," the man said.

Mei Ling looked at the man sharply. "The shadows?"

"The shadows," the man assured her. "We've long known about them, and dealt with them."

"But the shadows are gone," Mei Ling pointed out. "Shouldn't she be…better?"

"Unfortunately, she ran into something much worse than the shadows."

"Really," Mei Ling stated flatly. The way the shadows had eaten at her that night on the field, tainting her mind, wrapping her soul in sticky webs—she didn't believe there could be anything worse.

"Really."

Mei Ling raised one expectant eyebrow.

"She met us," the man breathed out.

Suddenly, Mei Ling found herself surrounded by tall men and women, all powerful, all wealthy.

All deadly.

The first man stepped closer. "This will hurt a bit. But there's no pain afterward. Only peace."

His eyes expanded, changing into dark holes from Hell that Mei Ling couldn't look away from. She struggled to move, to breathe, to call up her twin, but not even her teeth were as sharp as the soul eater's.

READ MORE!

Be sure to pick up all three books in the Shadow Wars Trilogy!

The Raven and the Dancing Tiger
The Guardian Hound
War Among the Crocodiles

All available at your favorite retailers!

About the Author

Leah R Cutter writes page-turning fiction in exotic locations, such as a magical New Orleans, the ancient Orient, Hungary, the Oregon coast, rural Kentucky, Seattle, Minneapolis, and many others.

She writes literary, fantasy, mystery, science fiction, and horror fiction. Her short fiction has been published in magazines like *Alfred Hitchcock's Mystery Magazine* and *Pulphouse*, anthologies like Fiction River, and on the web. Her long fiction has been published both by New York publishers as well as small presses.

Find Leah's books on Knotted Road Press at (www.KnottedRoadPress.com)

Follow her blog at www.LeahCutter.com.

Read her essays on her Patreon, get free stories, and more! www.Patreon.com/leahcutter

Reviews

It's true. Reviews help me sell more books. If you've enjoyed this story, please consider leaving a review of it on your favorite site.

Come someplace new…
Are you a traveler? Do you enjoy exploring strange new worlds, new cultures, new people?

Journey into the various lands envisioned by Leah R Cutter.

Sign up for my newsletter and I'll start you on your travels with a free copy of my book, *The Island Sampler*.

I will never spam you or use your email for nefarious purposes. You can also unsubscribe at any time.

http://www.LeahCutter.com/newsletter/

About Knotted Road Press

Knotted Road Press fiction specializes in dynamic writing set in mysterious, exotic locations.

Knotted Road Press non-fiction publishes autobiographies, business books, cookbooks, and how-to books with unique voices.

Knotted Road Press creates DRM-free ebooks as well as high-quality print books for readers around the world.

With authors in a variety of genres including literary, poetry, mystery, fantasy, and science fiction, Knotted Road Press has something for everyone.

Knotted Road Press
www.KnottedRoadPress.com